Moonbound Secrets

Frances Stillman

Contents

Chapter 1

I groaned as I hauled myself into my apartment, pulling off my thick black coat and gloves. I laid my bag down onto a nearby kitchen counter and groaned at its weight. Just thinking about the paperwork I had to fill out was stressing me out.

"Are you sure you aren't gonna come home this week? I miss you," my sister, Zaina, said through the phone that I had squeezed between my shoulder and my ear, I smiled as I switched on the lights in my kitchen and reached for a bottle of wine.

"You know I can't, I just finished my hours at the pet clinic which means I have to stay here to make sure that everything works out well with my little patients and our new apartment business. Plus, I haven't finished everything on your stupid checklist. Seriously, why do I have to buy your clothes? I'm not your assistant Zaina," I said as I poured myself a glass of wine before walking over to my windows. Snow had begun to fall this evening, littering the ground with specks of glittery fragments of ice. I took a sip of my wine before setting it down on a nearby table and sliding the windows open.

"But you live in the city and know it by heart... and I mean, you know, you could basically take over for me," Zaina said and I rolled my eyes.

"Not if I was the last woman on Earth." In a figure hugging grey sweater and jeans, I savored the cold against my skin and enjoyed the city.

"Not woman, she-wolf," Zaina corrected.

"Half-wolf. There's a reason I'm living a human life, Zaina. And we both know you just want to be the pampered princess you are," I countered as I leaned against the railings and peered down on the streets, savoring the serenity and calm of winter... Before I heard what sounded like a wince... A dog's wince.

"Hey, mom and dad called me Princess for a reason..." she trailed off and I paused, straining to hear more of whatever was happening.

"Um, Zaina, I'm gonna have to drop this call. I'll call you later." I didn't give her a chance to speak as I hung up on her.

Followed by a loud thud to my left.

I turned my head, the balconies were divided by a panel of thick concrete walls. So I see nothing... but that sound had definitely come from next door. And I was sure no one lived there. I paused for a moment before I heard another thud, followed by another, a muffled shout, and then a crash... and... I do believe I heard a growl. Shit.

I went back into my apartment, slid the door to my balcony closed, and walked over to the kitchen counter before opening the cabinet below the sink. I pulled out a silver pistol and checked the magazine - fifteen rounds. Okay... Maybe you're overreacting... I thought to myself but I shook my head. Either way, someone might need medical attention and I was the closest person here.

I took the gun in my hands and closed the sink before I placed my ear against the left wall of my apartment. I heard movement, a kind of dragging noise... But no voices - which meant either that someone was passed out. Then again... maybe an unexpected new neighbor got drunk and a friend was taking care of them.

Either way, I was gonna check. I tucked the gun in the waistband of my jeans and pulled on a loose black jacket before leaving my apartment and knocking on the next door. I knocked three times, paused, and then knocked harder.

"Hi! I live next door and I couldn't help but hear some trouble going on... Is everything okay?" I asked loudly before following it up with three loud knocks.

I heard it again. The sound of something whimpering followed by what seemed to me like muffled sobs... My doubts began to increase. I placed my right hand on my back, resting my palm on the gun's handle as I heard thudding footsteps come toward me. The door soon opened with a golden chain dangling between me and a man, who looked about thirty.

"Sorry, my friend's dog is getting a bit out of hand. A friend of ours just moved here and we were just gonna check it out-"

"Oh, well, I'm a vet, I can help you, if you'd like."

"I don't think that's a good idea," he said. He wanted me to leave.

"Listen, whatever is wrong with your dog, I can fix. Trust me," I said and he shook his head before pausing.

"Okay, give me a moment." He shut the door and I waited. I heard muffled noises that sort of sounded like "Behave" and "Shut up" and, it was as if the guy thought I was deaf. It took a while before the door opened again.

The door opened soon enough and the man moved aside as I went in. The apartment looked like an absolute mess, the walls were torn up with scratches, the furniture torn to bits and well... it looked like someone ransacked and tore the place up... I almost cursed. That and there was blood on the floor leading to a door and then I heard the wincing and panting. I heard the door close followed by the soft muted sound of something clicking - safety lever.

"You're kidding me," I mumbled before turning my neck, hearing it click. Before the man could open his mouth, I turned around pulled my gun out and aimed it at the man. He gave me a look of surprise.

"Where's the dog?" I asked and he simply gave me a stare. I rolled my eyes before taking a step forward the man placed his finger on the trigger.

"Four people live on this floor. No one lives to the right- but three people live within a close enough radius to hear your shitty pistol fire," I explained.

"They can hear you too," he said and I smiled. "You know this isn't any of your business."

"Yeah, well like I said, I'm a fucking vet," I said, not breaking my smile before my hands moved, I aimed at his right knee and shot, earning a loud scream before I aimed at his left shoulder and shot again, earning a satisfying and rather agonized scream out of him.

"Everyone... would've heard... that," he said in between pants as he fell to the ground, bleeding profusely on the floor. There goes another chunk of the budget... I thought to myself.

"Yeah, well, I was trying to scare you," I said as I patiently stood, took hold of the barrel of my gun and swung hard at his head. He fell with a thud and though I didn't exactly end him, he'd bleed out soon. I tucked the gun back into my waistband and ran towards the sound of the whining, not failing to notice the trail of blood on the floor, which led me into a tiny hallway and to a closed door.

I opened it up and sighed as I saw a large wolf breathing loosely. It looked at me and whined - realizing that I wasn't a threat.

"Hey, hey, stay with me," I said. I got up and turned on the lights. "Listen, I need you to stay like this, do not shift, no matter how bad it is," I said as I examined her, she was large, black and brown, with blood soaking the fur on her lower body.

I heard a vibrating noise from outside and watched as the wolf in front of me let out a soft whine. I got up and made my way out, searching for the phone and finding it in the pocket of a pair of torn up jeans - probably torn from shifting unexpectedly. I looked at it and saw the caller ID - which was labeled with just the letter "L," I didn't take the time to process that as I slid my finger across the screen.

"Where the hell are you?!" A man growled and I could feel the strength of that tone - Alpha... That and I felt a shudder run through me.

Mate. For a brief moment, that was all my brain registered until I shook myself out of it. Not fucking now... not ever.

"I'm sorry. Um, my name is Auden, I'm a... pack doctor and I found um, the girl, um yeah anyways - she's in an apartment and she's bleeding and losing consciousness. I need help getting her out of here safely and into the closest safe space you have," I said calmly.

"What? What the fuck happened?! How is she?!" He shouted, making me pull back the phone from my ear. Looks like he didn't notice.

"She's breathing, I'm trying to keep her conscious. I'm sorry, but I want to make sure that you're a person I can trust, I found some lunatic with a gun here before I got to her," I said and I heard a low mumbled curse come through the speaker.

"Put me on speaker," he said, but I hesitated. "I'm her brother. You can trust me, I swear. Our pack house is far, but if you can help her- I can have someone come and bring her back safely by morning." I pressed speaker on the phone.

"Lana! We'll bring you home soon. Stay calm. Xander will come get you," the Alpha's voice said. The wolf's eyes glossed over, forming tears, and I took that as a sign that I could trust him.

"I'll tell you the address," I said. Once I was done, I immediately switched into work mode.

"Okay, your brother is sending help, I'm gonna go get my medical kit in my apartment, whatever you do, just... Keep breathing, okay?" The wolf looked at me and whined weakly before I sprinted to my apartment. I picked up a toolkit and a medical bag before running back towards her, ignoring the body in the hallway.

I moved quickly, washing my hands in the kitchen sink and opening my bag, slipping my hands into gloves. I took out a sterile syringe and immediately got to numbing the wound. There was a deep wound, some kind of laceration, just above her left thigh that cut straight towards her stomach, which was probably why she was lying on her right side. Fortunately, wolves healed quickly, so it was no longer as deep as it probably was. But it still needed to stop bleeding - and to heal in the right form, otherwise she'd lose too much blood and I doubt we would be able to get her off this floor alive. I began to numb the area with an the injection, talking to her as I did this to make sure she was still conscious. I began to clean up the wound, washing it clean with what I had and moving the flesh around, making sure that most of the fur was out of the way.

I cut parts of the skin, wincing as she screamed and moved about, making me apply more anesthesia. I sighed as I continued to work, I placed a gauze against the wound and cut up the edges, numbing it along the way and making sure I had enough light.

It didn't take me too long- but I did finish with more than enough blood on my jeans, blood on the floor, blood on my hands, and basically enough blood to drown myself in. Okay, I'm exaggerating. But there was a lot even for a werewolf to bleed out from. Thankfully, my patient was still breathing, though she'd passed out a while ago. When I checked, the stitches I had placed had already started to pull everything together. All she needed now was to not shift until that healed up - because she could rip that whole thing apart and bleed to death if she shifted back into human form. Grotesque, but true.

I sighed in relief as I stood up and began cleaning. I took my stuff to a nearby bathroom and shoved all the bloody waste material into a trash bag. I checked on the wolf and smiled as she continued to breathe softly but in regular small pants. She would need to be on some meds to avoid infections - but until we got her to a better location, this would do. At least the bleeding stopped and her wounds were healing and all sutured up.

I was putting my tools back into my kit and sighed in relief as I let myself relax now that the job was done. The wolf had begun to breathe normally, her eyes slowly blinked awake, glazing over me as the anesthetia continued to numb her senses. I patted her head.

"You'll be fine now... I'll go grab you a blanket or something, okay?" I asked before I stood and grabbed my kit.

I made my way over to my apartment and made a few quick calls about clean up. Thankfully, werewolves were pretty good at cleaning up messes - and someone would come by to pick up the dead body rotting next door. I didn't exactly check if he was a werewolf, but I guessed he was, capturing a werewolf, as a human, was no easy business. I shook my head. The guy was dead, any problems he made would be dealt with by the pack.

I decided to take a shower - to wash off all the grime and blood from my body. I looked at myself in the mirror and groaned. My dark brown hair that I had tied in a ponytail looked like a mess, whatever mascara I had from yesterday was beginning to crumble, my lips were chapped, and I could already see the dark bags forming beneath my deep brown eyes. I shook my head.

My clothes would have to be disposed of, there was no way I was gonna try and wash off this much blood... I grimaced as I peeled my jeans off my legs and jumped into my shower for a quick wash. I pulled on a simple navy blue long-sleeved dress that fell just at the middle of my thighs before grabbing a spare blanket I didn't mind staining to give the wolf next door. Not that she would've needed it in terms of warmth, but I knew it would provide some comfort.

As I headed back into the room where the wolf was, I watched as she barked - well, attempted to bark anyways, but winced instead at my figure. I got close to her and placed the blanket on her.

"Okay, okay, I'm sure you'll be fine here- I don't think I can move you, so you'll have to stay here for the night, I can stay here if-"

Before I could even finish speaking, the wolf started to move, slowly and weakly pulling herself up. I was about to admonish her, but she looked so determined... I eyed her stitches and they looked pretty stable. I sighed in defeat.

"Okay, I get it. Come," I said as I walked over to her right side and helped lift her up with what strength I had left. I wrapped the blanket over her as she stood and I helped her maintain her balance as she limped out of the apartment.

She paused for a moment in front of the corpse of the man that I had killed and she released a loud growl. I patted her head and sighed as she stumbled and limped forward and I guided her into my apartment. Eventually she settled on a black carpet in the spacious apartment. I sighed as I lifted the blanket off of her back and covered her with it before I picked up my phone and finally called the front desk.

"Miss Breaux? Is there a problem-"

"I need you to run a check on all security cameras."

"Yes Miss Breaux."

I hung up and sighed spotting my wine and grabbing it. I gulped it down and leaned against the wall as the wolf on my carpet fell asleep...

What the actual fuck was going on?

Chapter 2

I checked on the wolf. It was only seven in the morning, but I had to report to the clinic by nine if I wanted to get any work done. The wolf, Lana, was healing well, which gave me great relief as I started to cut away the sutures I had placed. The internal sutures would be able to melt away - but I had to get rid of the external ones that were beginning to peek through.

"I'm guessing nothing's hurting," I said as I finished cutting off and pulling out the sutures. I'm sure she was still a little light headed from all that blood loss. But I'm sure she'd be fine. In response to my words, she simply barked.

"Unfortunately, though most of that's been healed, I can't have you shift for at least a few hours, wouldn't want you tearing up those internal stitches, now would we?" I said as I got up and made my way to the kitchen. I placed my tools on a clean white towel and threw my waste material into a metal bin before I washed my hands.

"I'll go ahead and make breakfast for you," I said as I took a pan and heated it up. I grabbed a large bowl and filled it with water before placing it down in front of the wolf, who slowly stood up and drank from it, wagging her tail. She was half my height in wolf form, which meant that she was probably a really young wolf - after all, most wolves could easily be my height... and I was almost at six feet - but the Goddess chickened out on my final two inches.

"Do you want music?" I asked loudly as I made my way back to the kitchen. The wolf barked and I smiled as I turned on my phone and used a nearby remote to turn on the sound system before playing one of my playlists. She seemed to enjoy my music, because she started wagging her tail and barking and howling to "Animal" by Neon Trees.

She soon came by me and wagged her tail as she pounced on the counter.

"Bacon?" I asked and she barked happily as I began to cook.

"This would probably be less awkward if you were human right now, wouldn't it?" I mused and she barked again as she made her way towards me and placed her paws on the counter.

"I wonder what pack you're from... You don't have a very familiar scent," I said just as I heard a knock on the door. The wolf got down from the counter and sprinted away. I went to the door and opened it up. I found myself staring at a man with long blonde hair tied in a ponytail at the back of his head.

"And you are?" I asked.

"My name's Xander, I'm one of the Umbra Pack's deltas," he greeted and I raised an eyebrow. "My Alpha informed me that you rescued his sister-"

"Right, have you had breakfast?" I asked, studying the man. He was definitely younger than me - probably fresh out of high school or something - and he had bags under his eyes - he'd probably been driving all night.

"I'm fine, I'm sure-" I shook my head.

"Eat and then go, the poor wolf hasn't even eaten yet and I still need to have her shift into human form to complete my check-up," I said as I moved aside, allowing him to enter. He made his way inside and I closed the door, continuing to cook.

"Make yourself at home." I began to continue cooking, toasting some bread in the toaster and getting out three plates.

"Xander, right?" I asked as I looked at him, he had gone to the windows to stare at the view of the city, he looked over at me.

"Yes?"

"My name's Auden. What pack are you from?" I asked.

"Umbra," Xander said. I placed the bacon into a plate and pulled out some peanut butter and jelly.

"Could you place these on the table? I'm just gonna grab Lana from wherever she's hiding," I said and Xander nodded as I went into my open bedroom. Spotting Lana's tail peeking out from under the large white bed.

"Lana, if you don't come out, you're not getting breakfast," I said and I watched as she crawled out from under the bed, the bed lifting off the ground a bit. How the hell did she even get under there?

Lana got out and started to pout at me. I stared into her now more noticeable green eyes and folded my arms over my chest.

"You know you have to go back home right?" I asked and she simply pulled the puppy dog eyes at me. I shook my head.

"Come on, breakfast is waiting and I'm not feeding you in my bedroom." That's unsanitary. I added in my head.

Lana eventually came out, but she growled the moment she spotted Xander, who bowed his head in her direction.

"Where do I put her-"

"On the floor, she probably won't mind, right?" I asked as I looked at Lana. She barked and wagged her tail at me but as Xander moved to put her food on the floor, she growled at him. He paused and I sighed as I took the plate from him and placed it on the floor right on the carpet she'd slept on last night.

She gladly began to eat as I fixed myself a peanut butter and jelly sandwich for breakfast. Meanwhile Xander seemed to try and resist the temptation to eat... either that or he was being pre-occupied by Lana through the mind-link.

"Please just eat, I'm not asking for much right?" I asked and Xander looked at me and nodded before picking up some toast and slowly eating.

I rolled my eyes before I continued to eat and began fixing up another sandwich. I wrapped it up in some paper towels and handed it over to him.

"Take it for the road if you're not eating now," I said as I looked over at Lana who had finished off her plate by licking every crumb and probably grease on her plate.

"Okay, now I'm gonna have you hop into the shower and bring you some clothes. And you," I said turning over to Xander, "Finish off the rest of the food on that table. Put everything in the dishwasher and we'll be good, okay?"

"Okay." He responded as I walked over to my bathroom, Lana following behind me with her tail wagging behind her.

I had her hop into my tub as I gave her a wash down. I had thankfully showered the night before and I sighed in relief as I got to her wounded area and washed down the blood that had begun to clump her hair. Some of the dead hair also fell away and she shed quite a bit of her brown and gold toned hair - which was definitely gonna be hell for me to clean up later. She barked as I rubbed her head with water.

"Now, I'm not gonna waste a liter of shampoo on your wolf, so you better give a shot at shifting. If anything hurts, I'll fix it after you've completely shifted back," I said and she licked my face, making me laugh as I stepped back, turning off the shower head. I then set up a towel and a robe, hanging it on a nearby ledge before walking out of the bathroom.

"How's she doing?" Xander asked as I saw him finish cleaning.

"She'll be fine... Hopefully she doesn't scream as she shifts, but I'm just letting her shower. I'm gonna grab her some clothes and then you guys can hit the road, I'll hand over some antibiotics that I have on hand and some pain medicine - her side might be a bit sore and she might have bruising, but it shouldn't be anything your pack doctor can't handle," I said and he nodded his head.

"Does your pack live in the city?" He asked and I laughed.

"Of course not, I'm only half a werewolf, consider me human," I said and deciding not to let him ask any further questions, I retreated into my room looking for clothes. I found a padded deep blue dress that could probably work for most sizes, unfortunately... the underwear side of things was a little difficult but I guess she could awkwardly ask to buy some...

I heard a knock come from the bathroom door and went over, opening it to find a young girl, probably only a little older than ten, standing in front of me. If she shifted this early... I can only guess what her kidnapper wanted from her. An Alpha's sister at that... I brushed the thoughts away and gazed at her. She had short dark curly brown hair that fell just above her shoulders and was probably only five feet tall, she was tanned - with lines indicating a sun burn and her nose slowly peeling.

"You're a lot younger than I thought you were," I commented and she smiled, the robe she had put on looked so large it made me chuckle. As I was about to give her the dress she gave me a huge hug, squeezing me tightly.

"Whoa..."

"Thank you, thank you, thank you!" She shouted as she hugged me and I suddenly felt my dress get damp. I looked down at her and noticed that she tears in her eyes but then she squeezed me even harder.

"You're... w-welcome..." I managed to squeak. I mean she had basically squeezed it out of me. She eventually let go and I handed her my clothes,. "Okay, okay, stop crying and go change before you squeeze my eyes out of my body," I said, as I rubbed the bottoms of her eyes gently with my thumbs and she released me smiling as she took my dress.

I left her alone in the bathroom and sighed as I pulled my dark brown hair into its usual ponytail. I got into my bedroom and changed as well, pulling on a white turtleneck sweater, a pair of slim-fitting jeans, and some black low cut boots. I prepared my handbag for the day, stuffing it full of my things and paperwork I needed to fill out yesterday. Just as I was about to open the door, I heard growling.

Not from one person, no. I didn't even hear two growls, I heard fucking three. I immediately opened my door and lo and behold - there were three people in my apartment. Two men and my patient.

"Okay, who invited-" I froze. I smelled something that was a little too... sweet for my liking. I instinctively stepped forward but logically held back.

As man number two almost turned to see me, I ran into my room and slammed the door shut.

"Oh hell fucking no..." I cursed. "No, no, no, no, no, no..."

Not today.

Not ever.

I was not gonna let something else govern my fucking life. I was not gonna let this happen-

Unfortunately for me, slamming a door shut doesn't mean it's locked.

And the door opened.

Chapter 3

I was awkwardly standing with my back against the wall as a tall werewolf that smelled a little too delectable for my liking stepped into the room.

"Lucien-" A girl's voice - Lana's - started and I immediately reached for the door to my balcony in the hopes that I would be able to at least escape to my living room.

But before I could even touch the knob, he had already used the classic werewolf move of running at the speed of fucking light and appearing right in front of me. I bit my bottom lip, earning a very low growl from the man in front of me and I tried to resist him but my body seemed to have a mind of his own... His right hand reached up and tucked a loose hair behind my ear, sending goosebumps down my arms and he traced his thumb against the side of my jaw, eventually ending his touch on my lips. My body felt like it had been put into an oven- my cheeks felt warm and I felt my legs go a little wobbly. I breathed air through my teeth and turned my head, avoiding his eyes - because a look into those... would verify what I was feeling...

But werewolves weren't known to be patient people... Or respectful ones apparently - because he placed his thumb beneath my chin and lifted it, my eyes immediately meeting his pair of hazel eyes - a mixture of green and brown that had darkened with lust and a possessiveness that whatever werewolf blood I had in me wanted to succumb to. I decided then and there to shamelessly stare at him. He had hair the same color as Lana's, a kind of dark brown styled to the side and slightly curled, thick brows framed a defined face of high cheekbones, a tall nose, and deep set eyes... His lips were slightly open and he looked like he was in the latter stage of growing a beard - though it still wasn't nearly as thick or burly as a 'beard' I guess would look. I should know, my dad had a huge beard that engulfed the lower half of his face.

I cleared my throat but the Alpha just stared into my eyes and now both of his hands were cradling my face, forcing me to look into his eyes. When I attempted to look away, he growled and I was made to stare into his eyes.

"Alpha Lucien we have to-" I heard Xander begin the Alpha turned around and I saw Xander bow his head.

I stepped aside but as soon as I did, the Alpha had his hand block my way.

"You're coming with me," he said pursed my lips, biting into my bottom lip and earning a growl from him. I took a deep breath.

"Okay..." I said as I looked into his eyes and challenged him, mustering as much strength as I could to resist his damned Alpha commanding voice. I stepped forward. "I have a job to do Alpha." I bowed my head.

"And... as a result of your sister's incident-" I said glancing over at Lana and then back at him, "I am going to be late for work, so if you would please move-" I froze.

He was way too close. Too fucking close I could feel his breath against my skin. I heard a gasp from Lana's direction and my hands basically became immobile. For a brief moment, my eyes wanted to fall shut - they really did - and my body had already leaned forward expecting some kind of magic to happen... I could almost feel him against my lips and I had to fight back.

There was only one thing I could do.

I took a quick breath and then I lifted my limp arm and slapped him and his stupid kiss-attempting face. Trying not to think or use any of my instincts, I stepped forward. In the mere moments that I had, I grabbed my handbag and strode past Lana by the door who was gawking at me and also past Xander who was doing the same. Needless to say, I ended up forcefully bumping into his shoulder as I made an escape from my own apartment and I made a run for the elevator.

I sighed in relief as it opened - probably because Alpha Kiss-Face had just stepped off of it. I jumped in and pressed the close button multiple times. And because technology sucks and we have a stupid regulation on these stupid buttons, the Alpha, his sister, and his Delta made it outside just as it closed. And because I'm even more of an idiot, the Alpha pressed the down button and the elevator doors opened up for him.

"I think you forgot something," the Alpha said in his deep and albeit sultry-sounding voice, I reluctantly turned my head as he lifted a set of keys in front of my face. I ignored him and turned my head, he was still standing in front of the elevator as I kept pressing the close button.

He chuckled.

"You do know these things won't close on a person entering, right?" He asked rhetorically.

"A girl can dream," I countered and he laughed as he stepped in, Lana stepped in silently behind him and Xander followed. Thus, the most awkward elevator trip of my life began, with an Alpha sniffing my hair as two other wolves stared at us.

"Lucien, is she your-"

"Yes. If it wasn't obvious by your brother's incessant need to sniff my hair from right behind me, yes, he seems to be my-"

"Mate." He gladly finished and I stood stiffly behind him as I felt his hand graze my back, the warmth from his hand seeping through my turtleneck. I immediately turned and swatted it away.

"You know, there are cameras in this elevator and what you're doing is basically harassment," I said turning around. "What are you? A horny teenager? Hands off." I said as the elevator doors opened and I stepped off into the parking lot. I heard something jingle from behind me and mentally groaned as I turned and found him holding my keys up.

"You're not leaving me," he said with a confident smile and I shook my head for a moment.

"Excuse me?"

"As my mate and as an Alpha... I have the right to take you with me."

"...I'm sorry did you just say you had a right to kidnap me or did my hearing just fail me?" I asked, folding my arms over my chest, my bag slightly hitting me a bit too hard. The Alpha smirked at me.

"Do I look like I'm gonna just let you take me wherever the hell you're going?" I asked, tilting my head and giving him a look of concern.

"Well, I'm not an idiot and I did bring back-up... So you either come with me willingly or..." I heard footsteps echo in the parking lot.

"This is ridiculous." I cursed as I looked around, spotting at least six men and women around me. I sniffed the air and groaned, they were very much a part of his pack.

I laughed at my misfortune.

"I save a werewolf, feed them in the morning, and here I am..." Why does the Goddess hate me so much? I cursed in my head as I held the back of my head with my arms, my bag hitting the back of my head.

I released a huge sigh.

"What time is it?" I asked out loud, before releasing my head and looking at the Alpha in front of me. He smiled and stepped forward.

"Half past eight," he said and I closed my eyes, trying to calm down.

"I need to go somewhere and then I'll go with you," I said looking straight into the Alpha's eyes.

"You say you that like I gave you a choice," he said and I mentally groaned. I thought of an idea - a disgusting one but an idea.

I lifted my free hand and traced his jaw this time, his eyes widened and I saw the goosebumps that formed on his arms.

"I need to go. If you let me go there, and you can escort me if you want, I'll give you a kiss," I said, batting my eyelashes at him. He chuckled.

"What makes you think I can't make you kiss me whenever I want-" He began but I had grabbed him and pulled him down slightly. Thankful that our heights weren't that different, I planted a kiss on the corner on the farthest side of his jaw.

"You can make me..." I said as I trailed my lips along his stubble, I wanted to half-vomit, half-continue but I needed to play a game with this Alpha if I wanted to win the human way because I can't for the love of me win the werewolf-fighting-way even if I wanted to.

"But let's both admit..." I continued as I kissed closer to his lips, I dropped my handbag and wrapped my free arm around his neck as I finally kissed the left corner of his lip, my lips were tingling themselves and my stomach was feeling like a rollercoaster had done six loops inside it. "It feels a lot better when a mate kisses willingly, doesn't it?" I asked as I pulled away for a moment, just far enough so that our noses barely touched. He smiled confidently at me, making me a little weak as I held my ground.

"Well I wouldn't know since my mate hasn't kissed-" he began and I decided to cut him off again. I kissed him.

But to hell with it if I opened my mouth, there was no way that was going to happen. I simply kissed him and maybe... maybe licked my lips in the process, causing him to part his own lips in response. I smirked as I pulled back.

"Now you know," I said as I took the keys from his hand, bent to grab my bag, and made my way to my car. I heard him release a breath and laugh to himself as the wolves around me made room, suggesting that he had already made his command.

He followed behind me and just as I thought I would've been able to get into my car, I was hoisted over his shoulder.

"We made a deal-"

"I think you should know to hold up the final part of your deal until I say yes," he answered and I groaned as I kicked and struggled against him.

"Stupid fucking Alphas and their stupid fucking egos-" I groaned as I kicked and squirmed in his grasp.

"Alpha Lucien, our flight for Vancouver is scheduled for this afternoon - would you like us to-"

"We're heading straight for the airport," Alpha Motherfucker said as he carried me off. I sighed before I felt my bag, I moved it to my left hand and reached for my phone.

I quickly looked for my sister's name and called her.

"Auden? What's up? You never followed up on last night's call-"

"Yeah, I'm in a bit of a situation... Do you think you can handle everything for a bit? I've got a surprise trip to hell-"

"What are you talking about?" Zaina asked and I rolled my eyes. I felt myself slip down onto the ground and I resisted the urge to sniff the fuck out of the Alpha in front of me as I slid down his body until my feet touched the ground.

I watched as the Alpha smirked and took my phone from my hands.

"This is Alpha Lucien of the Umbra Pack and Auden's mate." Zaina went silent on that and I groaned as I reached for my phone. But Alpha Lucien decided to dodge me and I swear if I could've growled I would've. I looked around and sighed in relief as the rest of the werewolves began to drive off.

Alpha Lucien had already started conversing with my sister and since I didn't want to bother talking to him, I took it upon myself to slowly walk away. Lana, who was about to enter her car in a very unhappy manner, caught my eye and smiled. I placed a finger on my lips before she nodded and I watched as she pulled her arm back and punched Xander in the face, effectively knocking him out. I heard some bones cracking and Lucien put my phone down before he began to yell an Alpha command.

"Lana!" He shouted and I stepped back until I got to the emergency exit, I heard something tear and I groaned - Lana had just shifted. I opened the door to the emergency exit and made a run for it.

Happy that Lucien would have to chase after Lana as well, I ran up to the lobby of my apartment building and sprinted to the front where I knew a line of taxis would be waiting. I immediately went into one of them.

"Good morning little missy! Where are we off to-"

"Port Authority, thanks," I said, looking through my bag - relieved that it was even with me. "Sorry." I added, smiling at the driver who simply shook his head and smiled back as he drove off.

"No problem missy, I know a girl when she got a problem. Wouldn't wanna make you talk about it if you don't wanna so I'm gonna go ahead and put on the radio - any requests?" He asks and I shake my head.

"Play anything you like," I replied before I began staring out the window. Considering I didn't have my phone on me... I'd have to make it either back to Carmine territory directly or I'd have to try and contact my sister through other means...

I rested my head against the cab window. There were only so many ways I could outrun a werewolf especially an Alpha - but I was willing to try.

Chapter 4

I walk through the halls and sigh as I get in and look for a ticket booth. I groan as I realize that the next bus to my location is at ten. Supposing the Alpha doesn't find me within the hour, then great. But we're talking werewolves and I know he'll be able to sniff me out - literally. I paused, re-thinking my options.

If I make it to the clinic - I won't really be able to hide because Zaina could've told him where I worked. Plus, I don't know what the Umbra Pack is but anyone that has their sister kidnapped by some kind of psychopath when they're not even remotely close to their territory - is absolute trouble. I sighed as I stepped away from the ticket lines and move to an empty hall. I've been doing a lot of sighing today.

I looked through my bag, groaning as I find my undone stack of paperwork, neatly clipped together inside yet the corners of the paper had already begun to fold because of all the moving I'd been doing. It was only then that I saw something else in my bag, another phone. I stared at it in surprise - it was on silent and it wasn't vibrating but... someone was calling-

"Auden!" Someone yelled from my left and I turned only to find my eyes meet a pair of vivid hazel. Oh shït.

I broke into a sprint, hiding myself in the crowds that were heading out as I zig-zagged through people. Thankful that werewolf genes let me be a little faster than the average human, I made my way out and ran towards Times Square. I began to smooth into a fast walking pace as I got further through the crowds. If I wanted to mask my scent, crowds were the way to go. I immediately went towards every crowd I could see before I took out Lana's phone. I slid my finger across the screen and sighed in relief - she didn't have a passcode. I dialed Zaina's number and cursed as I waited for her to answer.

"Hello?"

"Zaina, thank fücking god," I said as I continued to walk along.

"Auden? What the hell are you-"

"No time to explain, what did the guy who was talking to you earlier tell you?" I asked.

"He told me he was your mate - Auden, that guy's not a normal-" I sniffed the air and groaned, I could already sniff him which meant he could do the same with me. Glad that whatever werewolf genes I had left was still able to aid me in my escape, I decided to make it down to the subways, crinkling my nose in disgust at some of the scents I picked up - heightening my senses wasn't always a good thing. I wasn't going to go for a train - but I did need the crowds to just go through me - which happened as people got off the train - I simply needed to make it to the other side and get out again.

"Sorry, you might get a lot of interference. I need you to help me get out of this situation, Zaina, I can't just leave-"

"Auden, you have to listen to me, Alpha Lucien isn't a small-fry that I can just negotiate with-"

"Zaina- I have done everything in my power to keep my nose out of werewolf life and I'm not about to lose it because of a guy that was chosen for me by a goddess that has never ever decided to bless me with anything-"

"Auden, I'm sorry but I can't just-"

"You haven't even tried!" I yelled as I got out of the station. People had stopped to stare and I felt my heart thump in my chest as I shook my head and continued to walk forward. "You can't make me get back into this shït, Zaina, you just can't-"

"It's not for me to decide, Auden, come on, you know that mates are bound together-"

"What if I just reject him?"

"He'll have to accept and you know he won't-"

"If I tell him I'm practically human he will- what kind of werewolf would want a human mate, right?" I asked as I turned and I felt immediate regret as I caught a whiff of the scent. Just as I was about turn on my heel and go back I was pulled back with an iron grip.

I opened my mouth to scream but I felt him place a hand over my mouth and spin me around. I was inhaling his scent and it was driving me insane, plus the feeling of his body against mine was sending me sensations I did not want to feel at the moment.

"If I let go, will you please keep quiet?" Alpha Lucien asked and I nodded, he released me and I breathed a sigh, stepping away from him.

There was only so much of the tinglies I could handle. And yes, I'm going to call those warm tingling sensations from the mate touch tinglies - because why the hell not? I folded my arms over my chest.

"Auden? Auden are you-" I hung up on Zaina.

"Where's Lana?" I asked and Alpha Lucien sighed.

"She's sedated in the car."

"Do you normally do that to your sister?" I asked and he shook his head.

"Lana's only twelve, there's no way I'm gonna let her roam around the city like a wolf - and there's a lot more people looking for the two of our ässes than you think. I've talked to your sister, Zaina and I have her permission to take you to Vancouver and let you do whatever you want beforehand. She says you need to deliver some papers-"

"You have her permission?" I asked with incredulity. What about mine?

"Yes, I do. As your Alpha her word is absolute-"

"What kind of archaic society do we live in where someone else gets to determine my fücking-" He placed a hand on my mouth again and I froze.

"Please don't make a ruckus in public," he said and his eyes made it look like he was begging. I nodded and he released me again.

"I'm sorry. I'm trying my best to calm down."

"I can see that. Either way, your sister says that she needs some papers from you before she can-"

"She wants me to do her paperwork... In this situation?" I interrupt before looking at him and shaking my head. "God this is fücking awful..." I cursed as I stepped away and felt something inside me - it was rage - just pure fücking rage.

"Listen... I'll try not to be overbearing, but we need to get a move on, there are people looking for my sister and myself... And this city is far from familiar to us." I paused to think and stared into his eyes. He really did look worried - if not a little more tense. I peered into the bag that had somehow miraculously managed to stay with me through this entire chase.

"You know what? Fück it," I cursed as I took all the papers from my bag, I spotted a nearby garbage can and sighed. If any werewolf strength at all is in my hands, please let me do this one thing... I internally begged myself. I placed my hands on two sides of the thick stack of papers and pulled it apart. I hear the stack rip with a satisfying sound.

"Do you happen to smoke?" I asked Alpha Lucien and he shook his head. I groaned. Damn it.

"Close enough I guess," I muttered before I tore the stack into further shreds and threw it in the trashcan. "Do you have my phone?" I asked as I turned to him and he nodded this time as he produced it from his pocket.

I took it from him and dialed my clinic.

"Good morning Clarissa from-"

"Hey Clarissa, this is Doctor Auden Breaux. I'm quitting and when my sister calls you, which I suspect she will do sometime today, tell her to go fück herself."

"Doctor Auden I don't think I can-" I hung up and sighed.

"When's the flight, Alpha?" I asked and Alpha Lucien sighed in relief.

"You can just call me Lucien... As for the flight - time's not much of an issue if you need it to get other things done."

"What? Last time I checked planes don't wait for-"

"Private plane."

"Oh. Well that's convenient," I said just as I looked for some kind of my pin in my bag.

"What are you doing?"

"Abandoning my sister," I said with a smile before I found a safety pin. Lucien watched as I simply plugged the needle through my phone's sim holder and took it out. I shook it out and sighed in relief as I plugged it back in.

"You could've just destroyed it," he commented and I rolled my eyes.

"And waste a perfectly good phone? No fücking way."

———

"Where were you gonna go in the bus station?" Alpha Lucien asked as we boarded the plane. I didn't have many things to begin with, so I decided to comply.

"Carmine Territory. Two hours by bus and probably another hour's worth of walking on human legs," Supposing I was gonna be welcomed of course. I added in my head.

"How is Carmine as a pack?" He asked and I sighed before I took a look at the plane's interior. Mainly composed of leather reclined seats and an upholstered couch, with secured coffee tables - I basically gawked. Carmine wasn't poor by any means - but who the hell could be rich enough to have a private plane? Just what kind of pack was Umbra? I heard someone clear their throat and I shook my head as I took a seat nearby where a table was propped up in front of me and the couch was to my left.

"Oh, um, Carmine... well, I guess we're a small pack that just minds their own business. My sister Zaina is three years older than me and is learning the ropes of being Alpha," I explained as Lucien took a seat across me.

"I mean how is Carmine, to you, in terms of attitude," Lucien asked and I paused.

"I haven't really seen them in a while, but I would have to say that they mind their own business, just as much as I mind my own," I said freely. If Zaina wasn't gonna be by my side, I needed someone else - and maybe my mate would do for now.

"How often did they come see you?" Lucien asked and I paused for a moment.

That's strange.

"Um... well, I came to see them for Christmas-"

"They don't come see you? Not even your sister?"

"Um... I'm sure I'm getting it wrong..." I said and Lucien simply shook his head. Deciding not to really think about it, I spotted Xander as he carried someone in his arms and my eyes widened as I realized that it was Lana who was now dressed in a simple white T-shirt dress. He rested her on another chair and buckled her up before he bowed his head towards Alpha Lucien and then at me. I raised an eyebrow as he walked towards the back of the plane, taking a seat.

"Is he Lana's mate?" I asked and Alpha Lucien chuckled.

"She's not old enough to discern if that's true - but from what he tells me, it seems like it," he said before he looked over at his sister and smiled.

"How old is he?" I asked.

"He's seventeen, five years older than my sister."

"And you're okay with that?" I asked just as the airlock door shut and I buckled my seat - Alpha Lucien did the same.

"Lana isn't someone I can say no to, plus, Xander's been her friend for years before he figured out he'd been mated to her. I think that's enough to prove I can trust him, don't you?" He asked and I nodded.

"Though I guess that kind of justification doesn't work in our case." I paused.

"...Oh, you're referring to the fact that we literally don't know each other," I said and he nodded in response. I leaned back in my chair as take-off began.

"What exactly convinced you to come with me?"

"I'd rather not talk about the real reason so I'm gonna just say one of them. Having an Alpha chase me attracts attention and I'm guessing that if I had stayed and you chased me- while others chased you..." I trailed off, only spotting a hint of uncertainty in Alpha Lucien's eyes. "Well. My life would easily become a mess no matter what," I said, completing my answer.

"So that's it?" he said and I sighed.

"You didn't expect me to say that I did it because you were my mate right?" I asked before looking over at Lana.

"A wolf can dream," he said in response and I rolled my eyes as I took my bag back into my hands, sifting through the piles of paper.

"How long is the flight?" I asked.

"Five to six hours."

"Damn."

"So... more about you. How often do you go back to Carmine?" He asked and I chuckled.

"...Once, twice a year?" I admitted. "I haven't really seen anyone other than my parents and Zaina for... maybe seven years. Most of the time, I lock myself up in my room in the pack house- there's not much space for a human there-" I said stopping myself, I looked at Alpha Lucien, his hazel eyes had turned dark green and filled with concern.

"It's not like it's their fault though, I let my head talk me out of the pack," I tried to explain but he still gave me that worried look that made me feel uneasy. It was a look that I was used to - a look that I got from my parents when I said I was leaving - a look that I've come to really resent.

"Do you think your sister can handle your workload?" He asked and I nodded, appreciating the fact that he had changed the subject.

"I mean, it's not like I can run it from Vancouver. And it isn't that big of a business in the first place - I don't really even get paid to do it," I added, pausing for a moment.

"Does this plane not have wifi?" I asked, trying to get on a more easy subject, and he gave me a blank look.

"I wouldn't know, it isn't mine," Lucien said and I paused.

"Then who's is it?" I asked.

"A friend's."

"What? Who lends someone a private plane?"

"I went to New York for a reason, Auden. Speaking your langua ge... I went for a business reason," he said casually and I stared at him.

"What reason would have you drag your pack out here with your sister and get her almost bleeding to death beside my apartment?"

"I'm not inclined to tell you anything..." He trailed off and I folded my arms over my chest.

"Really? After I just spilled my beans?" I asked and he smirked. "Wow, okay, well, as your mate, I'd love to know the reason for your being in the city- you know, especially since I don't believe that fate has everything all planned out for us to meet," I said and he simply looked away, staring out the windows. I looked as well, smiling as I got a view of the clouds.

"We were hunting for some people, but another group found us instead," he explained plainly, like I was supposed to get his story.

"God, it's been a while since I've been on this side of things..." I murmured.

"We can talk about this later."

"I'd rather... not stay in my thoughts right now," I admitted honestly and he smiled.

"Then maybe I should let you ask other questions," he said kindly and I paused.

"But I just asked you one-"

"I said other questions."

"Stingy motherfücker." He laughed at me and I rolled my eyes.

"Do you have none?"

"...Fine, let me think about it."

Chapter 5

"**A**uden..." Someone called and I shook my head. I heard a slight laugh close to my left ear before I felt someone literally blow into it. I opened my eyes immediately and lifted my right hand to smack the shït out of someone when I saw a pair of hazel eyes stare into mine.

"You could've just woken me up like a normal person," I said, stretching out my arms and hit the ceiling. What- that can't be right because I'm in a plane-

"We're almost on Umbra territory," Lucien said and I looked around, there was nothing but trees everywhere - and a nice solid road. It took me a few moments to make my brain finally recognize that Lucien and I were seated in the back of a fairly spacious car. In front of us was Xander who was driving and right beside Lucien, leaning against the window and drawing on it was Lana.

"Where exactly are we?" I asked.

"Near a mountain trail, but we gotta get off in about two minutes," he said and I looked out at the snow-covered roads. "Need a jacket?"

"Do you have one?" I asked and he nodded in response, pulling something from underneath the chair. I took it from him and shrugged it on, it was a little too big but it was a good enough winter jacket - I guess.

"What about you guys?" I asked and Lucien smiled before Lana giggled.

"Can I take her? Please?" Lana asked and Lucien pet her head.

"I don't think that's a good idea."

"You just want her to ride your back, it's not fair, if you're mates you guys can do it whenever you want-"

I froze.

"Okay, taken completely out of context, this conversation can really fu- screw with my head," I said before taking a breath, "can someone just please tell me what the plan is and why?"

"Our main territory is found in the forest and we don't have any real roads there so we have to run," Lucien said simply and I stared at him.

"You mean-"

"We're gonna have you ride on my back until we get to the pack house," he said plainly as Xander stopped the car. I looked behind us and saw other cars stop as well, their drivers remaining inside.

"Who's gonna get rid of the cars?" I asked and Lucien smiled.

"There are a few others that are willing to drive it back. We run a few businesses in the main city too," he explained and I paused for a moment.

"Huh," I commented, not knowing what else to say just as Lana opened the door.

"Lana!" Xander yelled as he unbuckled his seatbelt and opened the car door. The cold had come in and despite having werewolf blood in me - I couldn't help but shiver. It was really fücking cold out there.

"Let her be, she won't leave until Auden here gets out," Lucien said calmly as he stepped out of the car. I shook my head as I took my phone and Lana's and opened the door to my side. Having just got out of the car, I stretched out my arms and felt the cold just straight up hit my legs.

I love winter, but goddamn sometimes too much cold can really bite you in the äss.

I closed the door behind me and shoved my hands into the pockets of the jacket. I bit into my bottom lip as I walked around the car, a bunch of other people had left their cars a few remained on the steering wheel and someone came up to our car.

"It's nice to meet you Luna," the person greeted, it was a girl with short cropped hair- she looked sixteen and had deep red hair that stood out against her pale skin and rosy cheeks from the cold.

"Nice to meet you too, you are?" I asked, ignoring the whole Luna honorific, and she grinned.

"My name's Freya, I live in the city but I'm part of the pack," she said and I nodded.

"Taking the car?" I asked and she nodded.

"Somebody's got to, right?" I smiled before I felt someone grab my arm.

"Let's go!" Lana said as she tugged me back to the edge of the road.

"Lana I think I should-" I froze as I saw Lucien tug off his shirt. He then proceeded to unbuckle his belt and I shook my head. You're a fücking doctor, grow a pair - okay - not exactly a doctor but you're a vet so-

I tore my eyes away and tugged my jacket on, zipping it all the way up. Multiple sounds of cracking bones, half-synchronized groans, and yelps later, I turned around found myself surrounded by wolves- except one of them - Lucien, was just about a foot below my neck when he was on all fours. I folded my arms over my chest.

"Well, I can't mind-link you so you better start barking boy," I said and he wagged his tail.

Aside from being insanely huge, Lucien's wolf was gorgeous and a totally different color from his sister who had brown and golden bundles of fur that faded to black... Lucien had brown and golden fur - sure, but the tips were black and his his fur was mostly light. He looked like a husky and as his pack disappeared - save for Lana who refused to leave and Xander who stood by her - he hopped along like one. I bit my bottom lip.

"Can you lie down at least?" I asked and Lucien barked as he did lay his body down, waiting for me to - well... ride his back. I shook my head. Let's just pretend we're riding a horse... A large furry horse that gives you the tinglies... Okay, not helping.

I stepped forward and just as I was about to grab hold of him and hoist myself over, he was tackled by Lana's dark wolf. Who barked at me and bowed down to have me sit.

"Lana, I don't think that's a good idea," I said with a smile and she whined at me. Lucien barked as he nudged Lana's stomach away with his nose and she only whined louder. I looked over at Xander and watched as he scratched the back of his head. The cars around us had already pulled away, leaving just us four - and from afar, I looked like a lunatic with three giant wolves around me.

"Lana, if I apply pressure on the wrong spot, you'll start bleeding internally," I threatened - and lied - she winced before bowing her head, her ears flopping downward as she backed away and pouted at me. Lucien barked and moved in her place, wagging his tail as he bowed down again. I glared at him.

"No funny business, otherwise I'm gonna pull your fur out and watch you bleed to death," I threatened, only earning a pant and a bark from my mate. I rolled my eyes as I touched his fur, sending shivers down the length of my arms before I grabbed hold of him and straddled his back. I lay against him and grabbed hold, making sure that I could hold onto his fur or his skin - or something.

Although by the time he stood up, I had wrapped my arms as far as I could around his neck. My nose had begun to freeze up and I appreciated the warmth that was reaching my hands and radiating off of his body. Lana whimpered as Xander barked at her. Lucien barked as well before he reared back.

"Oh God," I murmured just as Lucien broke into a sprint. My breath hitched as he began running through the forest.

I did my best to look up, but it really wasn't all that possible. It was like I was trying to open my eyes with a wind running through - and that wind happened to be frigid and cold and just harsh towards my nose and my face in general. I buried my face deep into Lucien's fur, getting close enough to bask in the smell of his wolf which smelled quite sweet - I don't know what this guy was wearing but damn was it unexpectedly good - and I don't mean musky like male perfume it was just... nice? I tried to put my finger on it... He smelled a little bit like cinnamon - and apples? Like the weird fruity kind-

Lucien barked and I looked up noticing that he had slowed down. He had climbed up a hill and we were now alone as he turned and I looked at the view he was showing me. It was a view of the mountains topped with quite a bit of snow, trees were topped in frost and layer after layer of forest covered the lower half of the mountain. My breath had now started coming out in large white tufts of mist. I took a breath before staring out at the view and just as I was about to appreciate the view, Lucien barked and turned, rearing back again and making me grip his wolf tighter as he continued to run.

He eventually began sprinting uphill and I could feel the strength that ran through his body as he leapt forward. I mean... he was also probably showing off his abilities but hey, a woman can appreciate the effort - actually considering he can leap more than three meters uphill - anyone can appreciate the shït out of that. But I wasn't gonna say that out loud. Alphas had bigger egos that I'd rather not feed.

I caught my breath as he leapt one more time, stones shifting beneath his feet as he finally seemed to make it to the pack house - a small house on what looked like the the edge of a hill. I paused for a moment, it looked like a very modern home with wooden panels all around it. It looked fairly small and really consisted of one floor but it extended over the edge of the hill. The plants around it made it difficult to see what views the house had - but I'm willing to bet that there was more to this house than it seemed. I mean, our pack house in Carmine wasn't something to boast anything of so it's not like I could really compare. I just expected pack houses to be very... cabin-like, the way my home looked.

Lucien eventually lay down. He began panting as I released him, sighing in relief as I finally got my feet on stable ground. There was a fine dirt path heading up to the home that seemed to have formed over years of people - or rather, werewolves - treading over it regularly. Lucien barked to gain my attention as he trotted, quite adorably, towards the front of the house which had a small wide wooden bridge made of smooth wooden panels.

"Nice house," I commented as we walked across and Lucien barked and it was only when I stepped onto the 'bridge' that I realized what this pack house really looked like.

The plants in the front hid it really well. The bridge wasn't much, it had a stable support of ground but... I walked over to the edge and felt my breath catch in my throat. There was whole set of three floors heading down, all beautifully made of rugged stone and wood. I gawked at the staircase that led down, concealed just out of my sight below the bridge. I went over to the other side and I saw a stream trickle down the edge of the hill. I heard a bark and immediately stepped away, following Lucien as he pawed the door, which swung open. I took a deep breath before I opened the door, mentally trying to prepare myself for the view.

Sure enough, the first floor consisted of half a real house and the other half just glass. A simple balcony revealed a beautiful view of the mountainside. A lake could be viewed but it was at a significant distance. Though I was relieved by the warmth of the pack house, I couldn't help but head out onto the balcony. I slid the thick glass door aside and caught my breath as I looked out. It looked like I was just in the forest, nothing but greenery and snow and a distant lake. It was like the ultimate getaway from my life in the city.

"Enjoying the view?" Lucien's voice asked from behind me and I turned to find him dressed in a black shirt and some jeans.

"Are you kidding? I literally thought you had dragged me into the middle of nowhere and then there's this..." I trailed off and he chuckled as he made his way towards me.

"A lot of our pack members live in the town nearby and I took the long way to show you the other side but, if you look closely, you'll find a few cabins hidden along the slope - a lot of my pack live around here and the others are spread throughout the place," he said as we walked over to the edge of the balcony. He pointed over to a patch of greenery just barely out of place and I squinted my eyes.

"That's a hidden cabin it's where Xander lives," he said and I realized that the patch was what made up the roof - so I turned around and looked up. I found that there was bits of green, vines creeping up throughout the sides of the house, and leaves stuck out from the rood.

"You guys sure know how to hide," I muttered and he laughed.

"We're called the Umbra pack for a reason," he commented and I raised an eyebrow.

"What does Umbra even mean?" I asked, actually unsure.

"It's the shadow on the moon- if I wanted to sound cool, it's the dark side of the moon-"

"Please don't go all Mulan on me," I said with a smirk and Lucien merely smiled.

"Well, that's what an umbra is, we're hidden from most packs for good reason. Few packs know our location," he said and I decided to just nod. "Anyways... your room is ready, you can head out if you'd like or you can go ahead and sleep." I stretched my arms out.

"Lead the way," I said. I had zero complaints right now, especially since I'd basically be on a vacation - although I do want to continue working... I'd have to discuss that later - I guess.

I followed Lucien as he led me down a flight of stairs and I simply kept staring at the house. Every step I took made me love the place. It was very simple but modern. There were apparently five floors and some extended further back into the mountain - indeed concealing most of its parts. I was just wondering who the hell built this place - because there isn't a single bit of road here - unless there is and I'm being ignorant. Lucien eventually brought me into a small hallway and opened a door to the right, which opened to a large and spacious room. It was half concealed into the hillside, but also held quite a view with large glass windows that showed off the forest. I finally peeled off the thick jacket I was wearing - I was beginning to sweat from the heat that radiated off the house. The floor was finely polished wood with a mix of plush carpets. Sleek black bookshelves were filled with books and glass frames of photographs. The room smelled of vanilla and a small modernist fireplace was lit by the door.

A large glass panel separated one half of the room from the other. The first half had bookshelves, some kind of leather couch covered in fluffy blankets and what looked to be a fur cover - though it had that glint that said it was fake - not that I would judge. Wolves were known to hunt after all. There was a black coffee table with a large glass surface and a single vase with a white and violet orchid decorating it. A TV was installed against the walls just above the fireplace and that was basically all that the first half was made of...

I walked over to the other side and almost had my jaw drop. All the other half contained was a king-sized bed with nothing but green and white sheets, large pillows, and a black leather bed frame. It sat a top a furry looking grey carpet and was pushed against the glass panel so that it faced the windows. Two large and simple lamps stood by each side, there were no nightstands but I spotted what looked to be a movable tray that was made of black and silver - it honestly looked like it belonged to a hotel. The walls were wooden with a nice mix of white and a hole-in-the-wall kind of arch led into a spacious hall that led into a well-concealed bathroom that had its own closet built in. There was nothing much in the closet- or rather closets- so I thought for sure that the room was mine - until I slid a drawer open.

I walked out and spotted Lucien with his arms folded over his chest.

"Like it?"

"Lucien. Be honest with me," I said, hoping to the goddess that I would growl - but of course that would never happen.

"What?" He asked a bemused grin immediately gracing his damned god-like face.

"Okay... Is this my room or yours?"

He smirked. He fücking smirked.

"It's both."

Chapter 6

"Just... try," My mom said, nudging me along and I bit my bottom lip as I hunched over, my fingers touching damp soil. I closed my eyes.

Please... please... I begged inside my head. But nothing happened. Zaina smiled as she got in front of me, she bent down and touched the ground - her bones began to crack and shift... Fur sprouted along her body until she had become a wolf. I got up from my position.

"Auden?" My mom called and I turned around and sighed.

"I can't."

"But you haven't even-"

"I can't! How many times do I have to tell you that?!" I screamed before seeing a scared look grace my mom's face- "Mom- I'm sorry I-"

I opened my eyes and groaned as I rubbed them. I had taken a 'nap' on the couch and I was having one of those moments where my eyes didn't know whether or not to go completely to bed or to stay up now that they were open. But apparently my nap had become a whole night's sleep and my eyes didn't know if they were tired from sleeping or tired in general. I looked around, the windows revealed to me that it was morning, surprising me. I stretched out my arms and stood from the couch before making my way into the bathroom on the other side.

The bath was simple, with black tiles all over it and some wooden embellishments. It honestly looked like a sauna. I looked at my reflection in the widespread mirror that basically took up one entire wall of the bathroom. My brown eyes looked pretty tired to me, my hair looked like a bird's nest and as I pulled it out of its shïtty ponytail, I almost screamed murder - it had tangled up in it and pissed me off. I stripped down and turned on the shower - not caring about what I would choose to wear after.

As I started to wash my hair, I realized exactly that Lucien's scent of cinnamon and apples came from this kind of shower set he had and considering that I actually did enjoy that smell, I let myself bathe in it. Washing my hair and body with the set and grinning as I hopped out clean and refreshed. I wrapped a towel around my body and picked up my clothes, folding them up in my hands before I padded my way out and headed for his closet. I opened one of the drawers and picked up one of his shirts, a plain crimson colored v-neck, and pulled it on. I searched through the rest of his drawers and did my best to look for something to wear underneath it - but alas - I found nothing. Unless I wanted to put his underwear on - and to be honest - I would - but we just weren't that close yet.

But feeling a little bit exposed down there, I searched the other drawers and opened up the cabinets until I sniffed him in the air. I turned around and found Lucien staring at me, his eyes looking from my legs up to my face.

"What?" I asked and he shook his head.

"Breakfast's ready," he said and I nodded.

"Okay, I'll be there in a sec." I continued to shuffle through the cabinets, coming up empty-handed - mostly because they were actually empty.

"What are you looking for?"

"Underwear," I replied simply before finally opening a bottom drawer and spotting loose boxers, "Do you wear these?" I asked and he paused.

"Not often-"

"Close enough," I said as I took a pair of grey ones with patterned lines, I held them up to my body and looked at him. "Turn." Lucien chuckled in response as he turned around and I slipped into the boxers, glad that they fit me like a pair of shorts. They were also kind of decent in length - so that was a relief.

"Good?"

"Good." I answered as he turned around and I ran my hand through my wet hair, running the towel through it this time. I followed him out the door and smiled as I spotted the propped up table of food. The table was one of those foldable ones and had two chairs on them. There were waffles, an assortment of toppings and syrup, and a pitcher of water along with another of orange juice.

"Did you make this while I was in the shower?" I asked and Lucien nodded. "Well, thanks," I said, not knowing what else to say as I took my seat. Lucien did the same and I poured some syrup into my waffles, adding some butter and a handful of blueberries.

"I wanted to talk to you about something," he said as he ate and I spied on his waffles, which were covered in a buttload of syrup and cream.

"Mmhmm..." I trailed off as I ate a forkful, I softly moaned at the taste of fresh waffles, earning a hint of a smile from Lucien.

"Xander told me you were human- and yesterday's 'ride' to the pack house seemed to confirm it. I wanted to hear if you had an explanation-"

"Do I need one?" I asked and he stared at me before I poured myself a glass of orange juice and drank from it.

"I do want to know more, considering you're my mate and all," he said simply.

"From what I know, I'm a full-bred werewolf. I can do just about everything other than shift - which makes me more like a special human rather than a werewolf," I said with a shrug, as I sliced into my waffle. Just as he was about to speak, a knock on the door stole his attention. Lucien wiped his mouth with a napkin before he stood up and walked over to the door and opened it.

In walked a girl with short curly black hair and bangs, she had painted red lips against a deep brown complexion, she wore a white shirt tucked into a pair of black flowy overalls - she looked like she was a vintage movie star. She also walked in with a bunch of bags- shopping bags.

"Okay, so I've gotten a couple dresses to spare and I asked Xander what size she looked like and he said to go with medium just in a case- I brought some loose pants and- I guess-" She spoke with a very... British accent. And then she froze- looking at me and then at Lucien.

"Oh, wow. You are so much prettier than Xander credits you for," she said as she dropped all the bags and walked over to me. She held her hand out and I quickly stood to shake it, she grasped my hand tightly and smiled at me.

"Katherine, Lucien's ever-so-underestimated Beta," she introduced and I smiled.

"Auden."

"Beautiful name, beautiful girl, tall height... Lucien you lucked the hell out of the mating pool," she said giddily before looking at me from head to toe. "But getting stuck with Lucien's wardrobe is an absolute pity for such a pretty woman."

"Noted, Katherine," Lucien said in a somewhat irritated tone. Katherine simply laughed before turning to me.

"Well, we girls gotta stick together- and as Beta, I think it'd be good for you to know that I live just on the opposite hall, all you need to do is walk out go down and then turn a left - Desmond and I have this agreement to have all guests take off their shoes before they enter our apartment."

"You have an apartment- in here?" I asked and she smiled.

"My mate and I need our privacy- and I'm not down for breakfast sëx where Lana or even Lucien can see."

"Desmond?"

"He's my husband and mate, he's the pack doctor-"

"I thought most Beta's-"

"Were men? I know right? Unfortunately, Desmond lacks the... social skills- but it is one of the things I love about him."

"Katherine-" She turned to Lucien and laughed.

"Oh, right, you wanted me out of here. Anyways- nice to meet you and I'll see you around - hopefully you enjoy the clothes - I know not everybody's into my style so I picked a... variety." She turned to Lucien and laughed. Man do I crave that mind-link. I thought to myself.

"Okay, bye bye for me, Desmond's linking the fück out of my brain," she said before she hit Lucien hard on the shoulder before walking out and closing the door behind her.

"Do you want to-" I got up and made my way towards him.

"Lucien, shut up," I said, as placed a hand on his chest, feeling the warmth radiate off his skin. "Listen, I'm not down for any exclusion - I know how that feels and I know you might not mean it- but take me into your pack." I felt a rumble come from is chest before he growled possessively.

"Are you sure?" He asked in a low voice and I nodded.

"The link with Carmine isn't much use all the way in Vancouver- and I've already tried running."

"I will never leave your head," he said and I smirked.

"It's a mind-link not a mate bond- we're not there yet, Alpha Lucien," I teased and Lucien wrapped his arms around my waist.

"I never thought I'd move this fast with my mate," he said and I laughed softly.

"Hm... well, you do have a human mate," I said and Lucien chuckled.

"I'll have to call your sister-" I ran my hands down his body, tracing his abdomen and earning a low groan. It made my stomach cave, hearing him do it against me.

"Or we could do it without her."

"She's your Alpha." I placed my hands underneath his shirt and he let out a low moan, I chuckled in his ear.

"Shame, I thought you were," I said low into his ear, before I traced the area around his waist.

"The only... reason I'm... not... stopping you-"

"Is because I'm your mate and trust me, this feeling is mutual... but since I'm not in 'tune' with my werewolf- it's a lot easier for me to control it." Lucien stepped forward before his hands traced my waist and lifted me up, my legs instantly wrapped around his lower torso.

"Do you rescind your link to the Carmine Pack?" He asked just as he lay me on the bed. "Then repeat after me..." He had his hand on my thigh and I resisted the urge to move.

"Oh...," I breathed out and I barely even felt anything else as he traced his hands along my body.

"I, Auden Breaux..."

"I, Auden... Breaux," I arched my back as he placed his hands on my hips.

"Renounce the Carmine Pack," he said as he lifted himself from me, placing his hands on either side of my face.

"Oh... Okay..." I looked into his eyes and he stared expectantly at them. "I... Auden Breaux, renounce the Carmine Pack."

Maybe it was because I hadn't seen my pack in a long time - or I was used to not being with them... But- I felt nothing as it-

"Then... I, Lucien de Martel-" I paused. Whoa.

"Hold on, your last name is de Martel?" I asked, gawking.

"Sorry, that was a little bit too cool for me not to comment on, please, go on," I said and he chuckled.

"I, Lucien de Martel, Alpha of the Umbra Pack, welcome you, Auden Breaux, as my mate and as the newest addition to my pack."

Now that I felt.

Chapter 7

<hr>

Lucien who's this? A voice asked in my head.

Bailey, this is our new Luna- my mate.

Nice to meet you Luna-

Auden. I answered and I looked up at Lucien.

Nice to meet you, I'm Bailey - not really much in this pack but I'm a good cook! I laughed.

Nice to meet you.

"So I take it, you've joined us," Lucien said with a smile as I lifted myself up, propping my body up on my elbows.

"It has been a long long time since I've linked with someone other than my family..." I said with a smile. I pressed a kiss on his cheek before I stood up.

"That's it?" He asked as I took my seat back.

"Did you want more?" I asked and he shrugged before he wrapped his arms around me- I turned to retort and he placed his lips against mine- just grazing it briefly before pulling away. He chuckled in response as he made his way out the door.

"And where are you going?" I asked.

Work.

And what about me? He turned.

Come.

I smiled before I picked up the last bit of my waffle and followed him out.

I watched as Lucien took a seat in his chair. I sat across him on a leather armchair and he opened up his drawer before he fished out a few papers. He handed them to me.

"These are a list of businesses we run in the main city, the next folder has some stuff in the nearby village. Pick one you're interested in and I'll give you a workload."

"...How many businesses does Umbra run?"

"To keep this place running and keep our pack fed - about four main ones - though we get some money for side-jobs and 'affiliations'..."

"What do you mean by affiliations?" I asked.

"We work with two other packs in the U.S.," he said, not clearing anything up for me.

"What packs?"

"Well, I guess one pack and one... strange little organization, but that's not something you should worry about just yet - so far we run back-end jobs and less... violent dealings."

"Okay, my mind is going wild, are you guys like the mafia or something?" Lucien laughed.

"Not us, but the other guys we work with may be."

"...Can you stop with the vague answers?"

"I don't think I can," he said with a smile and I glared at him.

"Do you guys run a veterinary clinic?" I asked and he thought for a moment.

"No, but I think Katherine can help you with that - speaking of Katherine... she's asking if you needed help setting up your phone, says she can do it for you no problem," Lucien said and I nodded.

"That'd help."

"Also, your bag- Freya will bring it over tomorrow. You didn't have to leave it."

"Didn't know where else to put it - I was kind of getting over the fact that I needed to ride my mate's back to get to the secret pack house," I said and Lucien smirked before he turned on his computer and began to, at least, look like he was working.

"Actually, Lucien, if you aren't busy, I wanted to know more about what happened in New York... with Lana and that guy that I, um-"

"The guy you killed?" He completed for me and I nodded.

"Yeah, I'd actually like that cleared up before I do any kind of work... you know, just so that I know what exactly I'm getting into."

"You're already in," Lucien tried to correct and I smiled.

"Right, that I'm already in." I almost forgot. I added with the mind-link and he smiled.

"Lana and I, as with most of my family are early shifters, which makes us great warriors to train as children... There's a kind of strength that stays with us from the moment we first shift - and it never really fades away. Lana's twelve - but she shifted three years ago. I shifted when I turned ten- our bones constantly break and shift. We're liable to deformation and we constantly face pain until the moment we mature, which is in four years for Lana. During these years - she'll have a large bounty on her head."

"And you thought bringing her out in New York was a good idea?" I asked and Lucien sighed.

"She hasn't left our territory since she turned, everywhere she went, she was stuck by my side- or Xander's- I left her in his care for whenever she would leave for school. I brought her into a stupidly expensive private school so that he could keep an eye on her. The rest of my pack do the same - she's always always with someone. I let Xander close to her because he and I have the highest bond to her- losing her would make us both go crazy."

"Smart move..." I commented and Lucien smiled.

"Xander was with her that night - she asked him for a cup of hot chocolate while she went ice skating... I've asked her what happened and she said her skates were still on when she was taken- before Xander went to your apartment, I asked him to check on the apartment you found her in - and the car she was probably moved in - one shoe in the car - the other at the edge of the parking lot. I asked your sister for any footage she had, come here," he said and I did, getting up and sitting on his arm rest as he loaded up the footage on his computer.

He opened up his e-mail - which was fairly empty - save for about three new messages - on of which had my sister's name - Zaina Breaux. Lucien opened it up and she had attached fairly small video files. He opened them revealing three videos, one of the parking lot, the elevator, and then the hallway. The videos rolled quickly, revealing the man coming through and it was only in the elevator that Lana began to shift. You could see her kicking and fighting to get out of his grasp as her legs began to shift, I watched as he made a run for the apartment. Like he knew that it was empty.

Knew? What the fuck? How could he possibly-

I replayed the videos again to make sure. The moment Lana would start shifting, the man stepped off the elevator and made his way past my room and immediately opened the door to the apartment.

It was left unlocked.

I replayed that moment again, watching if he had a keycard or anything- and despite the fact that I know there's at least one camera facing those doors - my sister hadn't sent any video files. But not once did I notice a single movement that would've indicated him picking his keycard from his pockets - and there was no way he was holding one with the way he was using his hands to secure his hold on Lana. I felt my heart pound in my chest. Keys to the apartments on my floor were only accessible to me and Zaina upon request - a lot of the apartments there weren't ready yet - and I was always there to assist any agent that wanted to give a tour or check it out... But Zaina had the extra set of keys - and I needed to know if she had been there without telling me.

"Lucien, I'm gonna need your phone."

I left Zaina a message with Lucien's approval. But that was three days ago. With any luck, I'd be able to have Lucien speak with her - because I wasn't about to. Not wanting to think anymore about that man - my apartment - and all that stuff - I mind-linked Katherine into meeting me about work. Hopefully working as a vet again.

"Okay, so most of the time Desmond works and manages over here, but I'm sure he wouldn't mind taking in a new experienced colleague," she told me as she drove into a small village.

"Why don't you guys live here?" I asked, admiring the snow topped houses and Katherine grinned.

"I like living in the pack house - it gives me a sense of calm and serenity not having any kind of sound that comes from some kind of machine - and not a single view of some kind of modern machine.

Sure - the pack house itself is pretty updated - but if you decide to take a step into our apartment - not a single television screen - and our phones are mainly on silent... Sorry, I tend to ramble," she said and I laughed.

"Well, I'm finally talking to someone other than Lucien after three days - meanwhile Lana asks me to play house with her and Lucien and Xander, can you imagine the amount of embarrassing moments I have to shame the two of those people with? I didn't even think twelve year olds were still into dress-up."

"Well, Lana thinks it's cool to pretend- you know, that they're just a normal family."

"There's a difference between normal and human," I said before playing with my fingers.

"True, but we can all hope and in cases like Lana and Lucien's, that kind of hope can only yield better people," Katherine replied before she stopped and parked at what looked to be the outskirts of the big city. "I'm gonna go grab a coffee, you'll find the clinic down this road to the right - literally just by the road - we make it so that people can spot us easily... Want anything?"

"An Americano?" Katherine grinned as she got out of her car and I sighed as I tugged the coat I had on a little harder. I shoved my hands into my pockets and sighed as I got out, closing the door behind me. I walked down the road as Katherine instructed, walked past a small home with a shop for a porch and then, behind a small set of trees, I found the clinic. I pushed the glass door open and stomped my feet on the ground to get rid of the snow.

As I took off my coat, I looked around. The place was brightly lit with pale blue walls and small plants in beautiful white pots. The front desk was simple, rounded and smooth with a glass cover on a white desk. The receptionist him/herself wasn't present, the room smelled of peppermint potpourri oil and I spotted a bright orange potpourri boiler on the shelves.

"Too overbearing?" A man asked and I turned to find a young man with tanned skin, he smiled at me. He had short black hair that had been slicked back on top,

"Nice to finally meet the Luna everyone's buzzed about."

"Funny, I don't see many others that buzz - but I hear them," I said and he grinned as he opened his arms and I gave him a hug.

"My name is Desmond," he said as he pulled away, "Although, I'm afraid Katherine might have already told you all about me." I laughed.

"I think I know more about your apartment than you, though I've heard you're the pack doctor."

"Indeed I am, and I run a clinic for the fun of it, come, meet the little ones- oh and feel free to hang your coat by the door- no one should come steal it - and if that happens, Katherine's willing to kill anyone that steals a gift."

"Gift?"

"Honey, once Katherine heard from Lucien about the new girl - she went on a spree for a whole two days, consider your outfits some well-thought out gifts from a girl that knows her shit. Anyways, down to see some kittens, hamsters? Dogs?"

"I'd love to," I said with a smile, following him into a hallway. I heard the sound of barking and the familiar scent of animals- funny how that smell could sometimes revolt you and sometimes just make you anticipate cute little faces.

We entered and I spotted a large - and might I add spacious - set of cages for pets that needed isolated care, a pen full excited little puppies, another pen nearby of kittens and cats, some larger cases for other animals - snakes and the like - and the amount of toys and food lying around was just incredible. I knelt down in front of the pen and placed my hand atop a little brown dog - probably a chow-chow mix, who licked my hand excitedly and nibbled on my sleeves.

"That one's Gus-Gus, Katherine named him after the Cinderella character, apparently chubby like him," Desmond said just as I heard a door open. Katherine walked in with a smile and a carrier box of coffee.

"I got Auden an Americano, myself a plain brewed coffee and you, my darling," she said as she walked up to Desmond and kissed him briefly on the lips, "Your favorite cup of tea."

"Always more British than you are," he said, grinning as he picked up his cup.

"With tea, yes, I'm surprised you haven't picked up the accent yet," she said, winking at him before handing over my coffee. Katherine's eyes widened upon seeing Gus-Gus. "Hello... Aw, how've you been baby boy?" I giggled as I stood and blew into my coffee before sipping it, savoring the bitterness.

"Do you have anything I can do for the day?" I asked Desmond and he nodded.

"Well, we have a small dog that's got this massive hernia - couldn't get surgery until she was much healthier. But she should be ready today. Think you can handle that for me?"

"Easy."

"Great, I'll observe you, help you out with equipment where's what, how some stuff you might not know works, and we'll be right on."

I was in the middle of completing the surgery when the door to the room open. Desmond chuckled and looked over at Lucien.

"Do we have a promising vet on the way?" Lucien asked and Desmond nodded.

"She's quick, accurate, and efficient. I'd say we've got a great one coming - though most of our work consists on check-ups, vaccines, and so on. I would've loved to have worked on that, but considering I'm out of practice - she'd probably be better at handling this stuff."

"Where's Katherine?" Lucien asked and Desmond chuckled.

"You know she doesn't like seeing surgery. She's all for the fighting but not standard medical procedure."

"Really?" I asked as I finished trimming excess skin and beginning to stitch the skin together.

"Finished most of your duties, Alpha?" Desmond asked and Lucien nudged him with his shoulder.

"Xander's busy at school and my other Delta's too busy making the rest of the pack do a run of the mountains before they train. Katherine won't let me touch the other business deals and my mate is doing work - I'm feeling all sorts of useless these days." I laughed as I finished, cutting the bit of the stitch and carefully wiping down the area to make sure the little dog was clean.

"Cone?" I asked and Desmond smiled.

"I can go get one and put it on the little guy. I'll also take care of the rest, I wouldn't want to keep an Alpha waiting."

"Thanks," I said with a smile before I went over to the sink, quickly washing off and sterilizing my tools before I slipped my gloves off, throwing them in a medical waste bin.

I took off my scrub and folded it neatly before putting it into the laundry basket that Desmond had told me about.

"Did you get an answer from my sister?" I asked and Lucien sighed.

"No, but I got a message from your dad," he said and I raised an eyebrow.

"Really?" Lucien nodded and I shook my head as we headed out to reception. I pulled on my coat and took a breath. "What'd he say?"

"He said he'd be here by this afternoon."

"What?" I fished out my phone and sighed in frustration.

"Auden-"

"Lucien... it's one in the afternoon." I was met with silence and I stared into Lucien's eyes.

Lucien... where is my dad? He folded his arms over his chest.

He's in his hotel room.

Fuck.

Chapter 8

"**W**hen was the last time you met him?" Lucien asked as he drove us into the city. Katherine and Desmond stayed over at the clinic saying that they had a few other things to settle for business.

"Not too long ago - almost a month - I guess... We don't talk much," I said and Lucien glanced over at me as he drove.

"Why not?"

"Lucien, an Alpha's daughter isn't gonna become an Omega- but I might as well have been. It's not like I was gonna let my parents live with that sort of shame so before that kind of shït could've gotten any worse... I left."

"But how does your dad feel?"

"I don't know," I answered simply before I lay back in my seat. "How'd you get into contact with my dad anyways?"

"Auden, he contacted me, not the other way around."

I sniffed out my dad the moment we walked towards the hotel. He smelled of Carmine and my sister's signature honey-scented perfume that had only slightly grazed his side. And yes, I could still smell all that - despite my human appearance. Lucien followed close behind me as I made my way to the piano bar, where I knew my dad would probably be drinking from his favorite kind of whiskey. And I was right.

He sat by the windows sipping a glass of whiskey with a ball of ice in the glass. I didn't bother looking over at Lucien or greeting my dad - I took a seat across him.

"Dad."

"Auden." My dad got up, his eyes were on Lucien's as he extended his hand. "Alpha Lucien."

"Dante, how was the flight?" Lucien said as he shook my dad's hand, he then took the seat next to mine.

"A little bumpy, but nothing unusual," my dad replied, taking his own seat. "Do you guys want anything?"

"No. We're fine," I answered before Lucien could say anything. "Why are you here?"

"I came to check on you-"

"You haven't checked on me since fall break of my freshman year at high school."

"Auden, darling, you know that I would've- but I had to take care of things with your sister-"

"Zaina went to school ten minutes away from my high school and our pack was smack in between the two," I breathed a sigh. "Anyways, we wanted to talk about the apartment attack, not me."

"You're my daughter."

"Really? I almost forgot," I said before I waved a waitress over, her eyes skimmed down Lucien before she even got to me. "Earl Grey tea, two sugars, and milk. Thanks." She nodded her head, her eyes glazing over Lucien and perhaps even more disgustingly so - my dad - before she left.

"Your co-workers were worried. We had to deal with calls all week," my dad said and leaned back in my chair.

"That's expected. I mentored most of the vets and dealt with some heavy-handed cases, but it's nothing that they couldn't handle," I said as the waitress returned, lingering a little too long as she placed my cup of tea in front of me.

"Ellis was asking about you."

Who's Ellis? Lucien immediately asked and I glared at him.

"No one."

"I see you've severed your ties with Carmine."

"Took me long enough, right?" I countered. "Listen, if you don't have any information about the night of the attack, why are you here?"

"I told you, I came to check on you, why is that so hard to believe?" He countered and I balled my right hand into a fist, earning a look of concern from Lucien as he reached over at traced a circle at my wrist.

"Okay, stop avoiding my questions, dad. I only contacted Zaina because I wanted to know how the hell that kidnapping fück that took Lucien's sister knew that the apartment beside mine was empty." My dad picked up his glass, swirling the liquid around it before he drank from it. I watched him with scrutinizing eyes.

"Zaina said that there was a series of people visiting a few weeks before the... event happened."

"There always are. I want to know how he opened the door knowing it'd be empty. One door and it would've been my apartment that he'd opened." My dad released a breath before he turned and picked up a brown leather bag and sifted through it. He then produced a fairly heavy-looking folder.

"These are all I can pick up from Zaina's office-"

"What- did she lock you out of-"

"I... also have a luggage bag with your things- I took as much as I could."

"Dad. What does Zaina know?" My dad's lips fell into a flat line and I found Lucien taking my hand and squeezing it reassuringly. I'm not sure if it was the mate bond, but I felt... calmer.

"I plan on returning to Carmine this evening, I just wanted to make sure you were alright. Your mom should've left you a few other things in the luggage bag - it's currently at the receptionist's desk," he said - a bit too fast for my liking.

"Dad. I asked you a question."

"It is no longer any of your concern," he said and I rolled my eyes.

"Cut the bullshït dad, If you're not gonna talk to me like I'm your daughter or at least some kind of ex-pack member - then talk to me like an old business partner because to be honest none of the things that we've established would've existed had I not been the one to start it all," I said, breathing deeply as I tried to regain my composure.

"There are things that I can say that I've yet to confirm. And as Zaina takes hold of Carmine, it becomes a bit harder to... get a hold of things. I will contact you or your new Alpha when I have more information," my dad answered simply and I felt some small bit of me relax.

"Thank you," I said and my dad shrugged before offering me a hint of a smile.

"All your life, I thought it was my fault that you weren't able to shift - my failure for looking after your sister more than you because she was my heir... But I'm glad you're able to help others in need."

"It's my job to help animals- and what could an Alpha do about his non-werewolf daughter? Bad enough that the pack saw you nurture and train me - no matter which of us you prioritized - I'm not sure which was worse, staying where I knew I wouldn't belong or trying to join those that think we don't exist."

"Um, excuse me, would any of you gentlemen want anything to drink?"

I turned my head to face the waitress that had been eyeballing both my- Lucien and my dad. My dad chuckled but before he could say anything I decided to speak.

"Sorry, we're having a serious conversation. If they want anything I'll call, darling," I said with a plastic smile.

"But I'm sure they'd at least have a glass of water-"

"Do you have any right now?" I asked, raising my eyebrows at her.

"I can go get them-"

"Aren't you supposed to serve them as soon as we get here?" I asked, folding my arms atop of each other. She stared at me and I returned it.

"Do you have a staring problem?" I asked, she shifted her weight between her legs.

"Sorry, um, do you guys still want water?"

"No." She froze before she offered a polite smile.

"Excuse me." I watched her turn and leave, the moment she caught the eye of her co-worker and opened her mouth, I rolled my eyes and averted my gaze.

"I'm guessing this conversation is over," Lucien said as he fished out his wallet and took out a set of bills and set them down on the table. "Excuse us."

My dad had to excuse himself, he said that he had a headache- although I was sure he only wanted to leave because he felt uncom- fortable. My dad was a strict Alpha - and I don't know how exactly he managed to keep a straight face when he found out I couldn't shift. But I'm glad that he didn't like to push questions. My only questions now were for my sister. It was like she became a whole different person - and maybe it's because I only saw her twice a year or something like that... but... I didn't think she was any different util my mate finally found me.

Which honestly begged the question.

What the hell does Zaina have to do with any of the events that transpired in New York? At this point... I doubt the 'attack' on Lucien's sister happened beside my apartment by coincidence. Like I said, I don't exactly believe that fate had a plan - because I don't see how an Alpha having a human daughter could be a part of any wolf goddess' plan. And I'm hardly the worst-case scenario for this kind of goddess' thing.

The morning after, I went onto the balcony of the pack house.

"You okay?" Lucien asked and I turned around, he walked close to me but not... close enough to let me feel the warmth off his body. So I stepped forward. I might as well savor the relief that this connection thing had to offer. Lucien stood stiffly as I lay my head on the crook of his neck.

"Do you wanna rest?" He asked and I nodded.

We made our way down to the room and as Lucien stepped forward to open it - as he had always left it unlocked - we heard footsteps. Confused, I watched as Lucien stepped back.

"Maybe we should-"

"Lucien, who the fück-"

The footsteps hurriedly made their way somewhere and I heard something hit the bed. I raised my eyebrows at him and walked to the door and opened it.

"Auden I don't think-"

"Lucien!" A woman yelped and I glowered in her direction. The woman wore a short black dress that was cut way too low to be decent and her hair was long, black, and curled.

I'm not gonna lie, she was pretty, but who the hell-

"I've missed you! Who's this?" She asked and Lucien cleared his throat.

"This is-"

"Oh, I don't care. I wanted to know when you'd be free for another meeting, papa wants to finalize a few things and I'd love to give you a private tour of our new hotel-"

"Sheila-"

"Sorry, did I interrupt you?" Lucien breathed a sigh, but before he could open his mouth, I tilted my head, smiled at the little talkative parrot in front of me, and turned on my heel, slamming the door behind me.

Auden- she's- Lucien began but I blocked him out of my head as I walked out the door.

I was not gonna be a part of some kind of shïtty love triangle.

Chapter 9

I made my way upstairs to the top floor. Katherine had just walked in with Desmond and was in the middle of taking off their snow boots when she spoke.

"Oh my goodness, Auden, you would not believe-" Katherine froze before she looked at me in a somewhat understanding way. "Oh dear, the demon's snuck her way into the lair."

"What demon?" Desmond asked as he put away their boots. "... Oh. Auden, she's really not-"

"I don't particularly care. It's not like Lucien's the only man I've had in my life either," I said with a smile. "I'm a particularly easy woman to understand. I don't like drama of any kind so I left. No biggie. Worst comes to worst, I can go out to town and find myself a good lay-"

"That's not gonna happen," Lucien's voice said from behind me and I turned around, folding my arms over my chest.

"You sure? I wouldn't wanna get in between you and Miss Pussycat," I said laughing, Katherine glanced over at Lucien before she made her way towards me and took my arm.

"That thing is absolutely disgusting," she hissed, looking over at Lucien. "Lucien took wooed the little bïtch because he thought he would gain a business partner and now we're stuck with a flea that actually knows where we are because her father's an influential man." Lucien rolled his eyes and I laughed.

"Well, business is business," I said, winking at Katherine who looked at me with surprise before she broke into laughter.

"You're a surprisingly un-jealous woman. I might've murdered the girl if I'd been in your position," Katherine commented and I rolled my eyes.

"Rather than jealous, I'm more pissed off at her attitude and I don't fight for things half-ässed-ly, no offense Lucien, we're not exactly 'there' yet relationship-wise," I said, folding my arms over my chest. "Besides, it's not like at twenty-something I expected Lucien to be some kind of virgin. I'm not a saint and I don't expect my mate to save himself for me either - hell, I didn't even expect a mate at all." Katherine and Desmond laughed, while Lucien remained silent.

"Back onto the topic, where on Earth did you send the wench?" Katherine asked Lucien, breaking his silence.

"She's on her way home. Her dad called and she had to leave."

"Great, because I was about to take a nap before little miss rude made her magical appearance," I said, stretching my arms out. "I'll see you guys later," I told Katherine and Desmond who nodded as I walked away. Lucien immediately began following behind me and I sighed in relief as I found myself inside a now-empty bedroom.

For the past few days, I had slept on the left side of the bed and Lucien slept on the other. After all, the bed was king-sized, allowing us more space than usual and sleeping on the same bed felt more like sleeping on two beds that were pushed together. I went into the closet to change before Lucien came in.

"Do you have a problem with me, Alpha?" I asked, as I looked through the clothes.

"You didn't let me explain things about Sheila," he said and I turned to glance at him.

"Lucien, I don't know what kind of relationships you've been in before but I don't normally discuss peoples' ex-bed warmers unless I catch them together 'in action'." I smiled as I picked out a simple silken black dress with a lace trim.

"I just wanted to make things clear, I don't plan on letting her stay. She's not anyone to concern yourself with, supposing you're concerned at all." I sighed as I carried the dress in my hands and made my way towards him. I placed a hand on the bottom of his jaw, feeling the warmth tingle from my finger tips until it sent shivers down my spine.

"Feel that?"

Lucien released a low growl in response and I smiled as I pressed myself against his body. I let the dress fall from my hand as I placed my hands at the side of his neck, trailing it down his arms, leaving goosebumps against his skin. His hands slowly snaked their way around my waist before they settled on the small of my back.

"You asked me something in the parking lot before, Lucien. I think you said, 'What makes you think I can't make you kiss me anytime I want'," I said in a low voice, leaning in to whisper in his ear. "Two can play at that game, Alpha."

Lucien groaned as I placed my hands on his chest, my left hand climbed up to his shoulder, my right went down, tracing his chest, his abdomen, before I lifted his shirt, my fingertips tracing every bit of bare carved skin. I bit my bottom lip as he released a subtle moan and I placed a soft kiss on his chin.

"How much would you like to feel today, Alpha?" I asked, smirking as I felt his chest rumble from a growl. "If you don't say anything, I might just go a little crazy..." I smirked and lowered myself kissing his neck.

"Auden, Lana's going to come home from-"

"Tell me, Lucien, have you ever had a dominant woman?" I asked as I kissed slipped both my hands under his shirt and lifted it. Lucien released a growl - an actual loud growl as I began kissing his side and the moving towards his stomach. He stepped back and I laughed as I stood up and pushed him against a wall.

How long has it actually been since I've gotten laid? I wondered before looking at Lucien, our eyes met and I smiled as I saw him mirror the same lust I had in my eyes...

"Lucien!" Someone yelled from outside. Lucien and I stared at each other and I resisted the urge to laugh. It was Lana.

"Lana, they might be busy," I heard Xander say and I covered my mouth to muffle my giggles.

"No, no, we'll be right out," I said loudly as I pulled Lucien's shirt back down. Lucien seemed to be dumbstruck by my actions as he held my hands to stop me.

Your sister's calling, Alpha. I mind-linked and he, quite adorably, lifted my right hand, kissed my palm and whined into it, his warm breath seeping into my skin. Lucien then stood straight and cleared his throat before turning.

A little more teasing wouldn't hurt, right? I asked myself before I hastily walked before him and just before we reached the door, I stepped in front of him and planted a kiss on his lips. Lucien growled into my mouth as I ran my hands through his hair.

You're driving me insane. I laughed before pulling away and winked at him.

"Hey Lana, how was school?" I asked, walking out and greeting her with a smile.

"It was fine, Xander got in trouble today," Lana tattled and Xander growled in response, making her laugh. Lucien cleared his throat behind me and I turned my head and grinned at him. Xander looked between the two of us and sighed.

"What happened at school?" I asked, facing Xander.

"Just a bit of trouble with some guys," Xander said with a shrug and I folded my arms over my chest.

"About what?"

"Xander quit basketball two weeks ago in favor of handling more trainees in the pack. Unfortunately, werewolves don't make up a majority in their school and they can't possibly know what reason Xander would have for quitting," Lucien explained and I sighed.

"Did you like playing?" I asked and Xander shrugged.

"I don't like it when Xander hangs out with the team, they're really really mean," Lana said before he could even respond and I smiled. So that's why.

Yeah. Xander replied, smiling at Lana before kneeling before her.

"Wanna go grab ice cream? I bought some yesterday and put it in the fridge," he said and she tilted her head.

"What flavor?" Xander rolled his eyes.

"Guess."

"Rocky road?" Xander smiled at Lana's response.

"And?"

"Cookie dough?!" She exclaimed before she squealed. "Does everyone else want ice cream?" She asked turning around and looking to Lucien and I.

"I'm in the mood for some kind of vanilla, but I doubt ice cream will fix that." Xander choked and coughed at my response and Lucien cleared his throat, earning a laugh from me as Lana gave me a look of confusion. I turned her around and opened the door.

"Go get some ice cream!" She giggled as I tickled her neck and Xander immediately stood up and followed her, Lucien coughed behind me and I'm guessing it was to catch my attention so I turned around and winked at him as I walked through the door, following Lana.

Problem, Alpha? I asked, turning to look at him as we made our way down to the kitchen area.

It really didn't take Lana long to prepare everything for ice cream. She brought out all the bowls and spoons and only waited for Xander to take the actual tubs out of the fridge. She climbed onto the tall stool and waited as Xander started scooping up ice cream and placing it into her bowl. To be honest, Xander's way of taking care of Lana was honestly adorable. I can't imagine how much patience you had to have and how much, well, control, I guess you'd hold over yourself, to just pretend that your mate was just some kid you had to babysit.

I felt Lucien touch me from behind, his hand resting at the small of my back before slipping beneath my shirt and tracing circles. I bit my bottom lip and chuckled, Xander rolled his eyes at us before he scooped some ice cream for himself and sat by Lana. I moved out of Lucien's reach as I got some ice cream as well. I couldn't help but laugh as Lucien maneuvered his way behind me and basically trapped me in as I served myself some ice cream.

Xander then cleared his throat and I smiled at him as I moved away from Lucien once more. I sat by Lana and grinned, shooting a smug look over at Lucien. We spent most of the hour then just chatting and relaxing with each other. I enjoyed watching Lucien play along with Lana and Xander seemed to enjoy it too. After our little ice cream session, Lucien disappeared into his office to work while Lana and Xander went off to do homework.

I, on the other hand, decided to look at the things that my dad had sent me. So I retreated back into the bedroom. I opened the luggage bag, shuffling through my things and spotting a couple clothes, some books, and soon found a strangely heavy sweater. I unfolded it to unveil a sleek black folder that seemed to be full of documents.

Intrigued, I brought it with me as I sat on the couch. It was filled with document after document of sales, contracts, scheduled meetings, printed e-mails and notes all being addressed to someone or some kind of organization I had never even heard of before. I skimmed through them as quickly as I could until I found some e-mails concerning deals in the apartment building I lived in. At first, there was nothing really strange about the fact that Zaina had accepted some new tenants in the purchase of the flat next to mine - or that she had given information on the number of available apartments on my floor. But the e-mails were dated months ago and not once did Zaina inform me about any kind of deal.

It also wouldn't have been strange had the person not signed such an insanely large amount of money - so much more than our apartments were being sold for.

To make things even creepier, one of my sister's last messages read:

Auden's information will come later - I'll see how much I can gather for you.

I rested my back against the couch as I continued searching through the documents, laying them out on the couch and arranging them by category of e-mails, contracts, notes, etcetera. Not a single time in any of the documents was there a signature other than the letter "I" stamped on with some kind of elaborate design in red ink. Even the e-mails seemed signed off with just an image of that insignia. I couldn't recognize it at all, even when I ran a quick search through my phone for any kind of logo. Though if this was a pack, I highly doubted I would've found it anyways. But the amount of money was just... off. But I just wasn't computer savvy enough to pull off some kind of global scan to figure out any of the exact details. So I decided to try and find more information by reading through the contracts, most of which simply officiated what was being said in the e-mails. The organization in question - probably a pack - would hold ownership over the apartment specifically beside mine. The contract also included a 'trade-off of information between parties' and that 'under no circumstances was information to be withheld from the 'investor'... I felt a shiver run down my spine and my lip quivered.

Something was wrong and my sister was hiding it from me. Some of the documents were dated up to four years ago when we first planned out the building and construction but what really had me unnerved was the fact that the most recent one that my dad had somehow gotten ahold of was a note dated from the day that I came across Lana. Zaina had e-mailed whoever-it-was my schedule for the day which I remember she'd asked for a week earlier. She said that she wanted me to run some important errands in advance - which apparently was a mere run for the paperwork that I threw in the waste-bin when I came across Lucien and she let go of me like nothing.

What the hell was my sister even thinking? We were making good money, she barely had to show up for meetings - what the hell did she want? How would helping anyone that would kidnap another person possibly motivate her actions?

Normally, I would give Zaina the benefit of the doubt - but she saw the footage. She even sent it to us -but she didn't offer any further information were it not for my dad's own meddling. Which means whatever she was doing was at least noticeable - and since Zaina was Alpha - there would be very little chance that she was doing anything innocently. Zaina knew something and despite being my sister - she refused to give me any kind of concern or to let me in.

I'd really like to think I'm being a little harsh - but not trying to contact me or ask about me was a pretty telling. Especially considering she had direct contact with Lucien and could could ask about me if she wanted to. Me asking about her was a whole other story. I don't think there's much to talk about with my sister other than her whining and moaning about not having her mate yet, the amount of money I've calculated into our account, and really her main concern of profit and what I could go get for her. I loved my sister, don't get me wrong - but it's not hard to lose touch when that's all I'd ever heard from her since I left and started working for her instead of with her.

"Auden?" I immediately lifted my eyes and spotted Lucien right in front of me, his eyes concerned. I didn't even notice that he'd gotten in here.

Was I really that lost in my thoughts?

Yeah, you were. Lucien mind-linked and I sighed as I held out my hand.

Well if I can't even hide my thoughts, I must be really lost. He pulled me up as I closed the folder and set it down.

"I need a favor," I said and Lucien raised his eyebrows.

"What kind of favor?"

"Dad left me a ton of information that surprisingly led me to no real clues - you're free to look at it but it doesn't give information about who exactly it is that was plotting to take Lana to the building and who the hell my sister is trying to make a business partner out of. But I'm sure they're connected."

"So you want me to find out who it is?"

"Did I have to ask?" Lucien shook his head.

"I would do anything to protect my sister- and it's not like I haven't been trying to do my own digging either. I'll see what more infor-mation I can get," he said, before taking my hand and squeezing it. "You should probably rest." I can practically feel the weight on your shoulders on mine. He added through the mind-link. I released a deep breath.

"True, let me just go grab-" Lucien then suddenly pulled me close to him and embraced me.

"I don't like feeling uneasy," he told me and I let myself relax into his embrace.

"Well, if this is how you'll make me feel happier then I think I'll forget about my problems in a bit," I said and he chuckled, his chest rumbling as I looked up. Lucien then looked down on me, his eyes making my legs feel a little weak. His left hand moved a little lower before his other hand reached behind neck, caressing the spot where my mark would be with his thumb. I instinctively leaned against his touch.

"Lucien..." I whispered and he released a low growl. I laughed softly before looking straight into his eyes and glancing down at his lips. I bit on my bottom lip before I decided to say what had been on my mind. "Don't you think it's about time you kissed me?"

Chapter 10

I woke up feeling a little too warm - before I realized that Lucien and I actually shared the bed tonight - in close proximity. Not that I minded a little physical touch. Besides, there was nothing sexual about him hugging me at the moment. It was actually kind of adorable. I cuddled into his embrace and turned my head to look out the windows. I'd have to go to work soon.

Just as I turned back to look at Lucien, his eyes fluttered open and he smiled at me.

Morning. He greeted and I smiled.

Good morning. Are you dropping me off at work today? I asked and he nodded, before turning his head and yawning, stretching his arms out.

"Sleep well?" I asked aloud and he smiled in my direction.

"Better than usual," he said before he turned to face me. "Breakfast?"

"Please," I said and he kissed my forehead before getting up.

After Lucien dropped me off, I checked up on several different dogs in the clinic, playing with some of them and filling all their water bottles. I then moved on to the kittens, playing with some that had just gotten de-wormed and would be picked up later today.

"You look happy," Katherine's voice greeted and I looked up to find her with a cup of hot coffee.

"I guess I'm alright, despite a few things," I said with a smile as I took the cup from her.

"So... I'm guessing things progressed with Lucien last night?" Katherine asked with a knowing smile as she sipped on her own coffee. I winked at her as I drank from my own cup.

"Not as much as you imagine," I said with a smile.

"But progress is progress nonetheless," she commented with a grin.

"If you say so," I replied as I got up. "Where's Desmond?"

"Busy, he said that he had to fetch some new supplies - he likes to run the clinic like everything's his responsibility."

"Well, I mean, this place seems to run on just him - why's that?" I asked and Katherine smiled.

"Our clinic's not exactly found near the main city, so we don't get many visitors other than those that really know us - we're quite good with canines after all." I laughed at that.

"Anyways, I'm gonna have to go pick Desmond up, he's just finished up and the bastard doesn't drive."

"What?" I asked, confused.

"Desmond never learned, so he walks here everyday - he doesn't even shift into his wolf- all he does is walk, walk, and walk everywhere he goes- rain or sun, snow or not. One of these days he's bound to get sick."

"You guys really love each other, don't you?" I asked and Katherine beamed in my direction.

"You'll get there," she said, winking and I rolled my eyes as I continued working. But a smile had definitely crept its way up to my cheeks. "Anyways, there shouldn't be much going on- but I'll try to be back as soon as possible- maybe even have a bit of a snack then."

"Sounds good to me," I said and she grinned as she turned to leave.

"See ya!" Katherine said one last time, I smiled before I got up and took a look at all of the pets. Desmond told me that most of them were going to be going to their forever homes soon, which gave me relief.

I went over to the front of the clinic and sat at the reception table. There really wasn't much I could do for the day - other than watch over the other animals of course. Not that the thought of spending the day just playing with puppies and kittens was a bad thing. But it's been the first time in months that I didn't have much paperwork to fill out or get called to show up for something or talk to a realtor interested in an apartment- or...

I breathed a sigh. I guess it's a relief though, plus, I'd rather be here than ignorant of whatever the fück my sister was planning. Just as I was about to pull out my phone to annoy Lucien into entertaining me- the door to the clinic opened. In walked a man that was carrying a limp looking husky in his hands. For a split second - I thought he had brought a wolf in - but it was much too small...

"Is the vet in?" He asked and I stood up.

"I'm new here, but I work with canines a lot. My name's Auden," I said quickly before asking, "So what happened?" I asked and he sighed.

"Probably ate something bad - I leave him at home sometimes and when I came back - the house was a mess and- I don't know, he's been vomiting and acting weak and this morning he just wouldn't get up," the man explained and I nodded.

"Okay, why don't you carry him to the back, we don't have anyone else in yet, so would you mind helping me out a bit?"

"Not at all, please," he paused, "Lead the way."

I walked to the back room where we had the counter for surgeries and check-ups. The man laid the black and white husky onto it and I put on a stethoscope.

"I'll just check on his breathing," I said and the man nodded. It was only then that our eyes met, and I found them to be of fascinating colors - one was brown and dark and the other a vivid green. To be honest, this guy was actually good looking if I say so myself - and that's coming from a werewolf. But he didn't smell off or anything - humans were pretty cute too, after all. Great... I'm checking out someone else- Lucien would probably kill me.

Relieved that Lucien and the other pack members weren't around to hear my thoughts, I began to work. There was nothing wrong with the husky's breathing or his heart.

"What's his name?" I asked as I moved the stethoscope around.

"Quietus."

"What?" I asked and the man smiled at me as he leaned forward.

"Quietus, like saying Why with a 'K' in front of it," he said and I raised an eyebrow.

"Interesting name - what does it mean?" I asked as I worked.

"I'd rather not say... Are you from around here?" He asked as I looked at the dogs eyes, they seemed fine - he just seemed fatigued for some reason.

"No... I flew in about a week ago from New York... Sorry, you haven't told me your name yet," I said and he chuckled.

"It's Ignus."

"That's... unique," I said, before looking up and noticing Ignus', well, intense stare. I coughed before speaking to break the awkwardness. "Oh, do you mind if I checked his blood?"

"Not at all," he said reassuringly as he pet the dog, "Do what you must." I smiled before I turned and looked through the drawers, finding a neatly sealed syringe and alcohol.

"Okay, um, just calm him down," I said. Not like he might react from how unresponsive he is right now... but you never know. I added in my head as I finished cleaning the area to draw blood, he pet Quietus' head as I performed the job.

"Do you mind if I ask where your name comes from?" I asked and he laughed. I looked at him and smiled. "It's a pretty unique name, after all."

"Take a guess."

"Isn't ignus related to a kind of rock?" I asked and he chuckled at my answer.

"Sort of, but it's more related to fire... it's not all that important." I thought for a moment.

"Well, Ignus, I should be able to get the blood results this week - I think, I'll have to check that over - in the meantime, if you have a calling card, I can tell you when they'll be ready... For now I think it's best to let Quietus rest, make sure he eats and drinks properly - and yeah, I think he should be fine," I said with a smile.

"I don't have a calling card- but I can leave you my number, if you have a pen-"

"I have my phone, here," I said as I pulled my phone out of my pockets, I unlocked it quickly and handed it to him. He smiled at me as he took it.

I pet Quietus for a bit before I noticed something a little odd...

"Hey um, Ignus... your dog's got a burn on his-"

"I found him just about a week ago - probably got beat up by his old owners..." Ignus responded sympathetically.

"Do you rescue dogs often?" I asked and he smiled.

"I guess I do, I rarely keep them around long enough... They usually go to another place."

"So you're like an independent shelter? That's pretty neat," I commented as Ignus handed me back my phone.

"Thank you for helping me, Doctor-"

"Auden. Just, Auden. Most people don't call vets doctors anyways," I said with a shrug. Besides, I'm too young to even think of being called Doctor - not that it'd be a problem though.

"But wouldn't you like to be recognized as one?"

"I don't mind. It's a title, just like so many other honorifics are. I think I can do just fine without being labeled anything, don't you think?" I asked with a smile, Ignus returned it kindly. "Well, anyways, I guess I'll see you sometime this week again."

"Of course, thank you for your help. How much will that be?"

I led Ignus out to the reception. He held the poor dog in his arms as he pulled out a few bills from his back pocket.

"Will this be fine? I can pay later-"

"It'll be fine, besides, I wasn't able to fix anything yet- I'm not done with the little pup," I said reassuringly. Ignus grinned and ran a hand through his deep brown hair.

"Thank you again."

The door to the clinic then opened and in walked Katherine and Desmond.

"Sorry we took a while- who's this?" Desmond asked as he walked in and looked at the dog.

"This is Ignus and his dog Quietus-"

"We were just about to leave actually," Ignus said, surprising me. "I'll be back soon though. Thank you again." Just as he was about to leave, I felt a strange feeling in my head. I watched as Ignus walked out the door and felt my vision haze.

"...Auden?" I heard Katherine call out but I couldn't focus on anything else.

It's a shame you don't know. A voice rang in my head. Except it was unmistakably Ignus' voice. I felt my senses come together as I ran out of the clinic, I stopped on the sidewalk and looked around. I sniffed the air- nothing. I looked around but there wasn't a trace of him - not a scent, not a footstep.

What are you talking about? I asked loudly in my head.

Auden, who are you talking to? Desmond's voice rang in my head just as a car pulled up and Lucien walked out. The doors to the clinic opened and out walked Katherine and Desmond. Katherine immediately made her way to me and wrapped my coat over my shoulders.

"Did anything happen?" Lucien asked.

"You heard me call out? All of you heard me, right?" I asked and the three of them nodded. "But did-" No, they wouldn't have heard- if it was a normal link then it was definitely directed at me a.

"Auden, what happened?"

"The guy that was in earlier- I- he smelled human- nothing about him was off and yet- I heard him-" Desmond and Katherine looked at each other.

"Did you see him?" Lucien asked and the two nodded.

"Briefly. He left as soon as we arrived. Though he said he'd come back."

"Something's wrong..." I trailed off. Remembering that I had handed my phone to Ignus earlier, I brought out my phone and looked into my contacts. I spotted the letter 'I' and felt my stomach drop as I opened it. There wasn't a number - not one I could use anyways - all he left was a note at the bottom of the list.

Shall we take a walk down memory lane? -I

Chapter 11

"**T**ell me when you find something," Lucien said, after about the twelfth call he'd made for the day.

"That was creepy as hell," Katherine cursed as she dipped a french fry into some ketchup.

We were all in a nearby restaurant sitting in a small booth for lunch all while Lucien made the decision to hasten the process of looking up who it was that my sister was collaborating with. I'd shown him what Ignus left on my phone and told him about what I had heard - in my head from the mysterious Ignus himself.

"I still don't understand how he could've mind-linked you," Desmond said. I nodded.

"Trust me, I'm confused as well." I looked to Lucien and placed my hand on his lap. He followed by placing his hand on mine.

"Though, I have to say, the man works pretty fast. Whatever he's planning seems to be going his way. He didn't even hesitate to talk to you... which is pretty fücking terrifying," Katherine pointed out. I bit my bottom lip.

"Have you contacted Zaina?" I asked and Lucien nodded.

"She hasn't responded and I don't think that's a coincidence."

"But how the hell does he know you? I mean cases of a human werewolf are rare but they're definitely not unheard of," Desmond said and Katherine rolled her eyes.

"Except, we all know she's the daughter of an Alpha- basically the strongest carriers of the werewolf gene," she countered and Desmond paused.

"But that doesn't make it an impossibility."

"Actually Auden, I was really wondering about that... and you can tell me if I'm being insensitive or crossing a line- but... when you say you're human, does that actually mean human or does that mean that you're wolf was traumatized in the past or something? And just, I don't know, can't come out?" Katherine asked. I paused for a moment and leaned back against the seat.

"When I turned sixteen, my family waited all day to see if anything would happen and nothing ever did. I didn't feel any different - and I still haven't. I mean, my parents tried to trigger it - shifted in front of me, trained me - made me drink all these weird supposedly magical concoctions made of like raw meat and wolf-like food, I guess... But in the end, nothing happened," I said with a shrug.

"Did your dad ever talk about it?" Lucien asked and I paused.

"Actually, out of everyone- my dad was probably the least conce rned..." I trailed off.

"But he's the Alpha-" Desmond said but I couldn't pay attention.

I sat on the grass and pulled at the plants around me. I felt my chest hiccup and heard someone behind me.

"Is there something wrong with me, daddy?" I remember asking my dad.

"There's nothing, nothing, wrong with you my darling," dad replied as he took a seat beside me, pulling me into his lap. "Don't let anyone tell you otherwise."

"I mean, I guess he was being supportive," I said, though I was unsure myself.

"I can call him and we can ask," Lucien said and I shook my head.

"Dad literally just came back from this place, I doubt he'd be able to make a flight back here without getting my sister on our backs... She already knows we're here in Vancouver," I explained.

"Something's oddly suspicious about this whole situation though..." Katherine added, leaning back against her seat.

"Yeah, tell me about it..." I trailed off.

"How do you think Carmine is doing?" Lucien asked as we hiked our way towards the pack house.

"I'd rather not really think about it... but I'm guessing it's running on a lot of secrets and suspicion these days - our pack's very close... but I haven't been a part of that pack in almost ten years so I guess my thoughts on how the pack is doing won't be anywhere near reality."

"Do you mind if I ask how it was for you- leaving your pack at sixteen and all?" Lucien asked as we finally made it to the house. I took off my coat and sighed as I stomped my feet to get rid of the gunk and snow beneath it.

"It isn't anything too dramatic... I guess. I didn't find it dramatic. One day, I just decided to take a hold of my life. If the Moon Goddess or whatever it is up there decided I couldn't be a werewolf – where else was I supposed to go? I thought it'd be better for me if I lived a human life – get out of the werewolf trap," I explained as I took a seat on a nearby couch as Lucien followed suit.

"Why'd you choose to become a vet?" He asked and I looked at him.

"I love animals – and if I couldn't be a werewolf, I guess, I thought it'd be good to be useful someday. Besides, even though I'm a full-on vet – I'm confident enough to say that I can pass for your average doctor, a surgeon even – just don't have the license or a degree to prove it... Not that I'd need one under our... packs and stuff," Lucien took my hand in his and gently traced a circle around my palm. I sighed as I leaned against him.

"What's it like being an early shifter?" I asked, thinking it only right for me to ask questions. Lucien paused before speaking.

"Weird. Painful."

"That's it?" I asked, turning to face him.

"I used to hate shifting – it hurt everywhere. Every time I shifted – something was always different. The older I became, the worse it hurt until I finally got used to the pain," Lucien explained, "Since our bodies are smaller and aren't as developed, it's harder for us to run or fight... It's better than fighting as humans but it's hard being a kid and having all these... senses. Though, we hit harder than most... And that lasts the rest of our lives... We'd be the perfect puppet dogs I guess, which is why we get hunted..." I simply nodded before I moved to straddle him, Lucien looked up into my eyes as I placed my hands on his chest.

"But... Lana seems to shift without a problem," I said and he smiled.

"Xander helps her get over it – though I'm not sure he thinks it was a good idea now that she shifts all the time. It didn't exactly play to his advantage when we were in New York." I giggled before peering into Lucien's hazel eyes. "Are you... usually this forward with men?" Lucien asked and I laughed.

"Would that bother or relieve you?" Lucien shrugged.

"I'd like to think we're at a good spot – even if I did act like a bit of an äss-"

"When exactly did you – oh. You're referring to the parking lot and that whole 'I can make you kiss me' thing," I said and Lucien chuckled before reaching up and caressing my cheek.

"Exactly." I smiled and just as I was about to pull forward to plant a kiss on Lucien's lips – his phone rang, causing me to sigh and Lucien to chuckle as he pulled out his phone.

"Alpha Lucien speaking," he answered. Knowing that I would be able to listen, he placed his phone in between us and pressed speaker.

"This is Dante of the Carmine Pack."

Why would dad call you? I asked and Lucien merely glanced at me in response.

"What is it?"

"Zaina is planning to visit Vancouver to meet with someone to-morrow-"

"We've already met 'I' who's probably that 'someone'," I said, causing my dad to pause for a fairly long period of time.

"Stay away from him Auden... Promise me," he said and I got off of Lucien's lap before taking the phone from him.

"Why?"

"He's not someone you want to take lightly... Trust me, Auden, I have spent a lifetime trying to lose him and his... 'kind'."

"What? Who is he?"

"Auden, you have to-"

The call ended. I swallowed a dry lump in my throat as the phone rang again. Another name displayed on the screen as I took a deep breath. Lucien gripped my free hand as I slid my finger across the screen to answer the call.

"Zaina," I greeted.

"So you've met him," Zaina said simply as I grit my teeth together.

"What the actual fück were you thinking?!" Zaina chuckled in response.

"I decided to make some benefit out of a complicated situation... Unfortunately, you were part of it," she said and Lucien and I looked at each other.

"What the hell is that supposed to mean?"

"It means you were the chip to bargain with. To be honest, I'd have thought the wolf was more important- I thought they were just using the poor little girl as an excuse to get your attention-"

"Give me a second to understand... You let them kidnap a little girl to get my attention, use our apartment complex, accept their money and didn't even stop to think for a moment to let me know that this was going on?" I asked, practically hissing my words.

"...You haven't really met him then."

"Can we stop talking like I'm supposed to know shït that I obviously don't?"

"Listen, Auden, I don't know what that man wants you for – but he's looking for you – and since you've obviously met him – or at least seen him... you better be saying your farewells."

"Who the hell is this guy?!"

"His name's Ignus and trust me, we'd be better off speaking in person."

"I don't think that's a good idea," Lucien said loudly, growling immediately after. I placed a hand on his leg to calm him down.

"Then you both better decide which one of you you'd be willing to lose- because he seems just as interested in your little family, Alpha." Lucien grit his teeth and his body tensed up. I reached for his hand, my fingers sneaking into his grip to make him relax a bit.

"I'll be in Vancouver until the day after tomorrow. I'll give you a location – meet me if you want."

And with that, Zaina hung up.

"You're not meeting her," Lucien growled. I put his phone aside and straddled his legs before placing my hands around his face.

"Lucien... I need to know what's going on," I said and Lucien shook his head, running his teeth against the pads of my finger.

"She's most likely going to meet that Ignus guy... I don't trust her."

"She's still my sister."

"I don't give a fück- she's bad news Auden."

"And so is Ignus – apparently... and according to what he said, he's still going to come back – whether it's to treat that dog I helped him with or... something else. He already knows where I work-"

"Then you're not working there anymore-"

"Lucien." He stared into my eyes and wrapped his arms around me, gripping me tightly.

"I can't lose anyone. I don't care how little we've known each other – I will not lose my mate."

"Then how about we let someone else meet her?" I suggested and Lucien paused for a moment. Lucien closed his eyes and I knew he was mind-linking someone. His grip loosened as I waited for whoever it was to respond.

"Katherine will meet with your sister tomorrow. I'll have the other pack members be on guard."

"Great," I said with relief. "Speaking of other pack members – how come I don't see anyone other than Katherine, Desmond, Xander – and... Well, you get the point, I haven't really seen anyone aside from when we were all in New York."

"They're spread out, we're not exactly an active pack. There are no packs coming after us – well, not my whole pack. Besides, we like having all this space to ourselves, when they wanna run in a safe place – they can run on this mountain. They don't live too far away from us, but for the most part, we like being a peaceful pack. Xander, Katherine, and I are basically the ones that lead training for members that want to be a part of our little 'army'."

"So you guys do have an offensive unit."

"Of course we do. I'm ready to protect my pack when I have to, I just hope that I won't need to resort to that." I nodded in response before resting on Lucien's shoulder.

"Tired?" He asked and I nodded, causing him to chuckle as he wrapped his arms around me and stood, carrying me as he went downstairs.

"If you drop me, I swear-" Lucien moved away from me and planted a kiss on my lips causing me to gasp.

"You swear what?"

"...Is my Alpha learning how to seduce me?"

"Your Alpha?"

"Well, if you don't let me call you mine, I'm sure I can find someone else to call-"

No way. He mind-linked.

Lucien leaned in once more and I laughed as I pressed a soft kiss against his lips.

"Auden!" My dad called, I turned to look at him and he smiled as he pulled me into his arms.

"Where's Zaina and mom?" I asked and he paused for a moment.

"They... took a trip, they'll be back soon," he said and I pouted.

"Why didn't they bring me?"

"Well, they didn't bring me either, so that makes two of us," he said as he squeezed my nose. I frowned before snuggling into the crook of his arm.

"Daddy... Why can't I hear the others?"

"What?" Dad asked.

"Why can't I hear the rest of the pack?"

You can hear me, though, can't you? I lifted myself from dad's shoulder and he smiled as he put me down and he pinched my cheeks.

"You'll hear them eventually Auden, you're just... too young right now," dad explained. I crossed my arms over my shoulders.

"But Zaina said she heard everyone as soon as she knew how to speak-"

"You just... learn slower, you'll hear them, Auden, just-"

"But why can't I? I'm already eight – I can speak, I can do every-thing else they can- I just-"

"Auden-"

"Auden." Someone called out and I opened my eyes. I felt a hand brush my face and realized that my face had gotten wet from tears. I looked to my right and found Lucien beside me, we were in bed together.

"Bad dream?" He asked and I snuggled into his arms.

"Yeah..." I trailed off as I sniffled.

After a few moments, I shifted about and looked at Lucien, who immediately looked back at me.

"I really think I need to meet my sister, Lucien."

"I can't let you do that, not when I don't know what she's up to-"

"Please."

"I can't. I can't lose someone I care about-"

"We haven't even known each other that long, Lucien-"

"I don't care. I'm not risking your life-"

"But you're willing to risk Katherine's?" I asked, getting up. Lucien sighed before he got up as well and wrapped his arm around me.

"Katherine isn't someone they want. And she's a wolf – she can fight her way through a bunch of enemies in that form-"

"And I can't fight because I'm not a wolf?" I asked and Lucien sighed once again.

"You know that's not what I meant."

I took a breath before I leaned against his frame. He pulled me closer and I wiped my eyes as I snuggled into him.

"I'm sorry... I just, I need to know..."

"I know... And you will, eventually. But we can't just rush in, we need to learn as much as we can before we push our limits," Lucien said and I turned to look at him. He stared at me, his hazel eyes revealing a swirl of emotions.

"Don't you wish you had a normal mate?" I asked and Lucien chuckled.

"Who cares about normal? I enjoy you and your... 'abnormal' self," he said and I smirked.

"Thanks... I guess," I muttered before I fell back on the bed. Lucien did the same and I caressed his cheek as I felt my eyes fall shut.

"Tell me everything that happens tomorrow," I said as I yawned.

"I'm bringing you with me," he said and I smiled as I snuggled into him.

"Great."

"...Good night, Auden," Lucien replied and I smiled before I opened my eyes briefly and kissed his cheek before resting my head on his arm again.

"Good night..."

Chapter 12

"This has got to be the worst kind of wire-tapping listening device ever," Katherine complained, her voice coming through the speaker on our phone. Lucien, Desmond, and I were in a tinted SUV about five blocks away.

"Just put it on the table, Katherine," Lucien said, rolling his eyes.

"Sure, as long as you guys keep silent," Katherine replied.

"We will," Desmond said.

"Actually... you guys know we could pull this off from the pack house right? It's not like we had to be out here," I pointed out and I heard Katherine breathe a sigh.

"My point exactly," she replied, "Okay, all of you shush, she's coming."

Just as Katherine spoke, I felt a strange feeling – it was like a pull to look a certain way. So I turned my head around and the doors of the building we parked in front of swung open and out came Ignus. He walked out casually, his hands tucked into the pockets of his thick and heavy-looking black coat.

"So you're the Beta." My sister's voice rang from the phone. But I couldn't focus as I saw Ignus stop and stand right beside the car.

I looked to Lucien and Desmond, but neither of them seemed to notice.

Come to take me up on the offer? I heard Ignus say and I turned my head to look at him once more. I was in the passenger's seat and he stood right by the door. His eyes looking straight through the tinted glass and into my eyes sending chills down my spine.

Lucien? I mind-linked.

What? He asked, just as I swallowed a dry lump in my throat.

Tell me you can see him too. I said as I lay back in my seat. Lucien turned his head and gave me a strange look,

Who? He asked and I turned my head only to find that Ignus had disappeared.

We don't need to cause a ruckus, Auden. Ignus said in my head. Though your sister might inevitably make a mess of things.

What the hell does that mean? I asked, hoping that it would reach Ignus, and apparently, it did.

You'll see. I'm not your worst enemy... Well, that would depend on the way you see things.

Auden? Lucien called me and I turned to look at him.

What? I asked.

"So, how's the half-ling?" Zaina's voice filtered through the phone.

"She's doing absolutely fine. Now quit changing the subject, I asked you about your involvements with this 'I' person," Katherine responded, Zaina sounded like she had laughed.

"The man was willing to pay for information on my sister. A few more digits to the bank account was more than welcome."

"You mean your bank account, the one you probably use to leech off of your sister's work?" Katherine hissed.

"Say what you want, but profit is profit. Auden got us started, but I made Carmine rich- and it's not like a human can take credit for raising our pack out of the wilderness and into... more modern interests." I heard a growl come from Katherine's mouth.

"She's your sister."

"She was a member of my pack and like the rest of them, they have to earn their keep. It only makes sense for a human to work for a... collective effort."

"You're a fücking lunatic," Katherine seethed.

"Auden's always been dad's favorite. Did you know that? Despite being the eldest child of the Alpha, my dad would rather dote on his failure of a daughter? The human lost cause? Poetic right?" Zaina paused. "And now she's wanted by people in higher places, mated to an Alpha of some rare bloodline – and she's being helped by my own father who's going around my authority to get information."

"Maybe it's karma for being a whiny bïtch." Another pause – a longer one.

And then there was a crash. The call ended. All three of us in the car looked at each other before we simultaneously rushed out of the car and sprinted for the restaurant where Zaina and Katherine were meeting. They were seated by the windows and Zaina's cold blue eyes immediately met mine. She had pale brown hair that fell to her chest and she grinned like a disgusting cat as she saw me. The glass in her hand had shattered and a waitress had begun to frantically offer first-aid – or to wipe her down. In my anger, I grabbed my sister's wrist and pulled her out of the restaurant, dragging her out into the streets until I found an alley that was safe and away from view.

"So you were listening in," she said as I pushed her towards a wall.

"What the hell are you thinking?!"

"I was trying to get rid of a nuisance and profit," she said with a smile.

"A girl – Zaina. You almost had a girl murdered in our building. Are you out of your mind?!"

"I'm getting real tired of hearing that," Zaina snarled. Her teeth began to morph and she bared her teeth at me as she released a louder growl and just as she seemed ready to strike, three growls resonated from behind me. I turned around and felt my breath relax at the sight of Lucien, Katherine, and Desmond.

"Oh, well if it isn't Alpha Lucien coming to the rescue...How's your special little sister doing?" Zaina asked with a smile and Lucien simply stared at her, his eyes had morphed into a vivid green with golden yellow orbs surrounding his pupils. I felt the strength of his Alpha command and had to fight the urge to bow my head as I watched Zaina do so. She clenched her jaw and grit her teeth as she bowed her head.

"You may be an Alpha, but we are not equals," Lucien said, his voice low and rough. As I turned to look around, I found Katherine and Desmond bowing their heads towards Lucien as well. "Kneel."

I watched as Zaina fell to her knees. Her lips quivered from fear and an instinctive sense of respect.

I felt the same feeling from earlier – a kind of pull that wanted me to look in a direction... So I turned my head and almost immediately, my eyes found Ignus across the street. *So I wasn't wrong about you.* Ignus' voice rang in my head. *Bow as you should Auden. Not many* can resist your mate's commands – not even his mate should be able to. I felt a lump in my throat as I turned my head back to face Lucien and then Zaina. I lowered my head.

"What business do you have in Vancouver?" Lucien asked, his voice still booming with the Alpha command.

"The final payment... it was going to be paid today," Zaina blurted aloud, I looked at her and watched as her body began to shiver. Lucien stepped forward, his steps crunching the gravel beneath his feet.

"Payment for what?" He asked.

"Her services," Ignus answered loudly. I heard him walk from behind me and Lucien growled as he approached. "The building rental and all that."

"Who are you?" Lucien asked and Ignus grinned.

"Just another wolf looking for a few things... However, I am not looking for trouble, Alpha Lucien," Ignus responded before he bowed his head, "Though it seems..." Ignus turned to look at me and smiled.

"Trouble is inevitable between us," Ignus commented before he turned to Zaina. "Lies don't do for good business, Zaina. But your business is none of my concern. Let's not make the mistake of framing innocents... I'd rather not deal with liars of your kind." Zaina looked down on the ground and Ignus' eyes landed on Lucien again.

"In all honesty, I meant no harm, Alpha Lucien." Ignus bowed his head, "I've merely been looking for something I need and I've found it. I will leave you alone."

"I have a feeling that isn't entirely true," Lucien replied and I looked between him and Ignus. In response, Ignus simply chuckled to himself.

"That depends on how much you get involved in my business, I suppose..." Lucien growled at that.

"Can the two of you call it quits for now? My sister's still on the ground while the two of you quarrel," I said with a sigh. Ignus looked to me and winked.

"Of course, I have places to be as well." Ignus walked right past me, his arm brushing mine as I felt something land in my hand. I turned to look at him but he had simply begun walking away casually...

"Take Alpha Zaina to Mila's house," Lucien said and Desmond nodded.

"Will do, will you send your commands to her?" Desmond asked and Lucien nodded briefly.

"You can't just-"

"We have enough evidence to mark you as a suspicious person and with your dad's cooperation, I'm sure he'll be alright with our 'handling' you and your petty little äss for a while," Katherine added.

Desmond walked over to Zaina and lifted her up from the ground before tugging her towards the street – probably to get into the car we were in earlier. I turned to Lucien and watched as his eyes returned to their usual color. Katherine and Desmond, on the other hand, moved silently and efficiently. To be honest, it was like their usual personalities had faded.

You okay? Lucien asked and I sighed as I walked over to him. I shoved my hands into my pockets, placing the paper into one of them before raising my right hand and caressing Lucien's face.

Are you? I asked, it was his turn to sigh as he turned and kissed the palm of my hand.

"Ignus isn't done with us, is he?"

"I doubt it," I said before stepping close to Lucien. "Thank you."

"For what? We haven't found anything yet-"

"For stepping in, dumbäss," I said, rolling my eyes.

"Your sister's... certainly strange," he said and I folded my arms over my chest.

"Strange? She's insane. She basically took part in your sister's kidnapping and she got involved with Ignus... Whatever the hell he is," I said and Lucien chuckled before moving forward and kissing the top of my forehead and then released me.

"Speaking of Ignus... That guy was even weirder than your sister."

"Tell me about it," I muttered as I shoved my hands back in my pockets, feeling the piece of paper concealed in my pocket.

"And you were right... he doesn't smell like a wolf – but he said that he was..."

"Well, he also said he wasn't looking for trouble-" Lucien laughed before looking at me.

"I've a feeling he likes you," he said and I raised an eyebrow.

"What- where the hell did you get that idea?"

"Call it a mate's intuition." I rolled my eyes and nudged him with my elbow.

"Whatever, can we just go back to the house?"

"Unfortunately, I can't. I have to go finish some business and... I promised Mila I'd go there to... follow-up on my orders."

"Who's Mila?" I asked and Lucien laughed as we made our way out to the sidewalk.

"She's... the pack's interrogator."

"I thought you said you guys were peaceful-"

"For the most part... Peace always has a cost – and we'd rather be safe than sorry."

"Oh." Guess that makes sense. "You... aren't going to hurt Zaina right?"

"...Concerned?"

"Well, I wouldn't want her to lose a body part-" Lucien laughed.

"I don't think we need to interrogate her that far. She seems to listen to my command."

"Speaking of command, you need to explain that to me- I've never seen or felt anything like that."

"I'll tell you later. Lana and Xander are heading home, right now, if you'd like to join them."

"You really are getting rid of me, aren't you?" I asked and Lucien sighed. I smiled at him and planted a kiss on his cheek. "If you don't mind, I'd like to go around... Maybe check a bit on the clinic."

"I'm a little bit worried about that Ignus guy-"

"I'll be fine, I'll mind-link you if I come across him," I said and Lucien opened his mouth in protest, but instead, I lifted my hands and pulled his face just a little lower as I kissed him.

Fine. As soon as you see him, Auden. He linked and I smirked as I pulled away.

"Thank you," I said as a sleek silver car pulled up in front of us. The windows rolled down and revealed the driver to be Freya – the young wolf I had met early on.

"Alpha, Luna," she greeted, bowing her head.

"Right on time, Freya," Lucien greeted before kissing my lips quickly and smiling as he got into the car.

"Bye," I muttered as I lifted a hand to wave goodbye. Lucien winked before Freya bowed her head again and drove off.

I took a breath and shoved my hands into my pockets. The paper still felt crisp as I walked in the direction of the clinic. After walking past about the fourth trashcan along the road, I pulled the piece of paper from my pocket and stared at it. It'd probably be best to throw it away... I thought to myself. The less secrets I keep, the better. I sighed as I threw the piece of paper into the bin and walked away, not bothering to look at it.

"It's a good thing that was just a piece of blank paper," A voice said from behind me and I froze. "But I'm afraid I do have business with you."

I mentally groaned as I turned around to face the person behind me.

And of course, Ignus stood right there, a wide grin stuck on his face.

Great.

Chapter 13

"What business?" I asked, folding my arms over my chest.

"I'd rather not say it somewhere... so public," he replied.

"...Fine, we can talk in the clinic. Come," I said. Better tell Lucien about this later...

Our walk to the clinic was done in silence. And thankfully, Ignus kept himself out of my damned head. I'm also guessing Lucien and the others were a bit busy... Since no one was speaking or really, linking me, at all today – no one was even bothering to leave any messages via phone. I unlocked the clinic and Ignus walked in as I shut the door.

"I'm gonna go do my work, so go ahead and talk as I go," I said and Ignus nodded as he followed behind me.

"I'm surprised you trust me so much," he commented as I lifted a bag of dog food.

"Carry this," I muttered as I handed the dog food to him, Ignus took it in his arms and I grabbed a cup to measure out the food preparing to serve them to the pups. "You give me the creeps- but something tells me you aren't here to hurt me and I'm willing, and perhaps stupid enough, to trust that something." Ignus simply shrugged in response as I began unlocking the first cage, petting the little shih tzu inside before placing half a cup of food in.

"Well, I'm not surprised. After all, why would a psychopath pay your sister money to hurt you when he could do it right here, right now?" He commented. I turned and stared at him, and from the casual look on his face, it seemed obvious that he was joking. It still didn't sit well with me though. "Too soon?" He asked.

"Definitely," I said as I continued to feed the rest of the dogs. "...Why did Quietus have a burn mark?" I asked.

"So that they don't kill him," Ignus replied in a relaxed tone.

"They?" I asked as I emptied yet another cup into a bowl, patting the head of the dogs as I also checked on their water bottles. "I'm beginning to get very confused."

"I would be too, if I spent my life growing up with the wrong species," Ignus said as he put his fingers into a cage and one of the smaller dogs came to lick him.

"At least the dogs don't hate you. Also, species? What's wrong with the werewolf-"

"Nothing's wrong with them, explaining would take quite a bit of time and I don't think I'd have enough."

"Okay..." I murmured as I filled the last bowl. "Put the bag back where we got it and grab the cat kibble – oh and two cans," I said.

"I'm beginning to feel like I work here," Ignus commented as he turned around and placed the food down.

"Thank you for being cooperative."

"You're welcome, although, I bet you have a ton of questions you aren't asking," he said as I heard him pick up the bag of kibble. He walked over to me and handed me the cans.

"Thank you," I said as I took them from his hands.

"Why canned?"

"The kittens we got aren't quite used to kibble – and one of the other cats have a hard time digesting the food," I explained, not really knowing why.

"You've got a really good eye for detail, that's a good sign," Ignus said and I raised an eyebrow as I began filling bowls again.

"I think that's normal... for a vet," I said, shaking my head, "And what does that even mean?"

"Tell me, Auden, do I smell like a werewolf?" He asked and I turned to face him. I sniffed the air and sighed as I turned around and set the cans down on a table.

"No, you don't," I said as I opened the cans up and distributed them into the spare bowls we had.

"I think you only smell like one because you've lived with them for so long," Ignus said with a shrug as he watched me work. His brown and green eyes staring at me – I cleared my throat.

"So you're telling me I'm a different kind of werewolf?" I asked as I took the bowls and placed them in the proper cages.

"Good. You understand, partially. That makes things easier." I stood up and looked over at him. I stared into his eyes, trying my best to judge his character.

"You know... if you stare any more than that, I might think you actually like me," he said and I sighed before running a hand through my hair.

"What do you want me to do?" I asked. "And please don't say anything freaky." Ignus smiled.

"I'd like you to meet me regularly – tell your Alpha if you'd like, though I doubt he'd respond well. He might just kill me... But I'd very much like to inform you of your abilities, what you are- your friend was right when she asked about how an Alpha could birth a human-"

"Hold on... You heard that? That was after we met you..."

"I tracked you. No worries, I didn't bother spiraling into your mate's territory. I wouldn't like to get jumped by a bunch of were-wolves, no matter how confident I am," he said with a shrug, smiling at me. "Would you agree to my... mentoring?"

"There's no reason for me to really trust you – and Lucien would never let me go, he suspects you too much of-"

"Of what? What did I possibly do?"

"How about stalking me? Creepily visiting me at my workplace? Leaving a weird note in my contacts? Paying my sister for informa-tion? Those things aren't exactly trustworthy material."

"Then it's a good thing I only aim to gain your trust. I care very little for Umbra and its supposedly rare breed of werewolf – we're not human Auden. But if you'd like to remain an ignorant 'human' under the wing of her Alpha... then be my guest," Ignus said, saying the word human as if it was a disgusting thing.

"Not that there's anything wrong with my little ignorant human life, Ignus, but if we aren't human -then what are we?" I asked.

"Tell me, Auden, what creatures do you think exist outside the mundane world of humans?" I raised an eyebrow.

"The usual array, werewolves, witches, vampires... those are the only ones I hear of," I said. Not that we meet many of them or any outliers for that matter...

"And say I call these creatures, 'species'... which one would we fit under?"

"Well, if we aren't werewolves, we've only got witches and vampires, and I can tell you that I'm neither of those two," I said, folding my arms over my chest. Ignus smiled.

"Exactly," A phone rang and I watched as Ignus reached into his pockets, pulling out his phone. "I will wait for you tomorrow, if you choose not to appear, I will take it as a rejection of my offer and a... decision of yours to be the... 'human' mate you believe you are."

"Wait for me where? What time?" I asked as Ignus turned around and placed the phone to his ear. Ignus raised his right hand and I saw a flash of images race through my mind.

A lake. The sun barely up as mist crept over it. From a distance – I could sense... It was across Lucien's territory. Far away but close enough to view it partially from the pack house.

By the time I had gotten back to my senses, Ignus had disappeared though I still heard his footsteps. My breath hitched as I went to the reception to catch him and ask him more questions. But he was gone. The door to the clinic opened and Lucien walked in with a bag.

"I figured you'd still be here. Took a while to crack your sister into speaking- by the way I got you some..." I couldn't hear the rest of Lucien's words. My vision blurred and hazed as I felt my legs go weak.

Darkness.

My eyes fluttered open just as I smelt Lucien's familiar scent. He was carrying me into the bedroom and I heard people talking in the background. Lucien's eyes looked over at me and I saw a hint of relief in them.

You okay? He asked and I nodded as he lay me down on the couch. I was wondering why he hadn't put me on the bed, but then I saw Xander, Lana, Katherine and Desmond as they came into the room.

"What's everyone doing here?"

"Zaina just told us what Ignus was- and aside from your sister being a terrible bïtch- I'd have to say I believe her about this," Katherine said.

"What'd she say?" I asked. Xander took Lana's hand.

"Zaina called Ignus a 'bloodsucking bastard' but to us, that term's better known for those we call 'bloodhounds'."

"Like the-"

"Unfortunately this isn't the time for jokes," Desmond said and I immediately shut my mouth.

"And just so we're clear, they're not at all related to those beautiful dogs..." Katherine trailed off.

"Most people know them better as-"

"Cannibalistic blood suckers." Katherine finished, interrupting Lucien's sentence.

"What?" I asked, looking at Lana's fearful face as Xander squeezed her hand.

"We don't know much about them- just the stories, the rumors that circulate among packs- they're a particularly secretive kind of pack, I guess, though I'm not sure they really are a 'pack', but no one knows much at all about their kind-"

"Species," I muttered.

"What?" Lucien asked.

"Nothing. Continue."

"Anyways, whatever his interest in you – you, out of all of us, have to be cautious, you still have werewolf blood in you – and..." Lucien said, but I had practically muted his voice in my head.

"Do they kill werewolves?" I asked.

"...They're known to do worse, but supposedly yes. Not much else is known about them, so best to assume that these are just rumors right now, we'll do our own digging for information," Desmond said and I looked over at Lucien.

"Rumors always have some kind of root to the truth, better to be cautious in case this guy's more trouble than he's worth dealing with," Katherine commented. And if I wasn't mistaken, Katherine looked like she really believed in all the rumors that they were talking about- Lucien seemed even more so.

"...Would you guys mind leaving us alone for a moment? I- I need a bit of time to process what you all just said." All of them nodded and I watched as they turned to leave, each saying their goodnight's while Lana walked over to me and kissed my cheek as she walked away.

"I'm sorry, that was probably a little too much to take in," Lucien said as the door shut.

"No, I wanted to know."

"Do you wanna talk about it?" Lucien asked.

"Actually, Lucien-"

It'd be a terrible idea to tell him now, Auden. Ignus' voice said. His tone ringing in my head.

"What is it?" Lucien asked and I shook my head as I raised my hand. He smiled as he took it with his own hand and I pulled him down to me.

"Let me just... relax," I said quietly, my voice hushed.

People have always thought the worst of us.

"Any idea why you fainted?" Lucien asked as he sat by me. I shook my head as I rested it against his shoulder. For some reason, I knew that Ignus was somewhere... chuckling at Lucien's question.

"Are you afraid of him? Ignus, I mean... and his kind?" I asked and Lucien paused, causing me to look at him.

"We know very little about their kind, but we have stories. Legends and myths, old stories that are probably overly exaggerated... So from what I hear, I should definitely be afraid – for my sister, for my pack, for my mate who's being targeted by one..." Lucien trailed off and I found myself turning and pulling myself onto his lap.

"What do you think he's up to?" I asked.

"I'm not sure- but he wants you- and according to your dad... it seems he and his kind have really been looking for you," Lucien said.

"Maybe my dad did something... you know, some kind of tres-passing or rivalry or- the usual thing packs fight about," I said with a shrug and Lucien caressed my cheek. He stared into my eyes before pulling me down gently, placing his forehead against mine. He definitely stopped listening earlier.

"I would never let anyone hurt you," Lucien whispered and I smiled as I pressed a kiss on his lips.

"I know," I said with a smile.

After about an hour of cuddling and soft talk – mainly with us avoiding the topic of Ignus or his um, bloodsucking kind... Lucien finally fell asleep. I watched him as I lay in the crook of his arm.

You know- what you said about your dad isn't necessarily... false.

I refused to link Ignus back. I had no idea how to direct it to him – he wasn't my pack and I had no connection to him. Not one that I knew of anyways – other than his suggestion that I was... disturbingly one of his kind.

The monsters of this world believe that we are monsters... How ironic. Ignus said and I really wished that I knew how he was 'linking' me. I bit my lip as I slowly moved away from Lucien and stepped off the bed. I padded my way over to the fireplace and sat in front of it.

What do you think Auden? Surely you've figured out how to talk to me by now. You've already spoken to me once today... it isn't that difficult to figure out.

I ran a hand through my hair. If only the bastard would shut the hell up.

And she speaks! Ignus celebrated. But I see you haven't completely figured it out yet... I'll leave it at that then, good night Auden.

And then there was silence. I sighed as I stood up. I heard something vibrate somewhere in the room and I sighed as I walked around, looking for the source. I eventually found it to be on Lucien's nightstand. On it, was Zaina's name. I slid my thumb across the screen and placed the phone to my ear.

"She's boarding the plane back to New York, right now. She's a little dizzy but she'll survive. I'm leaving the phone with her now," An unknown female's voice said. "I'll see what I can find out about the bloodhounds she was talking about. Hate to see trouble stir up. We don't need wolf hunters of that breed around here," she said just before she hung up.

Lucien stirred in his sleep as I placed the phone back down.

Ignus? I attempted to call out, trying to... 'think' to myself.

I thought we said our good night's? He responded.

Do you actually hunt werewolves? Again, I knew he was laughing. I closed my eyes and I could almost feel it – he was somewhere warm and smelt of pine... Probably a cabin – a small one...

I'll see you tomorrow then.

I bit my bottom lip.

Bastard. I said, hoping that he heard it. Though I had a definite feeling he had.

Chapter 14

I kissed Lucien's cheek as he slept. I then left him a note that I was going for a run. It wasn't like I was going far enough that the link wouldn't work – so he had no real reason to worry. Besides, it was going to take me a while to get to the spot Ignus had "showed" me. I zipped up my coat and made my way outside, choosing to take the lower exit of the house. Glad that I'd worn boots with a decent grip, I navigated my way through the forest, the lake serving as my guide.

This would probably be a lot better if I was an actual werewolf. Walking all the way is a real pain in the äss – and the sun's still asleep. I thought to myself- or at least I thought I was- until Ignus responded.

So you're on your way? Fantastic.

Get out of my head Ignus.

Can't do. It's something we have to live with.

Then why can't I hear anyone else? Also, the distance on this um, link thing, is amazing – considering we aren't a pack.

Link thing? Ignus was definitely laughing at that one. Anyways, Auden, most of us can hear each other, all you need to do is meet another one of our kind.

Sounds freaky. I replied as I cut through the forest.

You know, if you drove here you would've spent a lot less time. Ignus replied.

It'd take me even longer to find out how and where to get a car. Finally having made my way around the lake, I began to jog. My breath came out in streams of mist as I finally made it to the clearing that Ignus had somehow showed me yesterday.

"Finally," Ignus commented and I found him wrapped up in a crimson coat, his hands shoved into his pockets as he greeted me with a smile. I raised an eyebrow as I spotted two other people. "They're other members of our little group, Hera and Dalton." Hera and Dalton looked like they were only teenagers, definitely younger than Xander. They waved at me from their spot by the lake.

"Little group?" I asked as I waved back.

Ignus calls us that. But we're not very little. A female voice said in my head, probably belonging to Hera.

Nice to meet you, by the way. Dalton said. Well, I guess 'linked'.

"Yeah, um nice to meet you guys too," I said loudly before turning to Ignus. "And you brought more people because?"

"Thought it might help with your... choices if you knew there were more of us," he said with a shrug, his eyes shining brightly now that the sun had begun to rise. "So, how has the pack reacted to the mutt's accusations?"

"Mutt?" I repeated before I realized he was talking about Zaina, "I don't think they're reacting all that well, Katherine in particular seems pretty unnerved." I'd have to talk to her about that.

"It'd be good if you did. We aren't the bad guys-" I scoffed.

"You do realize you guys are part of the group that kidnapped Lucien's sister, right?"

What? Dalton asked.

That wasn't us. Hera echoed in my mind. I looked over at Ignus, confused as I watched Hera march her way over to us, Dalton followed. The two of them had pitch-black hair and glistening blue eyes – siblings, I'm guessing.

"I told you not to trust that woman," Hera hissed as she walked over to me. "The three of us were planning to legitimately live there until your sister decided to ruin the plan and used it for her own devices."

"Half-sister," Dalton added and I raised an eyebrow.

"What?"

"Our kind doesn't breed werewolves... technically speaking, so it's obvious that Zaina's not completely related to you," Hera pointed out and I looked over at Ignus.

"I'm sorry... But you do know how ridiculous this sounds right?" I asked and Ignus nodded.

"Unfortunately ridiculous doesn't mean false. Bloodhounds breed bloodhounds, whether or not they're sired by werewolves."

"And why exactly did you guys want to live beside my apartment?"

"We were gonna try and ease into your life, but your sister ruined everything and your mate came into the picture," Ignus explained as I bit my bottom lip.

"Why are we, and I'm using that word carefully... called bloodhounds?" I asked.

"Because-" Dalton began but Ignus stopped him.

"When are you planning to have your mating ceremony?" Ignus asked and I stared at him.

"And why is that important?" I asked, Hera and Dalton then stared at each other.

"You'll have to bite your mate, inevitably drawing his blood," Dalton said as he walked over to me. There's a reason we have blood attached to our name...

We shift at the taste of werewolf blood – and the first shift –

Involves some severe bloodlust. Ignus completed for Hera.

"You're telling me, we're the equivalent of werewolf vampires?" I asked, incredulous.

"We... don't just feed on blood, Auden," Ignus said grimly. "It's... just a trigger."

Katherine called us 'cannibalistic blood suckers', I thought to myself. Everyone seemed to have heard my thoughts as they looked at each other.

Monsters. Hera said in her head before walking over to me.

"That's one of the reasons why we're here. We need your help and you'll definitely need ours. Your mate can't be your first..." She said and I swallowed a lump in my throat.

"And how exactly are we supposed to 'fix' that? How exactly are you supposed to help me deal with that?" I asked.

"We hunt- as we should," Ignus said. "Rogues are usually our... target. But should you really need a first blood volunteer, I would gladly offer up my-"

"Stop weirding her out, Ignus," Hera said. "But it yeah, it works both ways, you can taste the blood of a werewolf – or one of our own."

"If that's the case, why would I have to meet any of you more than once? Why don't I just drink blood from you and go?" I asked.

"Considering how old you are- we'd be here for a while..." Ignus commented.

"Also... we weren't the only ones looking for you..." Dalton said. "Ignus has been taking information and getting rid of it – you're not difficult to find when you're the daughter of an Alpha. That and you don't know what'll happen when you shift for the first time-"

"Okay, now we're getting weird. Who else would look for me?"

"Our-"

Auden? Lucien's voice rang in my head.

Yeah? I linked back.

Where are you? He asked and Ignus looked around and shook his head.

"If he's asking you where you are-" Dalton began but Ignus spoke up.

You can't tell him. Ignus said. Not until you win his trust. Completely win his trust. I felt my lips fall into a thin line.

Just going for a run- I left a note.

Just wanted to check, any requests for breakfast?

Anything, really. I'll be back soon.

Can you come in five minutes?

Um... I'll try?

"Mates. Always so attached," Ignus muttered. "Unfortunately... this was, unexpectedly brief. But we'll see each other again. If not, Dalton and Hera will talk to you," Ignus said and I simply nodded as I turned to get back to the pack house. I turned around and the three of them seemed to be talking, whispering really – because I couldn't really make out what they were saying... But I caught the words 'worry' and 'shift' quite often before they stopped and stared as I ran off.

"So... are you going to tell me what else Zaina told you?" I asked Lucien as he stared at his computer. I was in his office – particularly because he was a bit wary of Ignus... Not that it helps that I met him earlier this morning.

"Well, we couldn't exactly... follow interrogation procedures with her," Lucien said as he glanced up at me. I sighed and got up from my position before walking over to Lucien and wrapping my arms around him, resting my head on his shoulder. I look at the screen and found that Lucien had really begun to research all he could about bloodhounds.

"You get to work pretty fast," I said as I looked at the amount of tabs he had open.

"Not really. Desmond and Katherine are on the search for information and yet we have nothing. We're asking just about everyone we know," Lucien said, sighing as he turned to look at me. I lifted my head off of his shoulder.

You absolutely cannot tell him. Ignus said and I wanted to smack him out of my brain. Instead, I chose to ignore him.

"Lucien... what if I could find out?"

"No."

I stared at him.

"What do you mean, 'no'? You have no other information on these guys." Lucien shook his head.

"I'm not going to risk your life-"

"You don't even know what they want from me. How are you so sure they're a threat?"

"How are you so sure they aren't?" He countered and I rolled my eyes.

"Ignus went out of his way to locate me, do you really think he's out to kill me? He's already met me when I least expected him. Wouldn't it make sense for him to kill me then?" I tried to explain.

"Some people like to meet their prey beforehand – what makes you so sure he isn't planning anything worse?"

"Well why would he turn on my sister if they were all in on it?"

"To make himself look like a good guy. You don't know them, Auden."

"And neither do you! Neither do any of us!"

"Why are you so defensive of them?"

"And why do you hate them so much? You don't even know anything!" That was when I noticed that my voice had risen. Shït.

"And what do you know that I don't?" He asked and I bit my lip, refusing to look into his eyes.

Lucien then held my chin and lifted it up so that I would look at him. But as soon as our eyes met, I looked away.

"Auden. What do you know and how do you know it?" Lucien asked, his voice dead serious. I tried to pull my face away from his grip but he grabbed my shoulders and I felt the sudden weight in the air. He was using his command and the grip on his shoulders had increased in strength. I grit my teeth and looked down.

"Look at me." He commanded and though I felt ease in resisting – I knew better. I looked up into his eyes.

"Let go of me, Alpha," I said, my jaw clenched and tense.

"Auden." I balled my hands into fists. Alphas and their stupid freaking commands-

Submit for now, Auden. He can't know – not now. Just... avoid answering- Ignus said, invading my head.

Shut up! I hissed in my head – and suddenly silence came, my thoughts now mine alone. I looked up into Lucien's eyes.

"Let go of me," I repeated and I could already see Lucien's wolf threatening to come out- questioning an Alpha's command was pretty much the worst thing you could do to a wolf's ego.

"Or what?" Lucien growled.

The door slammed open and Katherine stormed in.

"Xander's injured," she said before looking between the two of us. "Sorry... Was I interrupting something?" Lucien immediately released me and I stood up, touching my shoulders that had gone sore from his hold.

"Lana?" Lucien asked.

"She's fine, we got Xander to the living room. Desmond's patching him up but Lana's screaming bloody murder, so you better get your big brotherly äss over there and care for the poor thing," Katherine said. Lucien nodded before looking at me and without another moment's hesitation, he walked out.

"Get into a fight?" Katherine asked me and I sighed.

"Something like that," I said with a shrug.

"Show me your shoulders," Katherine said and I gave her a weird look.

"Though I know you're part werewolf, it worries me when Lucien does that whole Alpha thing, best to make sure you're not bruised."

"Wouldn't be surprised if I was," I muttered garnering a chuckle from Katherine as I sat on the corner of Lucien's desk. I tugged on my shirt and Katherine pressed it lightly, I winced once she pressed a little further. She repeated it on my right shoulder and the same pain passed.

"He'll regret that later, for now, you might wanna ice that," Katherine instructed.

"Thanks nurse, Katherine. Gonna join me and Desmond in the medicine job?"

"Hell no, but I know how to do the basic shït, can't exactly have a geek like Desmond for a mate and not learn a few things, Doctor Auden," she mocked and I rolled my eyes. "What'd you guys fight about anyways?"

"I was suggesting I meet Ignus to learn more about the bloodhounds for you guys, which obviously didn't sit well with the angry Alpha, out there," I said and Katherine paused for a moment.

"Well... hopefully we can discuss it amongst each other – for now, we should go to the living room – Lucien should've calmed down a bit," Katherine said.

"Hopefully," I mumbled, as I rubbed my shoulders, following Katherine out of the office.

"What happened?" I asked as Desmond wrapped Xander's chest up in a bandage. Lana had her hands stuck on Xander's as Lucien rubbed her shoulder. I almost winced just from the sight of Lucien touching her shoulders – I mean he did just hurt me.

"We were on the way back here- only half-way through the hike and Lana was about to get tackled – the scent wasn't familiar," Xander said, his voice hoarse.

"He got clawed on the chest and partially bitten on the neck," Desmond said, sighing. "Had the guy been on target, you would've gotten seriously injured."

"Better me than her," Xander said, looking at Lana who seemed to be sobbing as Lucien patted her back.

"I'm guessing the wolf escaped?" Lucien asked and Xander nodded, his face revealing a sense of guilt – I don't know why though, considering he did what he could to protect Lana. "We'll do a sweep of the territory. We can't let the perpetrator escape – not when it could be one of those bloodhounds." I rolled my eyes, Lucien practically spit the word out.

Don't get angry, Auden. I don't know how you managed to block me out of your head. But- I sighed.

"I thought they weren't werewolves," Desmond said and I folded my arms over my chest.

"Yeah, they aren't. But Lucien's getting a little overprotective because he doesn't want me to-" Lucien growled loudly, interrupting me.

"Fine," I looked over at Xander. "I'm sure Desmond has you covered." Xander nodded in response before everyone looked between me and Lucien. It didn't take a genius to figure out that we were pissed at each other. Even Lana looked worried. I took a breath then turned on my heel.

Lucien could go find somewhere else to sleep. I walked in and slammed the door shut, locking it this time.

Meet me tomorrow. I said, hoping that Ignus received it.

So soon?

I need to know more. I'll tell you where to go by morning.

Alright. Goodnight Auden.

Goodnight my äss. I cursed before I shut him out and everyone else out of my head.

Chapter 15

I woke up early the next morning and crept out of the room before sunrise. When I made it out, Xander was still asleep on the couch with Lana holding onto his hand as she slept beside him. I smiled before I crept upstairs. I walked up to the top of the cabin and shoved on my boots before making my way outside. I hadn't spotted Lucien anywhere, which made me feel a little nervous. He could be anywhere. But it's not like I was going to sit still when I had the opportunity to learn more about... I guess, myself. I took a deep breath before I threw my hair into a ponytail and headed outdoors. I jogged my way out of the forest, feeling relief as the cold wind hit my face.

The sun was barely even up as I got to the nearest town. I walked quickly, occasionally switching to a run as I moved through the town. I eventually reached the beach side, after my cheeks had felt like they were made of ice and I had to run into a small, and thankfully open, store for some warmth.

You up? I asked, as I served myself a cup of coffee, quickly paying for it at the counter.

The beach front, huh? Ignus asked and I rolled my eyes as I walked back outside.

Was it that easy to guess where I was going? I asked.

I could practically feel you run in the direction. I will be there soon.

Good. I said before as I quietly sipped my coffee. I walked down and sighed as I saw my breath scatter in a thick mist before my eyes. I continued my walk until I found myself right in front of the beach. I took a seat on one of the benches and watched as the sky turned into a brighter shade of blue as the sun began to rise, giving enough light to at least color the sky.

I heard a car park nearby and turned my head. Sure enough, Ignus walked out of the car, making his way over to me and taking a seat beside me.

"Things didn't go down well with your Alpha friend, I suppose," he said with a chuckle.

"Someone was on Umbra territory after that conversation. I'd say having permission to meet you is off the table... But I have questions I need answers to."

"Then ask away," he said and I turned to face him. "Dalton and Hera scolded me for not taking our first meeting all too seriously."

"Right..." I muttered. "Anyways, I want you to tell me as much as possible- and I mean it. If you want to, you can tell me what I can and cannot share with Umbra or Lucien for that matter."

"Some things are better seen than explained," Ignus commented. "But I'll tell you everything you want to know and more."

In silence, of course. Ignus said and I nodded.

Of course.

Ignus walked away just as the sun had risen to a fair peak. It was much later in the morning now. People were beginning to appear, cars were driving by, and it became clear that our conversation was no longer safely private. But I learned enough for today. I turned just as Ignus started the car. He nodded and waved and I did the same as he disappeared. I tapped my empty coffee cup against the bench before standing up. I threw my cup away and sighed as I shoved my hands into my pocket and walked off.

It was only then that I acknowledged as certain someone's gaze and turned around. If I could've growled, I seriously would've. I sniffed the air and walked in the direction it led me. Sure enough, I found myself face to face with Lucien, who was growling at me.

"I thought I told you-"

"You did. But what choice did I have?" I hissed.

"Xander was attacked yesterday, my sister was in-" I rolled my eyes and Lucien growled even louder.

"Growl at me again and I swear to the goddess I will-"

"You'll what? You have nowhere else to go," Lucien said and I felt my jaw clench.

"What is your problem? I'm trying to get information, trying to learn why I'm being looked for, trying to understand what the fück has happened to my life- and you threaten me?" I asked, exasperated. "Are you for real Lucien? Do you want me to sit down and be content with living my entire life as a little toy in a werewolf's home?"

"I want you to wait until I decide what's best for you, for my pack, for everyone," he explained and I sighed.

"Everyone has already told you that everything they know about the bloodhounds is based off of rumors. But I can speak to them, I can get you the facts you need!" I said, my voice growing louder.

"And how do you know they aren't lying to you?!" Lucien yelled and I grit my teeth.

"I... I know they aren't," I said.

"And how could you know that? Can you read their minds? You're-"

"Fine," I said, interrupting him. My mind was already getting exhausted over fighting about this and Lucien was determined to not listen to me.

"What?" Lucien asked, confused.

"I met him once. You've seen it. I'm done." Lucien paused and I folded my arms over my chest. "I'm done. I won't see him anymore. Not unless you want me to. Happy?" I asked and Lucien paused.

"Is that all?"

"Take me back to the pack house," I said simply and Lucien looked at me. He raised his hand and I turned my face away from his touch. "Take me back, Alpha."

He stared at me first, his eyes searching my face for any kind of clue to my thoughts. But I stared back at him plainly.

"Your mate is here," Ignus said.

"I know."

"You know you'll have to make a choice..."

"Then I'll make it when I have to. I'll contact you if I need anything else."

"Alright." Ignus said before he stood up. "Stay... sane." He joked, smirking at me.

"I'll try."

I walked into the pack house and sighed as I found Lana and Xander still on the couch. This time, Lana seemed to be bearing with the fact that she had to watch some kind of TV show that she didn't seem to enjoy. Xander, however, was laughing along to the show as Lana sat by him. She turned around almost as soon as I got to the last step.

"Hey Auden!"

"Hey, enjoying your Saturday?" I asked and Lana nodded.

"...Yeah," Lana said, making me laugh at her hesitation. "Xander won't change the channel."

"Well, I think he deserves it. You've been taking care of him, though, right?" I asked and Lana looked at Xander.

"Have you?" He asked and Lana stuck her tongue out before Xander moved his hands to tickle her, causing Lana to hop off the couch, laughing.

"Glad to see you two are doing fine," Lucien said from behind me.

"At least someone knows how to handle his mate correctly," I said, earning a raised eyebrow from Xander and Lana's own sideways glance. I smiled at them. "Anyways, I'm gonna go get changed." I said and Lana nodded as she hopped back onto the couch and I made my way to the room.

I opened the door and sighed as I took out my ponytail and unzipped my jacket. I hung it up and watched Lucien through the mirror as he closed the door and leaned against it.

"Lunch?" He asked as I stripped out of the outer layers of my clothing.

"No thanks," I said as I got down to my tank top and a pair of thick leggings. My back felt disgustingly damp from all the sweat this morning- which unsurprisingly didn't go away while I spoke to Ignus. But the bruise on my shoulder from last night's... 'quarrel' with Lucien had almost completely disappeared, save for some pink and pale purple skin. Werewolves were fast healers... and I guess bloodhounds were too.

"How about a-"

"You don't have to be nice to me, I think we both established that from all the growling that's been going on," I said as I folded all my clothes away. Lucien folded his arms over his chest before he walked over to me. I moved away from him and went into the walk-in closet. He watched me as I moved about, picking clothes for the day.

"Are you going to stare at me all day?" I asked.

"I could." I rolled my eyes at his response. I made my way into the bathroom and sighed as I moved to close the door, but Lucien stopped me. I stared into his eyes and he did the same to me.

"Fine, be my fücking guest, Alpha," I said as I ran the shower and placed the clothes I'd picked onto the counter.

I took my top off, standing with my back to Lucien as I undid my underwear and fully stripped down. I heard a growl from behind me and I glanced at him through the mirror. His eyes immediately met mine as I tore my gaze from his and went into the shower. Thankful for the steam that shielded me from his gaze, I was able to at least shower in peace. But Lucien literally didn't leave me alone, I could see his shape through the steamed glass.

Once I finished my shower, I took hold of the towel that was right outside the glass door. Lucien now had his back facing me and he made sure to look away from the mirrors. I smiled at that, only remembering that I was supposed to be pissed at him as I ran the towel through my hair and wrapped myself in it afterwards.

"Am I being puppy guarded as my punishment?" I asked, deciding it'd be better to be sarcastic than awkwardly tense... There was no point when his eyes screamed lust and I was practically bared to him.

"Yes," Lucien replied and I rolled my eyes.

"I think it'd be worse if you actually watched me the whole time," I said, smirking and really testing to see if he'd turn around.

"I wouldn't want to amuse you," he said and I frowned. Instead of dressing up, I moved my clothes aside and took my seat on the countertop and rested my head between my hands. I took a towel nearby and continued to dry my hair.

"Did I hurt you?" Lucien asked, making me pause.

"What do you mean?"

"Let's start by physically. Did I physically-"

"Yeah, you did. But it's nothing but a bruise now," I said and I watched as Lucien's shoulders seem to relax and settle with relief.

"I'm... sorry."

"Pardon?"

"I'm not saying it again." Lucien said quickly before pausing. "But I didn't mean to-"

"To?" I asked as I got off the counter.

"I haven't gotten into any real trouble for years, Auden," Lucien said quietly and I nodded, even though I knew he couldn't see me.

"Uh huh," I muttered as I stepped closer to him, dropping the spare towel in my hands.

"I don't want to make any rash decisions-" Lucien began but I had pressed my fingers against the back of his shirt.

"Mmhmm..." I trailed off.

"Are you still listening to me?" Lucien asked as I just lifted myself a bit off the ground.

"I am," I whispered into his ear and I could practically feel the goosebumps on his skin. Lucien took a deep breath and his body tensed beneath my touch.

"You're barely clothed," Lucien said.

"I know," I whispered again.

"And we haven't exactly talked about everything..." He trailed off.

"So what do you wanna talk about?" I asked as my fingers ran up and down his back.

"Are you still angry?" I didn't answer that, instead I kissed his neck, earning a low lustful growl. "I guess not." Lucien muttered.

"A little..." I said in a hushed voice before Lucien turned around and cornered me against the counter. He stared into my eyes before one of his hands raised and caressed my cheek.

"What did he tell you?" He asked and I turned and kissed his palm.

"Do you want me to tell you now?" I asked before I gently sucked the skin on his wrist. "Or later?" Lucien watched me with dark eyes before he bit into his bottom lip, I grinned before he moved forward and kissed me. I felt my stomach flutter as a heat ran down my body and my hands wrapped themselves around his neck. His hands wrapped around my waist, feeling me through the damp towel wrapped carelessly around my body.

"Do you trust him?" He asked me as he pulled away and I pressed a soft kiss onto his lips.

"Do you trust me?" I asked and Lucien's hand came up behind me, touching my neck and rubbing the spot where he would mark me. I shivered as he pressed a kiss there, sucking and grazing his teeth before he made his way to my shoulders. He hesitated and I knew he was staring at the faint bruises that had tainted my skin. He brushed his thumb against them before lifting his head and looking into my eyes. He then pressed his forehead against mine.

"I'm sorry," He said in a hushed voice and I closed my eyes as I relaxed and took deep breaths. "I trust you, but I don't know how to trust-"

"I know," I said, opening my eyes and staring into his. "But I have to help you somehow... and I can't do it by sitting around." Lucien sighed as I raised my hand and caressed his cheek this time. He leaned into my touch and sighed once more.

"Then we'll talk. If we're doing this- if you're doing this for us – then we have to let everyone know. You're one of us now-" I placed a finger on his lips before I raised my right foot, rubbing it against his inner thigh and earning a groan from Lucien.

"I think we've got something else to take care of before we talk..." I trailed off, my inner switch obviously flipped by how Lucien had been touching and looking at me.

"You know this teasing thing has to end at some point, right?" He asked in a hoarse voice. I smirked.

"And where exactly would that point be?" I asked with a smirk. Lucien growled before he took off his shirt and immediately kissed my lips.

Lucien lifted me up and my legs instinctively wrapped around him and my hands found their way around his neck, the actions earning a growl from him as the towel began to loosen up, revealing even more of my skin.

"So I'm guessing... we'll talk... later..." Lucien said, his words break-ing apart as he began pressing kisses against my neck. He walked us out of the bathroom like that, kissing and holding on another. I gently bit on his lower lip, pulling it away as Lucien lay me down on the bed.

"Talk. Later. Right," I blurted as pulled him back down for another kiss. His kisses turned from soft pecks into deeper kisses as he reached behind my neck and gently tilted my head, sucking and licking ever so slightly. Tantalizing me as his free hand moved and I felt it slip beneath the towel that was barely clinging onto my skin.

"Pants. Off," I said as we briefly parted, earning a chuckle as Lucien unbuttoned his jeans, parting from me as he did away with them. He returned to me, still wearing his boxers. "So I'm guessing all the way isn't a part of this- 'not talking' thing," I muttered and Lucien chuckled. Before he slipped his hand beneath the towel...

"Oh... Oh..."

Chapter 16

I could smell something warm... and it isn't me mixing up my senses... I knew from the smell – something that was attracting my attention like a magnet. I sniffed the air looking for it, the smell of pine around me faded away – nothing else mattered. I could smell it – it was far away but I could sense just how far it was. I opened my eyes and found that the sun had just barely risen. The smell was there though and I couldn't find myself thinking of anything else.

I stood up and walked to the windows and pressed my hand against the cool glass. I traced my fingers across it... I dragged my fingers across the trail – locating the scent against the landscape of Umbra territory. I licked my lips as I located it drawing circles on the single spot against the window... I tapped on it lightly. Right... there...

"Auden?" I jumped awake, my eyes immediately looking to the source of the voice, only to find Lucien propped on his elbow beside me.

"What?" I asked and Lucien shook his head.

"You were mumbling in your sleep," he said and before I could react, he caressed my cheek. "You feeling okay?" I paused for a moment.

"...Oh," I murmured before placing a hand on his neck and pulling him down to me for a kiss. He growled against my kiss and I gently nibbled on his lower lip before tugging it lightly and releasing it.

"We better go before I lock us both in here," Lucien said in a low voice.

"Mmhmm... Doesn't sound like such a bad idea to me..." I trailed off and Lucien chuckled, kissing my neck lightly and peppering kisses across my collarbone before lifting himself off me. He touched my hands that were still on his neck, he sucked on my palm and kissed it, tracing his teeth across it before placing it down and walking away to the bathroom.

I grinned as I got up, suddenly realizing how sore I was.

"Oh I am not okay," I muttered earning a loud laugh from Lucien in the bathroom.

I got up and quickly tugged on Lucien's shirt before stretching my arms out. I walked over to the windows and smiled as I took in the view. I caught sight of a few running werewolves out on the territory and I followed their path. It was only then that I realized that there was a stream of fingerprints on the window that remained from the fogged up glass.

"Are you gonna shower or what?" Lucien asked from behind me as he kissed my neck and I jumped before I melted at his touch.

"Definitely shower. Wouldn't wanna have Lana ask about why I smell so much like her brother, now would we?" Lucien laughed before I skipped over to the bathroom.

I folded my arms as we gathered inside Lucien's office. Katherine, Desmond, Xander, Lana, Lucien, and I all stood around a large table that was set up. On it was a map that was laid down by Xander – it was of the entirety of Umbra territory. Usually I'd expect these maps to be dated – but the map looked like it was professionally graphed and marked.

"The attack happened around here," Xander said as he took a marker and encircled an area about a kilometer away from the pack house.

"We've had pack members circle this area," Desmond said, guiding his fingers along the outer edges of the map. "Came up with not a single trace-"

"Had the other pack members find as much as they could about bloodhounds – I'd say we've got nothing but rumors unless we count meeting Ignus himself," Katherine explained.

"So, nothing useful..." Lucien trailed off and I watched as Lana gripped Xander's hand.

"How's the wound?" I asked and Xander shrugged.

"Healing, though much slower than usual-"

"Side-effect of a bloodhound?" Desmond asked.

Definitely. Ignus said and I sighed.

"Yes," I confirmed and all eyes fell on me.

"I met with Ignus yesterday, Lucien saw me – and no, I did not have permission to do so – but I had no other choice," I explained with a sigh. "I'll tell you as much as I can." I looked to Lucien who nodded in response.

"According to Ignus, most bloodhounds are under one major 'pack' if you will," I explained. "Ignus said he only recently got away from that pack – but the truth to that statement is up to you all to discern."

"Well... we can always take caution," Katherine said with a shrug. I smiled briefly at her, earning a wink before I continued.

"Bloodhounds are harder to track – no matter what werewolf you use. If they leave a trail for werewolves, most of them do it on purpose," I said and I saw Desmond grimace. Katherine immediately put her hand on his and squeezed it.

"So how exactly do we prepare for them then?" Lucien asked.

"You use one of them," I said with a sigh. "Of course since we don't exactly know what the goal of both Ignus and the other 'enemy' is, we-"

"We blindly have to trust one to get possible false information about the other," Desmond said with an exasperated sigh. I took a breath and paused for a few moments.

"Not exactly." Desmond raised an eyebrow.

"From what Ignus has told me... it seems that I'm not exactly a werewolf-"

"We've already discussed this, you're human, no problem-" Katherine began but I shook my head.

"According to Ignus, I'm a bloodhound. And the only thing I can find that confirms this suspicion is my dad's actions towards Zaina and my situation – although he warned me about Ignus – he can't currently speak to me."

"But I can get that to happen," Lucien said, nodding his head.

"...Hold on, you can't possibly be a bloodhound," Katherine began.

"Yeah," Lana agreed and I smiled in response.

"When I was younger, the only member of my pack that I could link with was my dad. According to Ignus, bloodhounds don't breed werewolves – if I'm one of them I can help track... thing is, Ignus would have to teach me how to better do that," I explained.

"But you haven't shown any signs of... well, bloodlust," Desmond said.

"Apparently it doesn't happen to most... but the first taste of it can have its... negative side effects," I said with a sigh. "But I don't need to intake blood to get the most out of my abilities."

"And what abilities would that be?"

"I can track them – if you let Ignus teach me," I said, looking to Lucien for his approval before gauging everyone else's reactions.

"I don't think that's a good idea," Desmond said.

"He could be using you," Katherine added and I shook my head.

"Not if you guys watch over them – we can train close to territory – not necessarily here," I said, trying my best to persuade them. "Ignus has two kids with him – they're vulnerable."

"Kids?" Katherine asked.

"Bloodhounds like them- us," I said, quickly correcting myself. "Listen, I don't know for certain if what Ignus says is true – but I can say that I've been shown enough to believe him."

"What the hell did he show you?" Desmond asked.

"He spoke to me," I said with a shrug. "He linked me."

"How long has he been doing that?" Lucien asked.

"For a while now... the link goes a bit further... We can- we can almost sense each other's surroundings-"

You know they're gonna kill me if I get near them- right? Ignus said and I mentally groaned. Lucien stared at me before looking at everyone else in the room and sighing.

"Does Ignus know where this is?" Lucien asked.

"The pack house?" I asked.

Not that I do, but I can sniff you and your little bloodhound scent-but that's only because I know you. Ignus said, irritating me.

"Is he talking to you right now?" Lana asked, curiously. Aware that everyone was already watching me, I nodded my head.

"He says he can sniff me out – but that's because he knows I'm one of them," I said and Lucien folded his arms over his chest.

"Does he know who's hunting you?" He asked.

Yes and no. I know who gave the order. Ignus replied.

"He knows who gave the order – but not necessarily who it was that attacked." Lucien looked around the room.

"Where is he right now?" He asked and I waited for Ignus' reply.

Sorry, I didn't catch that. Ignus replied and I rolled my eyes.

He's asking where you are.

Oh. Well, I'm sure you can find that out.

Ignus.

We're roadside – we've been scouting the area outside your territory. Hera replied and I sighed.

"What?" Katherine asked, concerned.

"They're close by, they said they were scouting the area, probably to find out who got on in it in the first place," I replied.

"Tell them we're coming to bring them in," Lucien said. Katherine and Desmond's concerns showed on their faces but Xander and Lana seemed to stand by his decision. I nodded my head.

Lucien says he wants to bring you guys into the pack house.

Um... can we do it later? A little busy here. Ignus said and I raised an eyebrow.

What happened?

Look for yourself.

A quick flash of images filled my head. They were out on the highway close to territory – a trail of warm blood was dashed on the road. I saw Dalton and Hera kneeling down and covering it in snow.

What was that?

Your little attacker probably tried to get someone else – do me a favor and ask your Alpha if anyone else was injured or missing. We'll be there after we find out a bit more. Ignus said in a more serious tone.

"They found something they're investigating. Ignus is asking if you know of anyone that's injured or missing – aside from Xander," I informed and Lucien looked around the room. I knew that he was already sending a message to the pack members and I waited to see what Ignus would say next.

"We got nothing so far," Desmond responded, folding his arms over his chest. Katherine, on the other hand, pulled out her phone.

"...Alright, found something – there's a missing person reported just a few days ago," she said, showing her screen to everyone.

Got that? I asked Ignus.

Yeah, male or female?

Male. Jogger. I said as I read off of Katherine's screen. Late fifties.

It was then that I could smell it – rotting flesh – as if it was right in front of me.

What the hell is that? I asked.

See for yourself.

I closed my eyes and the image flashed around me. Hera was crouched down examining a mangled body lying in a pool of blood. Chunks of flesh lay scattered around, the body itself had been hidden on a caved in area on the side of a hill – they weren't far off from Umbra territory – but they weren't on it for sure.

"What's he saying?" Katherine asked.

"I think we just found the missing person."

Lucien rubbed his forehead.

"We'll meet Ignus there," he said before turning to me and nodding his head, "Lead the way, Auden."

I swallowed a lump in my throat.

"Let's go."

Chapter 17

I led the group towards Ignus and the others. We had to cross over a highway and into territory that was just barely outside of the border. I scrunched up my nose as the smell intensified – a human carcass never really appeals to anyone and it definitely doesn't appeal to anyone when it's not even recognizably human. I heard Katherine almost retch.

"Shït," Katherine cursed as she covered her mouth. Lucien grimaced and Desmond shook his head.

"Do you think they meant for us to find this?" Lucien asked, looking to Ignus, who looked to be buried deep within his thoughts.

"Probably," he replied before looking to me. "Smell anything different?" I shook my head.

"Would you mind if I tried something?" He asked, looking to me before looking to Lucien as well. The two of us glanced at one another before we nodded.

I watched as Ignus walked over to me and produced a small glass bottle, barely the size of his pinky, from his pocket. He opened it before handing it over.

"Take a whiff of that," he said and I stared at him for a moment before I proceeded to do as he asked of me.

The smell was heavy, despite being such a small bottle, I grimaced. It was a sickeningly musky kind of smell that reeked of cedar – deep and heavy – and definitely not my favorite smell.

"What is that?" I asked.

"An old acquaintance loved it," Ignus said with a shrug before he took the vial from me and closed it up. "Smell it anywhere else now?" I looked around and sniffed the air, feeling a little bit like an idiot as everyone watched me.

"No," I replied and Hera nodded.

"Good," Hera said, "That rules out one of our suspects."

"Not exactly, it rules out the possibility of him being here," Ignus said and Desmond cleared his throat.

"Who are we talking about?" He asked.

"Someone we're not quite... fond of."

"Well that's vague," Katherine said and Ignus shrugged.

"Can't exactly let us spill our guts to you just yet, we're not exactly best friends," Ignus said in his usual tone. "Anyways, we're gonna have to clean this mess up for now, we're not gonna find whoever killed him."

"How useful of you," Katherine commented and Ignus smiled at her.

"If Auden can't sniff it out – neither can we."

"And why's that?" Lucien asked and Ignus simply grinned.

"How about we tell you later?" He replied earning a sigh from Hera.

"He means we'll tell you when we're not around the body – it's not exactly appropriate or necessary – and we've been out here too long," Hera explained.

I stared at the body and sighed. Guy was innocent.

Probably. Ignus replied but when I looked at him, he was already talking to Lucien about something. Hera on the other hand had taken Dalton's hands and was talking to him. Desmond and Katherine walked over to me.

"You okay?"

"Yeah, I'm not exactly easily grossed out," I said and Desmond nodded.

"Yeah, well I am," Katherine said, grimacing.

It took a while before Ignus completed 'documenting' the body and getting some samples of the body's scent- which involved the rather grotesque process of Ignus taking a small plastic container and collecting blood samples and bits of flesh. Eventually, we had to return to the pack house, this time, Ignus, Hera, and Dalton followed behind us. Lucien then sent out an order to have someone from the pack get rid of the body.

"So if you had no result from that little encounter, what was the point of bringing us there?" Katherine asked as we entered Lucien's office once again.

"The point, was to show you that the attacker isn't scared of going after humans – and tearing people to shreds, it was also to show Auden the kind of things our kind are capable of doing when... we're not in tune with ourselves," Ignus explained.

"Meaning?"

"Bloodhounds don't have packs – but we have families – and those form clans of a very similar hierarchy. We lose control over our 'selves' in two main scenarios – from extreme hunger or from a command," he said and I folded my arms over my chest.

"And who gives out the command?" I asked.

"The main bloodline – they're our Alphas but a little... more condescending," Ignus said and I heard Hera scoff.

"So who exactly was behind the attack?" I asked, trying to keep Katherine and Lucien's faces somewhat amicable. Ignus could be a little overbearing.

"Well, we still think it's the guy we're thinking of, but he wasn't there – so it had to be a remote order – which means he's looking real hard for you," Ignus said with a sigh.

"Me? Why?" I asked and Lucien placed his hand on mine.

"Might wanna ask your dad about that one, it's not exactly my story to tell," Ignus said with a wink. "Anyways, about the tracking thing... We make sure that we get the right person by handing off a scent that belongs to the 'pack' – since the man didn't smell anything like that – it means the attacker wasn't a very highly ranked person – so he'll be manageable."

"Manageable? He hurt one of Umbra's guys," I said, glancing at Xander who kept a straight face.

"I never said he was manageable for werewolves. Unless you're trained to kill our kind – it'll be hard to murder predators like us," Ignus said with a shrug. "Especially when it's someone low-ranked and made for this kind of shït."

"You're gonna make all of our heads explode with this information," Katherine commented.

"Yes, but you were gonna come across it either way – and we're really the only ones that can help you out of this situation," Ignus said with a smile. "If you want to keep Auden here, of course." I raised an eyebrow.

"Of course," Lucien said, pressing his lips into a thin line. I squeezed his hand and sighed.

"I can't possibly be the only reason that whoever-it-is is hitting Umbra," I said and Ignus smirked.

"You'd be surprised how petty we bloodhounds can be."

"And now you're just freaking me out," I said, rolling my eyes.

"Does this mean we can stay here?" Dalton asked, looking around.

"What do you think?" Lucien asked, looking to Katherine who had her arms folded over her chest.

"Well, considering our little Auden here's involved, I'd say my decision's already made," she said, smiling in my direction. "And I can grow to enjoy sarcasm," she added, looking straight at Ignus who simply smiled in her direction. Hera and Dalton looked at each other and sighed in relief.

"Same here, but my trust is based on Auden's," Desmond said, looking to me and bowing his head briefly, I did the same. Lucien ran his fingers along the top of my knuckles.

"I admit, I'm not sure how exactly things will go. But I'm willing to take them in if it helps us out," Lucien commented, "We have rooms upstairs, someone will show you around the house later on." Ignus and Hera looked at each other before they walked over to Lucien. Dalton followed behind them before they pulled out something from their pockets.

"Since bloodhounds aren't bonded by packs – we usually offer something in exchange for 'trust', if you will," Ignus explained. Lucien held out his hand and Ignus smiled before he placed a ring in his hand. It looked like an engagement ring, silver with small intricate vines that all joined to hold the large diamond that sat comfortably in the vines.

Looks special. I said and Ignus smirked.

It was.

It still is. Hera countered. Hera then walked over and placed a small glass stone with a flower settled inside of it. The flower was a beautiful sapphire color with dark edges around its petals. The stone itself was the size of a pebble and Hera ran her thumb over it before placing it on Lucien's hand as well.

"It's not as fancy as Ignus', but I'd fight for that to stay where I can count on it," she said, looking Lucien straight in the eyes. "I'll trust that we can count on your pack." Lucien nodded before Hera stepped back and Dalton walked over to us. He shifted a bit before he sighed. Dalton bit his lip before bringing out a thin silver brooch shaped in a butterfly form and inlaid with diamonds, sapphires, and rubies.

"They're all from someone we cared about," Dalton said before looking at Lucien and then at me.

"One person?" I asked but Dalton didn't answer and Ignus simply cleared his throat.

"We'll talk tomorrow – the three of us have spent all day tracking," he said with a smile and I nodded.

"Aren't you guys supposed to be trackers?" Katherine asked and Ignus grinned.

"Did any of you smell that body before you got there?" He asked in turn. Not getting a response other than a solemn stare, Ignus excused himself and their group walked away – but not before Dalton turned and gave me a soft smile.

"What was that about?" Desmond asked.

"I don't know, but I've a feeling I should know," I said before turning to Lucien. He showed me the objects before he turned to the rest.

"We should all rest for the day. Try not to get too hostile, you two," Lucien said. Desmond and Katherine shrugged.

"We can be civil," Katherine said with a wink. "I'm just a little too overloaded with info."

"Ignus tends to stuff it into people's heads like that," I said with a sigh.

"They seem like reasonable people – I'm only concerned with what exactly they eat," Desmond said and I bit my bottom lip.

"Well, it doesn't seem like they're total monsters, so let's give them a chance," Lucien said.

"Will do. Desmond and I have some other errands to run – time to give everyone a break about researching bloodhounds. Do you want us to do anything?"

"Run a warning through the pack – I'd like it to come from you in person if possible. We need everyone to be a little more cautious than usual." Katherine nodded.

"Will do Alpha. See you guys later."

As Katherine and Desmond exited the room, Lucien turned to me and used his free hand to run a hand through my hair.

"You okay?"

"Yeah, I guess," I answered just as Lucien pressed a kiss to my forehead.

"I really think I should set up a meeting with your dad."

"I think so as well," I said, pressing my lips into a thin line. "Where do you think you'll keep their things?"

"In a vault. It doesn't take much to understand that these things are worth more than money – they're sentimental," he said and I nodded. "Come, I'll show you where we'll put them."

We eventually made our way into our bedroom and it was only then that I realized how much time had passed – and having realized, I actually yawned in reaction to the fact that the sun was already sinking behind the mountains. We made our way into the closet and Lucien smiled as he opened one of the closets. He moved the hangers aside and pressed his hands lightly against the back wall. I watched as it popped up and Lucien gently slid it to the right to reveal a small vault. He then placed in a series of numbers and opened it up to reveal a black cardboard box sitting on the top level of the vault.

"What's that?" I asked as Lucien set the three sentimental objects on the bottom half of the vault.

"A few files, some memories..." he said with a smirk before he picked it up and handed it to me.

"Whoa, you sure you want me to-"

"We can look at them together at some point. Get to know each other, you know?"

"I'm not even sure I know myself anymore," I said as I tucked the box back into the vault.

"Then we'll get to know you together," Lucien said as he pressed his hand against mine, closing the vault. I sighed and as Lucien finished closing the vault, he turned to me and pressed a kiss to my lips.

I felt relief course through me and I relaxed as he deepened the kiss. He placed his hands on the small of my back and pulled me into my arms.

"A little better?" He asked. "I can feel your uneasiness – and it's not a good feeling."

"Sorry," I muttered before looking up into his hazel eyes. I kissed the corners of his lips before pressing my forehead against his. "Man did I get lucky on the mate roulette." Lucien chuckled and I sighed before I pressed another kiss on his lips. The hunger in my stomach was growing and it wasn't for food. Lucien probably felt it to, his hands began to roam around my body as he pulled me closer. He growled into my mouth, tracing his teeth along my lips, before parting from me.

"I thought you were sore," he said hoarsely and I smirked.

"I'm a little better now," I said, batting my eyelashes and earning a hearty chuckle from Lucien before he lifted me up and I wrapped my legs around his waist. "I don't really wanna think anymore today."

"Understood," he said as he carried me to bed.

I could smell something again. The same scent as before... I got up...

I walked over to the window and tapped the glass, tracing a path... eventually circling around a spot. There... Right there... I tapped against the spot on the window.

I felt a cold shiver run down my spine and my legs felt weak in fear.

That's right. Right. There. Find me. A sharp whisper said and I immediately opened my eyes, gasping for air. Lucien immediately got up.

"What's wrong?"

"Nightmare... Bad... bad nightmare..."

I looked to the window – and felt my heart slow as I saw the clear line drawn against the fogged up glass until it created a circle that marked a particular area. Lucien's eyes followed my gaze and he took me in his arms, cradling me.

"We're gonna need Ignus to speed things up."

Chapter 18

"How many times has this happened?" Ignus asked me after he had finished pacing for the nth time around the room. We were in the living room now and Ignus had come down as quickly as I sent the message.

"Once," I said with a shrug.

"That's not possible. It takes a while for anyone to contact remotely," Ignus said, running a hand through his hair. "Do you remember any kind of similar experience?"

"No..." I trailed off.

"She's been mumbling in her sleep a lot. Though I haven't been able to make out exactly what she's been trying to say," Lucien pointed out, Ignus shook his head.

"Since when?"

"Just the past two days or so," Lucien said and Ignus groaned.

"Shït."

"What?" I asked. Ignus seemed to be lost in thought, his body had tensed up, a crease had formed between his eyebrows and his jaw was clenched.

"I'll be right back – I need to speak to Hera and Dalton."

"Okay-" I said just as Ignus walked off.

It didn't take long before Hera, Dalton, and Ignus appeared in our room. Ignus also seemed to have called Desmond and Katherine – and now we were all basically having a meeting in the mini-living area of our bedroom. Katherine stretched her arms up and yawned – she was dressed in some leggings and a large shirt – she had probably just woken up. Desmond was already dressed in a buttoned down shirt and some jeans – he looked like he was ready to go to work at the clinic. Hera and Dalton were wearing their clothes from yesterday – and now that I thought about it, so was Ignus.

"We didn't know whether or not to tell you or have your dad tell you himself – but since we're slowly running out of time..." Ignus said – but for some reason his voice seemed to be fading away.

I could feel a frigid cold hit my body, climbing up my arms and legs – paralyzing me. I could hear someone breathe slowly – saw flashes of a landscape of snow and forest. North.

Ignus can't hide you for long. A distinct deep male voice said. I shivered but felt something even stranger, a warmth spread out from my chest and the smell of something familiar – almost nostalgic – hit my nose.

Find me. You know you have to.

"Auden," Lucien boomed beside me. I jumped at the sound of his voice and turned to him. Despite the harshness in the call of his voice, his eyes revealed worry and concern. Ignus cursed under his breath. Lucien nodded in Ignus' direction – as if to give him permission for something. I watched as Ignus walked over to me.

"We're gonna need to buy a little time," Ignus said and I raised my eyebrows and looked to Lucien. "Keep an eye on her for now. Dalton,

Hera, and I will try to create a temporary barrier – we should be able to do it to hide her. Don't leave Auden alone."

"Got it," Lucien said understandingly, I raised an eyebrow as Ignus bowed his head respectfully and walked away.

"What the heck did you two talk about?" I asked.

"It's nothing too important, I'll tell you about it later," he said and I pressed my lips into a thin line. Lucien caressed my cheek and pressed a kiss against my forehead. "I promise."

"...Okay," I muttered just as his phone rang. Lucien looked at the screen briefly before picking it up.

"Alpha Frasier," Lucien greeted stiffly. Deciding that it wouldn't be good for me to eavesdrop, I walked away to shower.

As I let the water fall over me I felt a feeling of calm wash over me. Who the heck am I hiding from? No one's ever said it so far- but I'm definitely 'hiding' or at least being hidden. That's been made pretty clear by how Ignus acted this morning and Lucien's own 'hidey-hole' pack basically reinforces the whole idea. I sighed and leaned my head against the wall. What the hell have I gotten myself into?

I walked out of the bathroom now fully clothed in some loose pants and a white shirt and watched as Lucien typed away frantically on his laptop. I wrapped my arms around his shoulders. He turned his face and placed a quick kiss on my cheek before he resumed working.

"What are you working on?"

"Another Alpha just informed me of a killing on their territory. They're further up north – but apparently our case isn't the only one. Seems like someone's trying to get the northern packs rattled."

"And are they? Rattled, I mean?"

"Pretty much. I'm just writing up some e-mails and reports as to recent events. I'm not telling them about Ignus and the rest for now – I'm avoiding the subject of bloodhounds in the first place. Some of these packs aren't exactly as open to cooperating with, you know..."

"Yeah, I know," I said before pressing a kiss on his cheek as well. "Who's Alpha Frasier?"

"Welll... his territory is the closest to ours – and... well, he's Sheila's dad," Lucien said – and I don't know if it was just me – but he sounded a little shaky? Nervous even.

"Who's Sheila?" Lucien paused before looking at me.

"The girl. The one that was in this room-"

"Oh," I interrupted before I sighed and ran my fingers through my hair. "That Sheila."

"Mmhmm..." Lucien murmured as I saw him hit send on his laptop. As soon as he did so, I pulled the thing away from him and set it down behind me before I climbed into his lap and straddled him.

"Well... it's not like she'd make her way over here again, right?" I asked, staring into Lucien's eyes as I placed my hands on his chest.

"I don't think she would," he said as he placed his hands on mine, lifting my right hand to his mouth and kissing my palm and running his teeth along my skin. My belly warmed up and I could sense the hair on my arms stand at attention as I bit my bottom lip. "This'll never get old, will it?" He asked as his other hand fell on my neck and his thumb caressed my jaw.

"Probably not..." I trailed off as I turned my head and ran my own teeth along his thumb. I moved the hand he had held to his mouth and caressed his face. "Are you worried?" I asked.

"A little," he admitted before I leaned closer to him, resting myself on his right shoulder as he wrapped his arm around me.

"So am I," I commented as I snuggled into him.

What did you see? Hera's voice rang in my head.

What do you mean? I asked.

Ignus said your mate had to use a command to snap you out of it. You couldn't hear us, Auden. His voice was only loud enough because he was both your mate and your Alpha.

What?

Nevermind the details – what did you see?

I didn't see anything relevant – just another forest – colder. He said he'd find me.

...Okay. I'll talk to you more later. Hera said before her voice faded from my head. Lucien had now begun to play with my hair before I smelt something – the same exact thing that I had smelt before. But I wasn't having any voices through my head.

Guys- what is that? I asked, trying to make sure that it was one of Ignus' group and not whoever-the-fück-it-was. Lucien sighed before squeezing my hand.

"Your dad's here."

"What? How do you-" I began but I heard a loud thud come from the stairs.

I looked up and found Lana and Xander leading someone together. The person was limping, quite badly, behind them. Lana held his hand, Xander pulled him up, and as they made a turn – I caught a glimpse of my dad's face. He gripped a piece of white cloth in his hands. I immediately stood up to help him and he chuckled, his voice hoarse as I helped Xander bring him to the couch.

"What- why are you- how-" my dad cleared his throat, stopping me. He gave me a soft smile.

"Your mate here sent for me – ran into a bit of trouble with... well, you'll find out soon enough."

"What do you mean?" I asked, "When did you fly out here?"

"As soon as he could," Lucien said. He took my hand and gripped it.

Ignus said it'd be best if you two spent some time alone. Lucien said before he then got up and kissed my forehead. I'll see you later. He then nodded his head in a way of respectfuly bowing towards my dad, who did the same and smiled. My dad settled onto the couch and groaned as I lifted the leg that he was limping with onto the footstool in front of him. Lana then walked over to me and squeezed my hand before taking Xander's hand and walking off. The two of them disappeared into the hallway leading to Lana's bedroom – and if I wasn't mistaken, Lucien had gone into his office.

I then turned to my dad and sat down beside him. He sighed before handing me the white cloth.

"What is it?" I asked, as I realized that it was a delicate white handkerchief that was embroidered with small daisies.

"It's your mother's," he said plainly.

"Mom sent this? Well-" I caught a scent – and I looked to my dad.

"Do you smell that-"

It was sweet – like gardenias... I took the handkerchief and pressed it to my nose. A wave of nostalgia came over me but I had no idea where that sense came from.

"Your mother said that it'd be unavoidable – but that it was worth a try..."

"What are you talking about-"

My dad sighed before he brought out a small journal – it was basically falling apart. Its faux leather cover had begun to peel, a few loose papers peeked out of its form, and even the cover had large creases. I opened it and my dad watched as I leafed through the pages. There wasn't a single word written in it, only bits and pieces of newspaper clippings, magazines, a few leaves – collectibles that were hardly sticking to their pages anymore.

"Whose were these?" I asked.

"They belonged to this woman named Aurelia..."

Aurelia... I repeated in my head. I flipped one of the pages and this time – it contained a frail envelope that had slightly yellowed over time. It was still sealed with bit of wax – not red or anything – just like plain candle wax. There was a fingerprint over it instead of a seal and I placed my thumb against it.

Keep safe, Auden... and stay away. A woman's voice said in the back of my head and I found myself opening the envelope without another moment's hesitation.

Chapter 19

----

24 years ago...

Dante, we have trouble. Dante sighed as he sprinted forward. He was doing his final rounds around the territory. Days of nagging from his parents about his refusal to 'complete' the mating ceremony had been weighing him down – and though he really didn't have much reason to, well, not complete it – he felt like it wasn't right. It wasn't fair – Diana had met her mate and he hadn't. And yet-

Where do you want me? Dante asked, distracting himself.

East. It's really just some kind of brawl – I think they're just humans but it looks pretty serious.

Okay, I'll be there soon. Don't tell father.

Roger that.

Dante took deep breaths as he pressed on. Eventually the sound of a what seemed to be a large argument rang louder and louder in his ears.

Dante? Diana's voice rang in his ear.

Not now. I'll talk to you later.

But your parents are-

Not now, Diana. He shut her out – it wasn't that he didn't care about her. Sure, she was his childhood friend – but he wasn't exactly sure if he loved her or not. He'd always thought that he would reserve himself for his mate – and now he wasn't so sure if his duty was more important than what the goddess wanted him to do. And... well... the full moon last night guaranteed certain things that he wasn't so sure he could commit to either.

Dante slowed down – the smell of unfamiliar people had gotten stronger. They were close now.

"What the hell do you mean we can't hunt here?!" A man shouted. Someone snorted and Dante crept close behind a set of trees – he was still far away but just close enough to hear them.

"It's against your oath-"

"Fück those oaths! We haven't fed for months! We're blood-" A loud thud was followed by an agonized groan.

"Careful of what you say. We're on territory-"

Territory? How do they know? Dante wondered, his nose sniffing the air as he attempted to walk closer. He continued to sniff the air trying to figure out if he could sense a pack or a general kind of smell among them... They could be witches for all he knew – and witches and werewolves didn't necessarily mix too well together. Just as Dante was about to take another step, he felt someone grab his arm. He didn't even have time to gasp – whoever it was had a tight grip on him and had muffled his mouth.

"Well, lookie here- seems we're in luck," a man behind him said. Dante tried to scream – but nothing came through and the man simply tightened his grip on him.

"Charles... let the guy go-" Dante spotted another man speaking, he was tall, calm, and his eyes gleamed a vivid ice-blue color in the dark.

"Oh come on – lone wolves are easy prey- you should know that, or has this wolf-less diet made you soft?" Dante heard something crack from behind him – and he was almost certain the man behind him was shifting.

What the fu- Someone- Dante began but it was cut off.

"No use trying to contact your friends little guy. No offense – I don't have much against you personally – I just need a little bite of your-"

Dante felt a strong breeze blow behind him – the hands the restrained him had let go – he didn't even see what had happened. But he immediately fell forward and the tall man in front of him grabbed him, pulling him to his back. It was only then that Dante's senses were able to catch up with him. A woman with long black hair had appeared now and she exuded power from her body – almost like an Alpha... but for some reason, at that precise moment her power felt almost suffocating to Dante.

"Stand down, Charles," she said. The man spat at her feet but he could barely get up. She then turned and it was only then that Dante was able to get a clear look at her. In the dim light, he could make out her vivid green eyes that seemed to glow in the dark – and though she wasn't looking at him, he felt a pull so powerful that he couldn't have mistaken it for anything else.

His heart pounded against his chest. He barely registered what was being said as the man that stood in front of him moved forward, picking up Charles from the ground before disappearing in the blink of an eye. The woman remained and her eyes marked hesitation –

she didn't want to look at him. But Dante walked forward and when she didn't move – he pressed on until he stood a mere step away from her.

He reached out his hand and her breath hitched as she recoiled away from his touch. She bit her lip before she spoke.

"Aurelia," she said simply, stopping Dante's movements.

"What?" He asked.

"My name, it's Aurelia." Dante looked at her and she returned his stare this time. She was commanding, her eyes challenging him, studying him – and if he wasn't careful he would've revealed how intimidated he was. He cleared his throat, glancing away briefly before looking back into her eyes.

"Dante," he replied briefly before holding out his hand and she looked at it simply – Dante could swear he saw a hint of a smile on her cheek – but she quickly turned on her heel. The longing to touch her immediately intensified and Dante reached out to hold her but she moved before he even had the chance.

"I thought Alphas were supposed to be 'special'," she said before turning to glance at him.

"...What?" He asked and she shrugged before walking further into the forest. Dante followed behind her.

"Well, I guess the lore makes you all seem more interesting than you really are," she commented and Dante rolled his eyes, but before he could retort, she stopped.

"You've mated," she said as she placed her hand on a tree, running her fingers against its coarse surface. Dante swallowed a lump in his throat.

"I..." he trailed off but she immediately turned her head and smiled at him.

"I wouldn't have waited either," she said.

"Wouldn't? So you aren't-" he froze – and all that had caused it was a look she gave him. Piercing him with her emerald eyes as if she was staring right through to his core... and for a moment, he felt vulnerable.

"Why?" He asked, finally mustering up the courage to speak. She raised he eyebrows.

"Why, what?"

"Why did you wait then?" She chuckled, the sound making his heart flutter as she faced him fully now, allowing him to admire her, her pale skin, the long curly hair... she was tall, confident, and completely different from-

"Good night...Dante," she said simply before she turned again, this time stepping forward. And she was gone. Dante didn't even see which direction she'd turned. She left barely a trace, save for the leaves that had turned up from the ground and the soft breeze that swept across his face. She smelled of gardenias and her disappearance immediately left Dante feeling empty.

Dante... your father- Diana began, but he interrupted her.

I'm coming. Dante replied hastily. He dragged his feet in the direction of the pack house with a weight falling on his shoulders and a deep almost animalistic urge to find her. Aurelia. And had he paid hard attention, he would've noticed a pair of emerald green eyes watching him in amusement – before they disappeared into the night again.

I took the envelope, my hands shaking as I tried, as gently as I could, to open it up. Inside it was a series of photographs. One was of dad and a woman I had never seen before. She had black hair and a shy smile- as if she didn't really want the photo taken. Dad seemed happy though, his arm slung over her. They were both young and had a pair of matching black turtlenecks on. The next photo had them looking much more relaxed. She was laughing now and you could see that my dad had held the camera up and pressed it at a time where she wasn't really aware of it at all. It was the third photo that captivated me. It was of the woman sleeping, but she had fallen asleep caressing her stomach. She was wearing what looked to be a red shirt that was pulled up to reveal her enlarged stomach and she cradled it with a soft smile on her face. Although she looked peaceful – they were in what looked like a really tiny cabin – maybe even a garden shed of some sort. Hidden...

"Who-"

"That's Aurelia..." My dad trailed off. "I think you can guess what-"

"Is she my mom?" I turned to him and watched as he avoided my gaze. He nodded grimly before looking at me.

"I was already... I had to be with Diana before I met her. Her dad was a close business partner - it made sense to bring us together. She lost her mate in a car accident – and we grew up together. I hadn't met my mate and I wasn't getting any younger... I met – I met Aurelia-" my dad's voice had gotten shaky. So I placed a hand over his own and squeezed it in hopes of reassuring him. I moved closer to him and rested my head at the crook of his neck.

"I... I met her a few weeks after we'd finalized the ceremony I guess. I... I couldn't bring myself to mark her yet – to make her officially 'mine.' Something just didn't feel right. And I guess that was the goddess' way of saying I'd made a mistake. I... She... we stayed together. She would meet me and we'd talk... she'd never let me touch her," my dad laughed and I smiled at that. I smiled at how he spoke of her – even if I'd never known her.

"But... mom— I guess, Diana, now... she never treated me any-"

"Diana's the kindest soul I could ever had as a Luna... She knew... how could she not – and I know it was painful for her. An unmarked Luna despite a 'mating ceremony' pregnant with Zaina from a sudden 'duty.' But she understood how painful it was to be parted from a mate, she had lost hers and I hadn't found mine when we were... well... I couldn't hide Aurelia's existence from her. She never met her personally, I wouldn't let that pain happen. I asked her for a year and she gave it to me...

"We left Carmine together – she decided to 'explore' the world and Aurelia and I decided to stay at a small cabin far from anyone's reach. And... well... things just... things got..." My dad had a hard time speaking now so I rubbed his back and snuggled into him. "Aurelia was always too strong... too hardheaded... but we both had duties to fulfill – and she... she chose to keep you with me – she said that it'd be better off if you didn't know about the past... But she said that if it was unavoidable – she'd let you at least know a part of her..."

"So... she left?" I asked and my dad nodded.

"It wasn't... it wasn't easy... she never once marked me, asked for my blood, or anything of that sort. She wasn't a predator like the rumors say – but she told me that the others weren't like that. She always disappeared a few times into the night and she'd reappear in the morning, smiling... And then she had you – and for a time, she stopped leaving. We had the most wonderful time together."

"But...?" My dad gave me a woeful smile.

"We couldn't hide forever... and it was clear she was someone important to her group as much as I was to Carmine. When you were born – she refused to have anyone else around, she brought you with strength – and I was so scared for her. She only stayed a few days before she told me she couldn't stay anymore. That our time was up...

"You cried so much that day. Aurelia calmed you down and handed you to me – and then a man showed up to fetch her. It was the same guy I'd met before – the one that tried to protect me when she stepped in. I could still remember the look in his eyes. He looked sad for us – for all of us..."

"And you never heard from her again?"

He shook his head and I looked up at him, only noticing then that my dad had been crying. His cheeks wet with tears as he silently did so.

"Hey..." I murmured, rubbing back and hugging him.

23 years ago...

"You have to do it, Dante... please," Aurelia said, begging him with her eyes. Dante held the baby in his arms, looked at her and then back at Aurelia.

"I... I can't- we could- you and I could- we-" she placed a hand on his cheek and smiled. The baby began to hic, signaling that she was about to cry again. Aurelia hushed the little one and gently caressed the baby's cheek.

"She'll grow up strong and you'll love her... She'll grow up safe... as long as she's with you," she said and Dante shook his head.

"That's not tru-"

"Then you'll make it true, Dante... We promised a year and our time is up. You have a family, a real family waiting for you back there. You swore to her – to your pack, your family, that you'd come back."

"But you'll never-" She smiled at him and caressed his cheek this time.

"We can say it together then."

"But-" Her eyes stopped him again. Emerald and bright under the full moon he felt himself choke up.

"I... Aurelia-"

"I... Dante," She smiled at him and the two of them spoke together.

"Reject you, Dante-"

"Reject you, Aurelia-"

"As my mate."

"As my mate."

Dante let out an exasperated breath, a loud sob, as his tears fell from his eyes. He could see it in Aurelia's eyes as well, as her tears welled up and she gently pulled him in for a kiss. He held onto her desperately with his free hand, making sure that their child was alright. Aurelia closed her eyes and before her tears could fall, she parted from him, gently caressed the cheek of her child, and stepped away, as fast as she could.

She disappeared from him again.

And this time, she would never return.

Chapter 20

"How is she?" Ignus asked from outside the room.

"She's fine... just... quiet," Lucien answered as I buried myself underneath the sheets.

"She hasn't had any of those 'episodes' right?"

"No. She's been doing fine – though if it's because of a lack of sleep or because she's- well, shutting everyone out... I'm not sure. Have you tried to talk to her?"

"She shut me out too... I'm afraid you and Dante are the only ones that can talk to her for now. And yeah, I know you can hear me!" Ignus said, yelling that last part. I heard Lucien chuckle before I heard a clap- they probably shook hands. They'd gotten pretty friendly over the past few days – but who could blame them. Ignus and the others had been running non-stop, supposedly covering their tracks. Even Katherine and Desmond seemed to be better off with them. I'd hear them make jokes and talk over dinner – and though everyone has been more than kind, empathetic even, I couldn't bring myself to go out there just yet.

For some reason, every time I thought of Aurelia... my mother... I could see her so vividly, even hear her at certain points, and it made my heart ache in a way I had never felt before.

The door opened and my thoughts disappeared as I listened to Lucien's footsteps padding against the wooden floor. As soon as he got close to me, I reached my hand out and he took it, pressing his lips against the back of my hand before he took a seat by me and I brought myself out of the covers.

"Any chance you'd like to have dinner in the kitchen today?" he asked and I shook my head. He sighed before taking my hand and massaging it.

"What's she like?" He asked.

Lucien knew about what I'd learned. It was hard not to tell him. Not when he walked in on me staring at a bunch of photos all over the room of her. Tears would fall from my eyes without my control. I vaguely remember Ignus and Hera's voices trying to tell me something – but I shut them out. Not because I didn't want the comfort or the explanations they might've provided, but because I couldn't think and I didn't want to. My dad cried too, but I think he was more surprised when I began sobbing. I didn't know where it came from – it just washed over me.

"Auden?" Lucien called and I sighed as I sat up. Lucien then moved to sit beside me and I rested my head on his shoulder. "Feeling any better about things?"

You think? I asked earning a chuckle.

"Well, I was wondering if you wanted to join me- for a run."

Not really in the mood for exercise, Lucien. I said as I lifted my head off his shoulder.

"Then let me just show you something-"

I don't wanna put on-

"Please."

And maybe it was something about the way he said it, but I timidly got up, my feet feeling the cool floor for the first time in three days. I looked at him before I climbed onto his lap and pressed the tip of my nose gently against his.

"Okay," I said, my voice low and hoarse. Lucien smiled before he gave me a quick kiss.

"Go change. Quickly."

Considering how cold it still was, I shoved my body into the thickest clothes I had. Lucien had gone earlier, I walked out of the flat, watching the mist from my breath as I heard the panting sounds of Lucien's wolf – or really the giant golden hued husky in front of me. He came to me and pawed at the clothes that were neatly stacked on the ground. I rolled my eyes and picked them up as he lay on the ground waiting for me to climb on.

I sighed as I climbed over him, embracing his warm furry body for balance.

Try not to drop me. I joked.

Of course. Lucien responded as he got up abruptly, making me latch onto his back, wrapping my arms as far as I could. He barked in response and hopped around, making me squeal as I frantically held on for balance. Before I could say anything else, Lucien reared his body back and pushed forward. I did my best to bury my face beneath my clothes to keep warm as Lucien darted through the forest. Just as I thought Lucien had peaked his speed, he pushed even harder when we got to an uphill spot. My eyes could barely even stay open as I buried myself lower against his fur, eventually finding myself listening to Lucien's pants and his fast beating heart as he sprinted upwards.

Still alive back there?

Thankfully. I responded and Lucien would've barked if he had the energy – but he kept on pushing forward. I don't know what he was such in a hurry for – but I kept silent as he continued. The cold wind blew hard over my body and I struggled to keep hold of Lucien's damned clothes. Just as I felt them almost slip out of my reach – Lucien slowed down, allowing me to take them back into my grasp (I had been keeping them against my stomach while I held onto Lucien for dear life).

When Lucien finally came to a stop, his tail brushed against my back and I playfully swatted him before he barked.

This is our stop. I giggled before I climbed off of him and handed him his clothes. He took it with his mouth and nudged me with his snout until I turned to face the other way. I stopped.

The sun was setting behind a set of tall snow-covered mountains. It took me a few moments before I realized that this was a view that Lucien had showed me when he first took me to Umbra territory. I smiled and took a deep breath. I stretched my arms out and moaned as I did so. I felt the warmth radiating from Lucien's back as he stood silently behind me.

"Thank you," I said lowly as I leaned back against him. He placed his hands at the sides of my waist and pushed against me, support-ing me.

On an impulse, I whipped around, stunning Lucien as I reached around the back of his head and pulled him to my lips. He growled and I felt my stomach turn in delight. I beckoned him into my mouth and Lucien obliged, kissing me deep before peppering softer kisses against my lips and leaving me breathless as he deepened it once more. His hands had traveled up into my hair before he reached down and unzipped my coat, desperate to touch more. I traced his body through the thick shirt he'd just put on and I realized my hunger couldn't be satisfied.

"Take me... please," I begged in an almost breathless whisper. Lucien's eyes turned dark, he growled and radiated so much more heat than before.

"We're outside," he said, dangerously low.

"It's cold," I whined before I pulled him close to me again, this time by the waistband of his jeans. I kissed the edge of his jaw before I whispered into his ears. "I need something to warm me back up..." Lucien growled louder and before I knew it, he had me pressed against a tree.

"Someone might-" I didn't listen, I reached around to the back pocket of Lucien's jeans and pulled out what I knew would be there.

"I know you're always ready," I said, biting my lip as I took the packet and held it up in front of him.

"I-"

"Sshh..." I said as I rubbed my leg against him. "Please."

"Fuck... Auden-"

"Please..." I said, pouting as I let my hands wander his body from his neck to his abdomen, down to the V that led into deliciously dangerous territory. Lucien quieted down before his eyebrows furrowed and I laughed. He was warning everyone not to come near and my laughter caused his face to flush a beautiful cherry color. I ran my hands down his face and kissed his cheek.

"I need this."

"I know you do... God, Auden, your eyes are practically begging," he said and I smiled before I felt Lucien's hands against my abdomen. He popped the button of my jeans open and unzipped them. "Turn around."

Lucien carried me on his back – in human form – all the way back to the pack house. I asked him several times to put me down – the last time, Lucien made a point to sprint forward as fast as he could to show off that he was doing just fine with both of our weights. He seemed happy and to be fair, the main reason I couldn't handle him carrying me on his back was the fact that – well – I was a little too giddy. Lucien made me feel happy – and although cheesy – I like him. His joy was also pretty clear to me – the mate bond making the two of us high on our emotions.

"So... the plan worked," Lucien mused and I rolled my eyes.

"Did that plan involve us fuc-" Lucien jumped and adjusted me on his back and I squealed. He laughed before turning his head to glance at me. I gave him a peck on the cheek.

"Ignus said he needed to talk to you," Lucien said and I sighed.

"Well, can't run and hide forever."

"That and he says its about time to teach you what you can do." I raised an eyebrow at that.

"Okay..."

The sun just about to disappeared when we finally made it back to the pack house – reminding me that although sex feels absolutely amazing and time seems to stop a few times, it didn't take hours off my day... well, not usually.

When we opened the door to the pack house, the smell of baked brownies filled the air accompanied by some amazing smelling savory stuff. Ignus, Hera, and Dalton were all scurrying around the dining table and I watched as Hera ran off to the kitchen counter to slice up the brownies and arrange them. Lana and Xander sat down at the table happily chatting away while Desmond and Katherine started serving food.

"And they're finally here!" Ignus announced as Lucien put me down. And they smell astonishingly of each other. He commented in my head and I rolled my eyes.

Whatever Ignus.

He's just jealous because he hasn't seen his mate for a-

"Ssshh!" Ignus said aloud, interrupting Hera who rolled her eyes and laughed.

"Didn't know you guys were cooks," Katherine said as she sliced into some beef. I took my seat beside Lucien at the head of the table.

"Ignus likes cooking – and Dalton's the same," Hera said. "My dad was a novice baker."

"Huh," Desmond said.

"Not what you expected bloodhounds to do in their spare time right?"

"Where's dad?" I asked, having looked around for him.

"He said he wanted to go out and buy some things. Should be back some time soon," Ignus replied as he took his seat. I smiled and laughed along as they all made jokes and stories. None of them touched on the fact that I had practically been a hermit for the past three days – and none of them brought up anything that I'd learned. I was grateful for that. I wasn't sure I was ready yet – I didn't even know how to tell anyone what the thoughts were in my head.

It wasn't even that I was mourning the loss of a mother that I never knew. It was that she was suddenly there. I could see her – almost so clearly that it hurt me to know that I ever forgot she existed. And that couldn't have happened if I was just a baby when she left.

When dinner was over, Ignus immediately called me over. We were both cleaning up, I wiped the dishes and tucked them away as Ignus quickly washed them.

"Our memories are collective sometimes," Ignus suddenly said out of the blue as he handed me another plate.

"What?" I asked as I wiped it down and placed it up into a cupboard.

"When a certain kind of bloodhound wants to look for something, to know something about someone, remember them – they search through the memories of their group – that's why you can see her," Ignus said, smiling at me before he handed me a glass.

"So they're not really mine? The memories?"

"Some of them are – we're exceptional memory keepers. That's why searching through our heads is a great trait – not everyone can do it."

"And I can do it because?"

"You're her child, I'm sure you can gather why she couldn't stay around. There are rules to follow and even she couldn't break them," Ignus explained.

"How was she... after, everything..." I asked and Ignus gave me a half-smile.

"Sad. Horrific as our kind may sound to everyone – we bloodhounds mate for life. There's no one for us after – even if we convince ourselves that that may be the case – moving on is... well, it's not impossible – but it certainly isn't easy." I turned around and watched as Lucien fooled around with Lana. They were playing a game of charades and I could hear Katherine screaming random words at the top of her mouth as Lucien acted out the part.

"You love him, don't you?" Ignus asked. I looked over at Lucien and smiled. He must've instinctively known I was looking because he turned his head to face me and smiled back. "You don't have to answer that." I can already see the answer on your face anyways.

Shut up. I replied as I nudged him with my elbow.

"What about you, anyways? Hera going on and on about-" Ignus sighed loudly. It was only after a long pause that Ignus decided to speak up again.

"I need to go check on Dalton – I'll talk to you tomorrow – it's about time we get started."

"...Okay" I said, watching as Ignus' shoulders seemed to slump as he walked away.

What's his problem? I mused.

No clue. Come here. Lucien interrupted, reminding me that really, I wasn't alone in my head. It seemed like I never was. I made my way towards Lucien who laughed as Katherine puffed up her cheeks and walked around like a chicken.

"Chicken!" Lana yelled and Katherine shook her head.

Have you heard from dad? I asked and Lucien paused.

No, I haven't. He doesn't know his way back here – and I gave him a number to contact for when he wanted to come back.

Maybe he got lost? I asked.

But he could still call. Lucien said, pressing his lips into a thin line. Should I worry? I shook my head.

It's probably nothing. I told him.

After a long night of games and just fun – we all retired to our bedrooms to relax. I had just changed into one of Lucien's shirts when he wrapped his arms around my waist and nuzzled my neck, peppering kisses up to my jaw and around my back. I giggled as I felt the slight prick of his growing beard hit my back.

"You need to stop," I said as I turned around and pressed a kiss on his mouth.

"Can't I enjoy my happy little mate for a day?" He asked and I smirked as he kissed me once more. He lifted me up and I wrapped my legs around him as he brought me to the bed. I caressed his cheek and he leaned into my hand.

"I could really get used to this," he said as he kissed my palm, tracing his teeth along it before kissing each knuckle.

"So could I, but we need a break – preferably while sleeping," I said as I lay down. Lucien rolled his eyes before he moved beside me, propping himself on one elbow as he stared at me. I turned around to face him too. For a while, we just looked at each other. My brown eyes staring into his gorgeous hazel eyes that had me squirming from their intensity. He moved close to me and pressed a kiss to my forehead before wrapping his arm around me and bringing me in closer.

"I'm gonna be too warm-"

"Sshh..." he said, smiling and I smirked as I snuggled into him. And we stayed like that until we sent each other to sleep.

I don't know what it was that woke me – but my eyes opened in the middle of the night. Lucien was still asleep but I felt the need to get up. So I did.

The moment my feet touched the floor I heard a buzz that came from my phone. I looked around the room and eventually found it on the couch. It was from an unknown number. I slid my finger across the screen.

"Hello-"

"Don't look for me," my dad's voice rang through the phone, surprising me. He was panting – he had probably been running.

"What- dad-"

"Stay safe, Auden. She would've wanted that. I can't stay anymore. You'll understand," he said quickly and briefly. He was panicked, afraid even...

"Dad, calm down. I-"

"Is that her?" A male voice said, and I heard the quivering breath of my dad's filter through the phone. The voice itself was enough to freeze me into place, sending nervous shivers down my spine. "Tell her I said hi..."

Before I could say anything – the call dropped. But the feeling of dread in my stomach refused to leave me alone.

They can't hide you for long, darling...

I froze.

I'm so close... So... very... close...

Chapter 21

I stepped out, shivering as the cold held me in its embrace. It was still dark, but I had to try. Just as I made it to the kitchen, I heard a glass clink and found myself staring into Lana's eyes. She was drinking a glass of milk.

"Where are you-" I held a finger to my lips and she stopped. I need help. I told her.

But my brother-

I just need to get off territory. Please. I begged and Lana nodded. Follow me.

It didn't take long for me to get to the highway with Lana carrying me. I climbed off her and embraced her neck.

I'll be back soon. If... I'm not back in an hour, call Lucien. I told her and she whined.

Please be safe. She said and I nodded before she nuzzled me.

I'll be fine, I promise. Now go. I said and she nodded before she turned around and ran back into Umbra territory. I tugged on my jacket sleeves.

"I can do this..." I muttered under my breath as I stepped off and made my way towards the nearest village.

I sniffed the air. I wasn't hoping for a miracle – it wasn't like I was trained or anything... But the fact that I was a bloodhound and a werewolf had to mean something didn't it? The town was silent, the frigid winter air bit at the skin of my face, and I felt my ungloved fingers start to lock up. I clambered into the nearest pharmacy and sighed in relief at the warmth. No one inside - save for a sleepy-looking cashier sat at the counter watching something on his phone. He glanced up at me and I smiled as a greeting as he returned to his viewing pleasure. I walked around the aisles and sighed.

What am I doing here... I thought to myself. I should've told Lucien – maybe even Ignus... Either way, Lana would call Lucien to bring me back in about half an hour – and even then I would've caused trouble for the two of us. I sighed as I pulled out my phone – there was no point in calling. Dad had probably taken the precaution to call a-

A phone booth.

How many of those were still up around here? I checked my phone. The nearest working one was miles away. There was no way I'd be able to convince anyone to drive me out there – and hitchhiking wasn't exactly my forte.

I'd have to make a run for it... and hope that Lucien was going to try and find me on foot.

My lungs felt like they were gonna explode. My heart pounded against my chest as the phone booth finally came to view. I was beginning to get light-headed. I definitely wasn't built to run like a wolf... and even if I was, I was way out of shape for it. But I made it.

Without much time to spare. Lucien could find me at any moment. But I could smell him- my dad- he was here and with how much I could still smell- he had to still be here somewhere. I panted as I rested my hand against a brick wall.

A sudden weight fell over my shoulders and my legs shook with weakness. My vision hazed. I could feel my blood boil.

Auden. Where are you? Ignus asked but I couldn't even respond.

I felt warm, my clothes clung to my body uncomfortably, and I could feel the heat travel all over my body. I could smell my dad's shampoo wafting through the air – clearer than ever. I struggled to move forward, a pain constricted around my chest, and I bit into my lip. Oh my sweet, sweet darling... Come find us... A voice said clearly in my head. I grunted as I staggered forward. Your body's barely able to control itself now, isn't it?

I finally made it to the phone booth, my hands tracing its metal ridges and the glass that encased it. Suddenly, a sweet scent filled my nose. It was different from my dad's... it didn't belong to him- couldn't. It wasn't something I recognized- but it intrigued me all the same. Come to me, my darling... The weight on my shoulders lifted, my vision cleared, and I could feel a strong urge to chase that sweet smell. But my hand refused to leave the phone booth- my hand pressed softly against its side.

What was I doing here again? I ran a hand through my hair and paused. I stood on both feet and felt a warmth, hot and fiery, surge throughout my body. I turned around. A shadow hid behind the corner alley- the smell radiated from there, I just knew it. I stepped forward.

We're so close to each other- I can almost reach out and touch you... The voice said as I took another step. But we have to do this properly... so come to me-

Auden! A powerful voice rang in my head and then- warmth. I felt someone at my side embrace me and I turned to find myself face-to-face with Lucien. He smelled funny... like some kind of soft dessert. He placed his hands around my face and I found myself staring at his neck...

"Come back to me, please," he said... I could hear his pulse, throbbing and racing against his chest...

"Dalton," Ignus' voice rang from behind Lucien and I saw him exit the large car. How had I not heard that coming?

"We barely missed him," Dalton said before seemingly gritting his teeth. Lucien pulled me into his embrace and then I felt someone else hug me from behind. I turned to find Lana burying her face into my coat. I looked to Ignus and found him glaring at me, he began to walk menacingly towards me.

"Ignus don't-" Hera's voice began but he made his way towards me and immediately grabbed me out of Lucien's arms. He pulled me away with force as Lucien growled loudly. Ignus moved as if meaning to hurl me towards a wall- my feet skidded to a stop as my back bumped against the wall I'd rested on earlier.

"What the hell was that?!" Lucien growled out and Ignus clicked his tongue.

"Fuck, fuck, fuck," Ignus cursed. "You're turning." He cursed out.

"Turning?" Lucien asked, hissing the question.

"Look at her, she's barely even able to speak," Ignus hissed, "and it isn't because she can't."

"Auden-" Lucien began but before he could speak, I found myself in front of him again. His eyes seemed to look at me funny.

"What?" I asked as I trailed my fingers on his neck.

"Lucien... step away from her," Ignus warned.

"The hell do you mean-" Lucien began. He felt so warm, his body was radiating it and it was like my fingers would burn by just a single touch. It sent shivers down my spine...

"I'm sorry," Hera's voice said and I felt a small pain on my neck. I was about to turn when-

Darkness.

My eyes blinked awake and I found my head throbbing. My body felt heavy and weighted, I could hardly turn my head without feeling like my brain was going to explode. It was too hot. Everything was too hot... I needed water. I felt around and realized I was in bed- I blinked my eyes several times until finally my vision cleared. It was day. I pulled myself up and groaned as I sat up, my head felt like it suffered from an extreme concussion. My eyes still felt a little slow and hazed and I needed to force myself up. I grabbed onto the table, the wall, just to maintain my balance. My legs felt weak and I was dying for a drink.

Lucien? I called in my head.

Auden- you're up, give me a second- Lucien began as I limped towards the living area where I knew a pitcher of water was sitting. The door opened and Lucien immediately came towards me and hugged me. I have no idea what came over me but I froze in his grasp before a ringing pain entered my head. I pulled away from him and groaned as I felt my legs give way. Lucien caught me in his arms and I began to breathe heavily.

"What's happening?!" Lucien growled.

"As I explained before, she's being hit by multiple things-" Ignus' voice interrupted as I shivered.

"L-let go of me... I just need to rest..." I said and Lucien swallowed a lump in his throat before he rested me on the couch. I looked over at the water pitcher and Lucien followed my gaze. He poured me a glass before handing it to me and I struggled to lift my hand to even hold it.

"You didn't answer my question," Lucien said and Ignus sighed but stayed by the door. I took a sip of the water with a bit of Lucien's help.

"For starters, she's in heat and it looks to me like her bloodhound line is fighting hard to suppress it," Ignus explained. "Also- you might want her to stay away from everyone else for a while. Bloodhounds are... territorial."

"Meaning?"

"Well, depending on which side of her wins on the time of day- she might be strong enough to rip someone's arm off or even kill someone."

"What?" I snapped and Ignus chuckled.

"Don't worry. Both werewolf and bloodhound instincts will fight to keep Lucien alive- so that's not a problem. He's just gonna have to wait on your hand and foot."

"How do I fix this?" Lucien asked and Ignus paused.

"You're not seriously asking me how to fix a bitch in heat right?" Ignus paused, "Okay, I didn't mean to make a pun or be offensive. But hounds and wolves alike- there's only way to fix her- and if you don't want it to be temporary- you're gonna have to-"

"If I'm... in heat... why is he able to... resist me?" I asked and Ignus laughed.

"Well, he's not going to be able to for long. You're the one in charge here, Auden. Bloodhounds are a little better off in that sense... You choose your target and in fact, most of the time- well... bloodhounds feed better in heat. Though please don't bite him. I don't know what'll happen when that time comes."

"So what the hell do we do, she looks like she's in pain each time I hold her!" Lucien exclaimed and Ignus grinned as he stepped back.

"It's cause she's resisting. She'll get the hang of it eventually. Though please don't bite him, Auden. I'm actually begging you."

"Then what do I do?" Lucien asked, looking a little frazzled.

"Well if she shouldn't bite you, which one of you should?" Ignus asked and I gawked at him, earning a chuckle. "Try not to overwhelm him, Auden. When a bloodhound gets a little too thirsty... well, she can be a little more demanding than a wolf. Things can get intense fast." Ignus laughed before he stepped back once more and closed the door. Lucien looked at me and I bit my bottom lip.

You aren't seriously leaving me here to-

Oh please, you guys have already fucked haven't you? Why not finish the process?

That's different and you know it-

Then deal with your problems Auden. You're the one in charge- it's your body, your mate, your instincts... Now don't mind me muting your little voice for once- I'd rather not hear either one of you. I'll see you in a few days.

Days? I didn't get a response. Ignus shut me out of his mind and I looked to Lucien.

"Where- where does it hurt?" Lucien asked and I bit my lip.

"Everywhere," I said with a sigh.

"But you pushed me away when I held you so-" Lucien said, pausing before he decidedly sat beside me. He didn't touch me and I felt my migraine worsen.

"How the heck am I supposed to deal with this?" I asked aloud and Lucien gave me a worried look.

"Why did you go yesterday?" Lucien asked and I paused.

"I thought I'd be able to find dad... and that you'd find me before I got into any trouble," I said, surprised that I was able to manage. I reached out for his hand and Lucien watched me carefully as I traced his skin. My breath staggered from my weakness but I did my best to focus on him and I placed my hand on his... To my surprise, relief rushed to my head like a drug and I fell limp towards his body.

"So Ignus wasn't kidding about it being under your control," Lucien muttered and I lazily nodded my head, burying myself further into Lucien's chest. "Mind if I lift you back into the bed?" He asked and I nodded once more. I felt his arms around my body and though a few times it sent a prickly feeling down my spine, Lucien managed to bring me into his lap where I instinctively wrapped my legs around his waist. He stood up and carried me to the bed.

He lay me down and I sighed contently as he released me. My vision was getting a little better and my breathing had turned into small quick breaths. Lucien lay by my side and I waited as I took deeper breaths, trying to calm down, before I turned to face him. Just relax... I told myself as I moved closer to him. Lucien smiled as I snuggled into his body and I felt the pain subside.

"Better?" He asked and I nodded.

"Just let me... pace myself..." I said and he nodded in response as I guided his hand around my body. He rested it on my waist as I turned to him, allowing my body to adjust.

"You know this is starting to test my strength," Lucien said and I raised an eyebrow before I realized how tense he was. I had the urge to touch his skin and he grunted as I gently traced it like it was the first time I was exploring his body. "Auden-"

"Sshh..." I hushed as I put my hand under his shirt, his warmth feeding a sudden growing hunger inside me that felt unusually powerful.

"I'm guessing you aren't in pain anymore?" He asked and I nodded as I climbed on top of him, straddling his hips, my core turning warm and bubbly.

"I'm feeling light-headed... and hot... very... hot" I admitted as my hands pulled Lucien's shirt up.

"I don't know if I'm enjoying how slow we're going or if you're torturing me," he said and I smiled as he lifted his arms so that I could move the shirt off him as I kissed his toned chest. He groaned as I slowly nipped and sucked on his skin... I couldn't think of anything else anymore but his pleasure and mine... Whatever it was that was blocking our bond before had begun to fade and I could hardly contain myself.

"Shit, Auden your scent-" I smiled as I let the shirt sit just above his nose, hiding his eyes from mine.

"Close your eyes," I said and Lucien swallowed a lump in his throat. I kissed his throat and grazed my teeth along his collarbone, earning an animalistic growl from his mouth. He moved against me and I pushed his arms down. Lucien gasped in response.

"Auden your strength- it's-"

"Stay still..." I said as I let go of him and took off my shirt.

"Can I at least... free my arms-" I chuckled.

"Sure... But keep your eyes covered," I said and he pulled his arms away from the shirt and I took his hand and kissed his palm.

"Fuck, Auden-" I put his hands down before I moved lower. My hands moved to his belt and Lucien's hands immediately came around my shoulders. I traced the waistband of his jeans, kissing the left side of that V leading down to his crotch as I unbuckled his belt. I looked to Lucien and found him biting his lip though I could see his eyes try their best to peek through the small sliver of a view the shirt was giving him.

"No cheating..." I muttered as I caressed his groin.

Chapter 22

Ignus whistled loudly, his hands shoved deep into his pockets as he waited patiently for his dog. You can't hide her from me for long. The man said and Ignus rolled his eyes.

I can try. He responded before he whistled again before he finally heard, to his relief, the sound of a panting dog. Kneeling down, the husky immediately pounced on his knees licking at his face. Ignus chuckled as he ruffled its hair.

"Got anything for me?" He asked and the husky barked at him. Ignus placed his hand on the husky's forehead, his thumb caressing the space between its eyes.

Quick images flashed in Ignus' mind. A forest, a home, some food, water... Finally, a view of Auden as she made her way to the phone booth. Ignus sighed as he watched the scene unfold. Auden had begun to stumble towards the booth and in the distance, he could barely make out a figure in an alleyway. Ignus let go of the dog and pet him furiously, scratching the side of his belly.

"Good boy, Quietus, good boy," he said and the dog wagged its tail. "Let's go grab you some food."

Ignus sighed as he let the dog run free once again. He had made sure that it was completely uninjured and unnoticed. So far, it seemed that he hadn't noticed how his own specialities worked. Although Ignus was beginning to wonder what it was that Auden would be good at as a bloodhound – especially as a half-blood.

Her time's running out. Hera said and Ignus grunted.

I bet she's starting to realize the real reason she's so hungry for her mate. Ignus responded and he could feel the disgust in Hera's mind.

Yeah well... let's just hope she doesn't mix up which hunger is for what.

Have a little faith. Ignus said as he walked off in the direction of the pack house.

He hardly had to sniff the place to know just how intensely Auden was seducing her mate. Unlike werewolves, female scents didn't entice just anyone, they were specifically for their prey – or in this case, their mate. Ignus chuckled to himself, it was amusing to see just how much a blissfully ignorant pup was using her bloodhound talents to satisfy herself. Bloodhounds loved to monopolize their mates – which only made him admire Auden's mother even more. Aurelia had always chosen others over herself... And though it usually ended well- the fact that Auden was here today would undoubtedly lead to one heck of a mess. Ignus shook his head.

"What the heck is that smell?" Desmond said and Ignus chuckled as he poured himself a glass of whiskey.

"Auden's in heat," Ignus said, "Want some?" Desmond nodded as he massaged his neck. Ignus slid a glass towards him.

"Well, that's different," Desmond said and Ignus nodded.

"For you, for Lucien- well... he's probably caught up in all that," Ignus said as he sipped his whiskey, savoring a bit of its flavor before it traveled down his body, sending warmth to his stomach. Ignus raised a hand and the scent faded from his nose and he heard Desmond breathe a sigh of relief.

"What'd you do?"

"Just toned it down a little, if you can't tell, we bloodhounds operate a lot better on smell. So it makes sense for us to be able to tone down fellow hounds' scents. Otherwise it'd be a lot easier to hunt us down."

"I see..." Desmond trailed off. "How is... well everything?"

"Everything?"

"Well, have you gotten any luck at finding whoever it is that's hunting her down?" Desmond asked and Ignus sighed.

"I know who it is, but capturing him isn't easy considering we're four against his... group," Ignus explained. The two of them paused for a moment as they quietly drank from their glasses.

"Listen, I know we didn't exactly come up to a great start... but the pack's with you guys now." Ignus looked at Desmond in surprise before catching himself.

"...Thanks."

A door down the hallway opened and Desmond chuckled as Lucien came into view. Ignus did as well, after all, Lucien looked like an absolute mess, his shirt was rumpled and his hair all over the place and he smelled so much of Auden it was almost nauseating to Ignus.

"You doing okay in there?" Desmond asked jokingly as the two shared a brief handshake of some sort.

"I'm trying to," Lucien muttered before he opened one of the cupboards and fetched himself a glass. Ignus pushed the whiskey towards him and Lucien nodded his thanks as he poured himself a glass. "Are you all usually like that?" He asked and Ignus scoffed.

"Well, Auden's probably more intense than the rest of us – she's got werewolf in her too, you know?"

"Yeah, well, she's getting pretty strong," Lucien said as he rubbed his wrists. Ignus laughed at the red marks on his wrists.

"As long as she hasn't fed yet, it's fine," Ignus commented and Lucien nodded.

"Now that we're all together, could someone please explain to me what that means?" Desmond asked, "I mean I can gather, but I also want some specifics." Ignus gestured for Lucien to hand over the whiskey and he poured himself some more. After taking a drink, he released a large breath before looking to Desmond.

"If Auden was a pure werewolf she would've shifted like six years ago right?" Ignus asked and the men nodded. "But she didn't which means there's something blocking that part of her and because she's half bloodhound you can tell it's that part of her that's stop-ping it from happening."

"Why?" Lucien asked and Ignus shrugged.

"We've never had hybrids before. There's... usually some inherent hatred for you guys in our instincts – it takes a while before we get used to it, think about it like cats and dogs. But because Auden was raised amongst you and has half your blood, she can take it. Also, don't worry about the three of us hounds, we aren't like the others of our kind."

"Meaning?" Desmond asked this time.

"We can control our thirst and even then quenching it isn't a problem," Ignus explained as he fetched something out of his pocket that looked like a silver case. He opened it up and revealed a velvet interior that held several tiny glass vials of some kind of deep violet liquid. Desmond and Lucien looked at the case with interest as Ignus took one of the vials out and slipped it into the top of a thin silver tool.

"We used this earlier with Auden and since it isn't real blood, it's enough to stave off any kind of hunger she'll have without fully triggering a turn," Ignus said. "It's like a vaccine, except you just slip this little thing into the top of this and press the top. Barely takes any pressure, one tap and boom."

"How long do the effects last?" Lucien asked and Ignus shrugged as he put the vial and the tool back into the case.

"Depends on the bloodhound. For us it lasts a week, but since Auden's in heat... that hunger might come back in a matter of minutes," Ignus said and Lucien pressed his lips into a thin line.

"Is there any way to treat it permanently?" Lucien asked.

"Well... there's only one real way to heal both of our kind when we're in heat," Ignus said, winking at Lucien, "But if you bite her at the wrong moment, she might just rip your head off." Desmond and Lucien looked at Ignus with dumbfounded faces, earning a loud laugh from the man himself.

"This mating business isn't a joke to us hounds. If you think werewolf bonds are hard, try fighting the urge to kill your mate for doing what they're supposed to do," Ignus muttered.

"You've got to be kidding," Desmond said, laughing nervously as he nudged Lucien. Ignus smirked as he unbuttoned the top of his shirt and revealed his neck. Sure enough, he had a mark on his neck, but also several long welted scars that marked him down from his collarbone to his chest.

"Shit man." Desmond grimaced as he drank up all his whiskey. "The hell kind of mark is that?"

"A painful one," Ignus said with a shrug.

"She worth it?" Desmond asked and Ignus simply smiled.

Suddenly a loud crashing noise came from the room and Ignus sensed an intense wave of pain rush over the back of his mind. Auden, calm down. Ignus said. Lucien had already rushed into the room and Desmond froze.

"Come," Ignus said as he took the silver case back out from his pocket. He turned to look at Desmond, "He's gonna need some help for the first part of this." Desmond shivered before he gave himself a small pep-talk and followed behind Ignus who now had the strange tool in his hand.

"Are you good at darts?" Ignus asked.

"What?" Desmond responded and Ignus shook his head.

"You'll get why I asked in a little bit."

He barely even had to step into the room to know that Auden was beginning to get desperate. Her body needed more than physical reassurance – and the bloodhound inside her wanted two things: to mark and to be marked... The first being the riskier option – and the second...

Lucien stood close to the door as Auden stood dressed in nothing but in one of Lucien's shirts and had her eyes aglow with a deep crimson. At the sight of Ignus her eyes immediately went to his and he felt a cold shiver go down his spine. His instincts told him to bow, but while he could still resist, he handed Desmond the tool.

Desmond had a disconcerted look on his face before he took it into his hands.

"Auden," Lucien cooed and she looked at him. Ignus could practically feel the hunger and the thirst in her throat as she scanned Lucien's body for his weakest points. Ignus stepped forward and Auden's head snapped towards his direction.

"Calm down, your highness," Ignus said jokingly and he could swear he saw her eyes flicker back to their usual brown color.

"S-step away from m-me," Auden said and Ignus sighed in relief. She was still in control and he was kind of amazed.

"No can do, you'll do so much more damage if I leave you alone," Ignus said and everyone felt a sudden chill in the air. Lucien moved and Auden looked to him too. Everyone barely blinked before Auden suddenly had Lucien pressed against the wall, her right hand pinning his neck against it.

"Auden, calm down," Lucien said, in a surprisingly calm voice. Desmond shifted his weight between his feet.

"You smell... so... sweet," Auden said as she tilted her head and Ignus grunted as he stepped forward and barely even registering a single move, he had Auden pinned against the wall, holding her hands above her head with both his hands.

"Desmond!" Ignus yelled. Auden's eyes snapped towards Desmond and he froze on the spot, her eyes freezing him there. A smirk graced her face before she lifted her legs and kicked Ignus off of her. With a single step, she was in front of Lucien again and this time he couldn't take his eyes off her.

"Oh for fuck's sake," Ignus cursed. "Get here this time." Desmond let out a shaky breath as Ignus got up and stepped forward, he put a hand on Auden's shoulder and she let out a hiss before she turned on him.

"You're getting... in... my... way..." She said between sharp breaths as she gripped his shoulder and Ignus groaned at her strength. Auden was giving in.

"The 'dart' Desmond!"

"But how do I-"

"Oh for the love of," Katherine's voice said as she grabbed the tool from Desmond's hand and threw it towards Auden's leg. Ignus groaned loudly as he pushed Auden away with all of his strength, propelling her backwards until she hit a wall. But it was enough, the tool had managed to press against the smallest bit of pressure and Auden's leg went limp.

She let out a shaky breath as she slowly fell to the floor.

"Nice shot," Ignus said as he looked at Katherine, "Next time though, aim for the neck. Effects last longer that way." Katherine rolled her eyes.

"You're lucky I even came to help out."

"How did you-" Desmond began but Katherine hushed him.

"It was hard not to listen to you idiots. I was working in our living room and you left the door open," Katherine said and Desmond sighed. Lucien held Auden in his arms and Ignus placed a hand on his shoulder as Auden's eyes returned to normal. Her breathing fell into deep slow breaths.

"Auden, I think you know what has to happen." She looked at him and then at her mate. "You don't have a lot of time."

"Stay by the door... just in case," she said, pleading everyone with her eyes. Ignus nodded before he took out the case from his pocket and retrieved the tool from Auden's leg.

"You sure?" Lucien asked as Katherine and Desmond left the room. Ignus stepped slowly away and saw Auden nod her head weakly.

She should've dropped by now even if it did hit her in the leg. She's only had one shot before this. Hera said ominously.

Yeah, well let's hope Lucien's mark will do enough.

It won't for long. Dalton replied and Ignus wanted to groan as he closed the door behind him and stayed there.

It will have to do. We have no choice. Ignus replied.

...She'll feed soon enough. And then we'll have no choice. Hera warned.

Shut up. Ignus said before closing himself off. He grunted as he took out his case and the tool. He retrieved the glass vial and placed it on the other side of the case before tucking it away. He leaned against the door and stared at the ceiling.

When will you be back? That sweet sweet voice said to him. Ignus' eyes widened before he shook his head and regained his composure.

Get out of my head, Celia.

Please... Ignus... I just want you to-

Get out!

Chapter 23

"Stay by the door... just in case," I said and Ignus nodded before he moved quickly to retrieve the small thing stuck to my leg.

"You sure?" Lucien asked, his amber eyes searching mine, trying to ascertain whether or not I was really really certain that I would let him mark me. I nodded my head and watched as everyone turned to leave. Ignus closed the door behind him, but I knew he was there.

I looked back into Lucien's eyes and sighed. I pulled away from him slightly and smiled as I traced my fingers across his face.

"Please," I said, my voice sounding breathless as I felt that burning sensation fill my stomach slowly... I bit my lip and Lucien stared as he let out a growl, he pressed a kiss against my lips and I sighed into his kiss. He kissed down along my jawline and he held me in his arms as he tugged on the shirt I had on.

"Hold still," he said, his voice low and dangerous as he pressed kisses against my skin, sucking and teasing me as he went closer to the crook of my neck where my mark would be. I could feel his fangs graze my skin as he reached that spot. He kissed it sweetly, my lips quivered and I loosely placed my arms around him, trying to encourage him. He lifted his head suddenly and let out a soft breath against my ear.

"I love you," he whispered and before I could speak, Lucien dove in and I felt a pain surge from my neck. I let out a whimper as I felt tears sting my eyes, I closed them tight as Lucien released me but I hugged him close... I felt a burning sensation rile up inside me, my cheeks felt warm and my body seemed to jump awake. A sudden pain in my head made my close my eyes and I felt myself grab onto Lucien's shoulders, my nails digging into his skin.

Lucien grunted and held me closer to him. I felt my fingers dig into his flesh until they touched a warm liquid - blood. I felt something build inside my chest and it became hard to breathe.

"Auden? Auden, hey-" Lucien said and I found myself looking into his eyes. He gave me a surprised look before he held me in his arms even tighter. I moved my arms and placed them against his chest and pushed him down. Arms and legs around him, he stared into my eyes as my hair cascaded over his face.

"Hey," Lucien said as he reached up to touch my face with his left hand, I kissed it and smiled before I reached for his shirt and pulled it apart, it tore between my fingers and Lucien release a shaky breath. I paused and listened to his heart beat and I could see the goosebumps along Lucien's skin as I trailed my fingers across his chest, bits of crimson tracing themselves across his chest.

Don't hurt him too bad. Ignus' voice rang in my head and I felt a build up inside of me before I released a growl. Lucien looked surprised and I watched him swallow what seemed to be a lump in his throat.

"Is this normal?" Lucien yelled and I heard the door open. I growled at Ignus as he stepped in and he folded his arms over his chest.

"Calm down, I'm just watching to make sure you don't kill him," he said and I stared at him, a wave of anger and some kind of ego washed over me... I found Ignus slightly shaking, he was better at hiding it than Lucien for sure. I smirked as I bowed my head and for some reason I knew I was making an order.

Ignus bit into his bottom lip.

"Auden... you need to stop," Ignus said but I refused to listen. I stared at him until he finally knelt down on one knee. "Auden-" I glared at him and he shut up.

"Watch," I said, not even recognizing my own voice. Lucien looked at Ignus and I could sense the worry in him, I gently caressed his face before I lifted my right hand and I felt my bones shift and change in my fingertips. I heard a gasp escape Lucien's lips and I could see the surprise in Ignus' eyes. I looked at my hands and though I should've felt surprised, I wasn't. Something about it made me want to smile in some twisted way. My nails were long and claw-like, black as night, and my fingers had elongated, and though they weren't beautiful- just strange... they weren't anything like a werewolf's paw... But then again whose hands shifted into a paw?

"Does she have to do this?!" Lucien asked, bringing me out of my thoughts as he looked to Ignus. A few tense moments passed between them and I could sense a kind of doubt in Lucien's mind. I didn't like that. I didn't like that I could feel that. It wasn't fair... he had me- why shouldn't I go ahead and bite-

"No," Ignus said loudly. "You can't do that, Auden." I stared at him blankly and tilted my head. Ignus fell silent and I turned to Lucien who was still looking to Ignus for advice.

"...You don't trust me," I said almost breathlessly and Lucien looked into my eyes. I felt like I had been rejected, the power I had thought was building up suddenly lost momentum and got caught short.

"No, no, no, Auden- I was just..." he began to say as he pulled himself up but I wasn't listening, I felt the bones in my fingers shift and change back. Lucien cupped my face in his hands and I felt a sudden urge to cry as I sat up. I felt the tears well-up in my eyes before I looked to Ignus who still knelt before me.

"Auden, hey, hey, listen," Lucien said as he brought my face back to his. He took my hand and placed it on his chest before he turned to look at Ignus. After a few moments, Lucien spoke again, this time in a clear voice. "You can leave us." Ignus paused for a moment before he breathed a short sigh and smiled at me.

"It's not that I don't trust you. But I'll explain later." Ignus stood from his position and crept out of the room, closing the door behind him. "But I'll still be by the door!" After the door shut, Lucien turned to look at me.

"Are you okay?" Lucien asked.

I'm fine, I said with a smile and Lucien grinned.

"It's healing already," Lucien said and my eyes widened.

"Really?" Lucien nodded as he moved his head towards my mark and he pressed a soft kiss against it. I flinched thinking it would hurt, but felt pleasure and warmth take over as I mewled. Lucien chuckled and I felt my cheeks warm up as he turned and looked at my eyes.

"You okay?" He asked and I nodded before I pressed a kiss on his lips. But even though I was feeling content I still had an aching feeling in my stomach. My mind knew not to mark him- but I wanted to- I needed to have something that said he was mine and mine alone. Lucien seemed to notice my shaking hands and to my surprise, he tore off the remains of his shirt and lay back down on the floor.

"All yours," Lucien said and I looked at him in surprise. "To be fair, though, I did not think you could shift any part of your body..." It was only then that it hit me that I had partially shifted. Lucien noticed my surprise and smiled as he took my hand in his and placed it on his chest. A heat bloomed in my chest and travelled throughout my body, this time, my touch left goosebumps on Lucien's skin that I knew wasn't just fear- it might've even been excitement.

"This'll hurt," I said as I lifted my right hand and it clicked and shifted into its form. I thought Lucien would look, I thought I would- seeing as it was the second time this had ever happened in my life. But his eyes captured mine and refused to let them go. A sweet scent wafted into my nose and Lucien seemed to smell it to as he breathed it in deeply and groaned beneath me. I extended my fingers far apart and curled them in a scratching position. I pressed a brief kiss against Lucien's lips and he sighed into it before biting down onto his lower lip and I quickly pulled away and my hand swept down.

My head was throbbing and I groaned as I turned around. I knew I was in the bed but I could barely recall how I'd gotten there, I felt a sudden touch- faint and gentle- trace my wrist up to my shoulder and I smiled as I felt butterflies in my stomach and opened my eyes. Lucien pressed his nose against mine and chuckled, his breath smelled of peppermint – he had gotten up earlier for sure. It was only then that I could feel our connection- my lips quivered as I looked into Lucien's eyes and smiled.

"You okay?" He asked and I nodded, feeling a sudden soreness on my neck. I suddenly looked over at Lucien's body – he wasn't wearing a shirt, just a pair of loose black jeans, and his hair was damp... My eyes immediately stared at his chest and I knew Lucien could sense my stare. I could feel a small sense of embarrassment as well as pride and it made me feel giddy.

I didn't think my claws were that big- or would cause such welts... I felt a bit bad and Lucien immediately tilted my chin up. But I glanced down and bit my bottom lip. The scars weren't perfectly healed, in fact they looked fairly tender and still healing.

"Did it hurt?" I asked and Lucien smirked.

"Yes... but I'm willing to bet that hurt too," he said, glancing at my mark. I felt my cheeks warm up.

"I'm hungry," I said, feeling that gnawing sensation in my stomach and Lucien chuckled.

"Breakfast is ready, though you might wanna clean up a bit," he said as he kissed my lips and I grumbled. Not fair, I haven't brushed yet. I thought as I 'attempted' to lick my teeth clean. Lucien chuckled and I felt my cheeks warm up.

"Don't listen in!" I said as I chucked a pillow towards him. Lucien laughed as he took me in his arms and pressed a kiss against my mark. I let out a shaky breath and he released a playful growl.

"Breakfast first," he said with a wink.

I freshened up with a quick shower, relieved to wash off the tiny bits of dried blood around my neck. Wrapped in my towel, I stared at my reflection in the mirror. Lucien's mark was large and though he said it had already healed, I didn't believe him until I saw how much of a faint scar the mark turned out to be. It was so light- lighter than even most-

That's because you're a hound. We heal quicker and our marks are more smell than sight. Hera said.

What?

Well, you might not notice it now but since half the marking ceremony has been fulfilled every hound will know you're marked... and you'll probably compensate with your own scent over Lucien's...

Compensate?

Well, you haven't completely marked Lucien yet so when your instincts kick in and you get possessive you'll literally overwhelm everyone in the room – not just in scent but-

But I gave him a scar-

She'll get it sooner or later. Ignus interrupted.

"You okay in there?" Lucien asked and I immediately snapped out of it.

"Yeah! I'll be out in a sec!" I yelled and just as I stepped forward I heard a loud ringing noise run through my ears.

I saw images flash in my head of someone standing at the edge of a forest. I could feel the cold and I watched as their gaze shifted around the forest until it spotted something – a house... I felt a shiver run down my spine and my stomach sank. I wanted to scream but I couldn't.

Found you.

Chapter 24

- -

gnus, did you hear any of that? I asked but I received no response. The ringing in my ears increased in volume and I rushed out of the room. Lucien turned to look at me with a smile but I couldn't hear a thing. I opened my voice and felt the vibrations come out of my mouth. I kept trying to say He's here but I couldn't hear myself. Lucien's face immediately turned serious and I knew he was mind-linking people. I felt a wetness drop from my nose and wiped it immediately, only to find that I'd smeared blood everywhere. I felt a heat race through my body and I tried to fight the ringing to my ears. I sat myself on the bed and held my head in my hands, attempting to gain some sense of sanity.

I felt a hand on my arm and saw Hera looking into my eyes. She was mouthing something to me- though I couldn't make it out. I felt like I was going insane. Hera took something out of her pocket – a thin silver tool like that of Ignus' – I barely even saw as she flicked her wrist and pressed it against my neck. I felt the heat leave my body and she squinted her eyes at me.

"How long will it take you to get her out of here?" Hera asked, her head turning towards Lucien.

"Not long," he replied simply.

"Then get going. Dalton will guide you to a safe house."

"What about Umbra?" I asked.

"They'll be fine. Ignus and I will be here. They won't bother with werewolves – not if we can do anything about it. We don't hunt anymore and it's more trouble than it's worth to shed blood. Your hunter isn't stupid."

"Hunter?" I asked, I was clueless about everything.

"Well, there's no better word for it. Get dressed and get going. We'll keep you updated," Hera said and I nodded as I got up to change. She suddenly cleared her throat and turned to me, handing me a silver case. "This is full of that stuff I used on you a while ago. Lucien will get one from me too. Just in case. Use it when you feel anything... weird." I nodded as I took the case into my hands and rushed into the bathroom to change.

I climbed onto Lucien's back and savored the wave of relief that ran over me as I felt the warmth radiate off of his body. His wolf seemed to relax under my touch too and I embraced him as he moved forward. A bark behind me showed that Lana and Xander were also both with us. Another wolf stayed behind and I stared at it and smiled as Katherine came out to pat it. It was Desmond. She looked at me and nodded as Lucien reared back and ran forward.

Good luck. I mind-linked.

Thanks. Stay safe, Luna. Katherine replied.

Lucien, Lana, Xander, and I all spotted Dalton quite quickly. He was simply standing by the lake in a calm fashion. He turned to face us and nodded before he took off. It honestly still surprised me how quickly bloodhounds could move. It was like they barely even had to step forward before they traveled several meters. We continued following him until he came to a stop. He turned to face us and pressed a finger to his lips.

He was about to step forward when something crashed into him from his left. Lucien released a loud growl before rearing back and pushing forward. Lana and Xander moved alongside us.

Dalton are you okay? I asked.

I'll be fine. Go here. He replied and a series of images flashed in my head. I could see the paths he took in the forest and the images appeared as if they were my own memories. I swallowed a lump in my throat.

Keep going forward, I'll tell you when to move otherwise. I mind-linked Lucien, Lana, and Xander. They barked in response before rushing forward even faster than before.

You know this would be easier if you didn't run... A deep voice whispered in my head and I shivered from the sheer sound of it. I closed my eyes and gripped onto Lucien tighter as I closed him off of my mind.

Turn right over here. I mind-linked and everyone followed. I felt my fingers turn cold and my breathing slow as we pushed on, weaving through trees and hidden pathways in the forest. A distinct smell filled my nose and I felt a sick feeling run in my gut. Something was wrong.

They know you aren't here. Ignus said.

We have a problem. Katherine's voice quickly followed.

Fuck! They're all heading in your direction! Hera said in a panicked voice.

"Keep moving!" I yelled and Lucien let out a loud bark as I re-adjusted myself on his back. I caught a glimpse of something in the corner of my eye.

Watch out! I mind-linked. Lucien barely even turned his head when something, or more likely, someone, crashed into us. I lost my grip on Lucien and a sharp pain raised from my back, the air was knocked out of my lungs before I slumped down and hit cold damp ground. I blinked my eyes several times, a ringing noise filled my head, I could hear nothing but growling as my vision came to me. A feral roar brought me back to my senses, my head still rung and I could hardly get up before I felt a warm bundle of fur in front of me – Lana.

We gotta go... She said weakly and it took me a moment to realize that Lucien and Xander were both handling enemies – I could barely even keep track of their figures. I got up and climbed onto Lana's back, wincing as I heard my bones shift and click into position – I had definitely broken something but it must've healed but I had no time to be in awe.

Run. Lucien said and Lana reared back but just as she was doing so she released a loud whimper and I fell off of her. She continued to whimper as she limped, her right hind leg had gotten hit by something – a small tranquilizer-like item. I crawled towards her and yanked it off.

I felt a sharp pain on my left arm and I groaned as my eyes snapped towards Lucien's direction. His left leg was bathed crimson in his own blood but he had his mouth wrapped around someone and Xander tackled the attacker. I felt cold rush run through my system and I heard a series of clicks and snaps in my body. I took the tranquilizer and sniffed it briefly before turning my head in the direction I could smell it in. I gripped it tightly and walked towards the smell's direction.

Where are you going? Lucien asked as he flung a body away from him and pounced towards me only to get hurled off to the side.

Can you hear me? I asked and I heard everything stop around me. Figures, men and women, stood around us, wearing a uniform of sleek black outfits and each carrying a weapon of some sort. Each one looked to me wide-eyed and I turned to where the smell took me. A woman stood there with her firing gun in her hand, she lifted it and aimed in my direction. I felt a fiery strength build in me and when I opened my mouth, I released a sound I could've never recognized as my own – I let out a loud growl. I stepped forward and found myself standing right in front of her with the gun pressed against my chest. I could hear her heart beat and her shaky breath and I took hold of her hands and aimed the gun right underneath her jaw. I released her hands and tilted my head. She looked around at her but no other person moved as she held the tranquilizer in her hands, her finger resting on the trigger.

Probably figuring out that no one would help her, she looked into my eyes, swallowed a lump in her throat and just as she was about to press the trigger, I felt a sharp pain in my neck and hissed through my teeth. I yanked the gun from her hands and stepped back before running towards Lucien's direction- my feet feeling almost weightless with every move I made. As soon as I got there, though, Lucien's attacker turned his attention to me and I could barely even register Lucien's limping form behind the man before he got to me. I fired the tranquilizer quickly but missed his face. The man was different from the others, the lower half of his face was masked by a thick crimson lining, his eyes the only thing peering out at me were an intense grey almost silver shade.

I couldn't reload the tranquilizer fast enough so I tried to use it to attack him but he merely stepped back, which to a bloodhound meant quite a leap. I grunted as I fumbled with the gun, ultimately throwing it down as I stepped towards him. He leapt sideways and I tried to follow, but I was always behind. I could sense the smile on his face and the frustration built up inside me. A few muffled voices started entering my head but I could only block them out. As I followed the man I was whipped backwards when someone grabbed onto my right arm, sending me recoiling around their body until another person grabbed my left arm.

They dragged me backwards, my heels digging into the ground to try and stop them. I heard Lucien and felt his anger course through me as well as his pain, I saw him as he was running towards the man. But he had picked up the tranquilizer I had dropped and he took out its contents replacing it with something else and I felt my stomach drop.

Lucien, please, don't let him hit you. He's not holding a tranquilizer. Please. I begged and I could sense a feeling of understanding from him. Lucien must've used all of his strength to gain that much speed as he clashed with the man before he could fire. I strained against the hold of my captors and I tried to gain strength as I saw Lucien engage in another battle. He took hold of the tranquilizer with his teeth and shook it, his wolf fighting hard to keep up. But just as Lucien got a grip on it, the man slipped one of his hands into his side and I could see the hilt of what I just knew was a knife. My bones shifted and clicked into place again and this time I could barely register any events as I felt myself ground my feet and yank my arms away.

I saw Lucien's eyes glance at me in confusion before I pushed him away hurling him in the opposite direction and I felt a sharp stinging pain slash against my body. Lucien whimpered in response. I fell to the ground and gasped as I felt my body grow cold. My side immediately felt damp and wet, my breathing broke into pants. Someone turned me over and I found that it was the same man but I didn't want to move. If I did, I probably risked making the wound hurt. A group of people suddenly surrounded me – they were in the same uniform and I felt my vision slowly fade.

"She's going to-" Someone began.

"She won't," the man in front of me said and he looked around. "Give me a vial."

I heard Lucien whimper but his pain was no longer as strong as it was. The stinging sensation in my body wouldn't stop – wouldn't let anything else in. I couldn't make a sound other than small hushed winces as I felt the ground beneath me turn soft and the smell of blood filled my nose. I could barely register the small noises, the fumbling, until the man pulled me up and pulled down his mask revealing his face.

"Make sure no one gets close," he said and I heard a few people move, a light breeze signifying that they had left. He then took out a glass vial and yanked out its lid with his teeth, spitting it away before facing me, he took the vial and placed its edge around my lips.

"Take it, come on, you won't heal otherwise," he said and before I could even react, someone else parted my lips for me as he tipped the vial in.

Chapter 25

He could just barely feel her now. Fuck. He cursed in his head. He groaned as he tried as best as he could to get up from the couch. The pain was unbearable, but his loss was too much. His whole body was in pain, but his wolf's own pain over losing his mate, unable to protect her was even more excruciating. What kind of mate was he if he couldn't even get up to save her? He coughed and tasted the tang of blood in his mouth. A hand came from behind him and he couldn't help but release a loud growl. Katherine rolled her eyes.

"Lucien- for the love of- You need to calm down, you're not healing as fast as we thought you would," she explained and he grunted before turning his head and spitting into a nearby trashcan. He was right, he spat out bright red blood.

"Where are they?" He asked, his voice low and coarse.

"Ignus? They're searching everywhere. Dalton's still here, he's doing his best to coordinate with them. If you need someone to talk to, he's your best bet," Katherine said with a sigh. "What happened?"

"I lost her," Lucien said, his voice filled with sadness. His and his wolf's emotions were in a turmoil. He wanted to howl, cry, rage...

"We'll find her," Katherine said reassuringly. Lucien decided not to take note of that, he looked down at his body and clicked his tongue.

"How are the rest of the pack?"

"They're fine. Most of them weren't too badly injured. I'm guessing they went all out on you because you had her," Katherine explained with a sigh.

"Do we have anything on how they got here?"

"Nothing so far, no one noticed a thing and... Ignus doesn't look good." Lucien raised a brow, Katherine studied his face before breathing a sigh.

"You can't pin this on him-"

"If he had done his job right- if he had-"

"Yeah, yeah, I get it," Ignus' voice said from above them. He came down from the stairs and it was only then that Lucien realized how different he looked.

"Anything?" Katherine asked, trying to break the palpable tension in the air. Ignus glanced over at Lucien before shaking his head.

"Nothing." Ignus said, almost spitting the words out, the disgust in his voice was clear, and Lucien saw the tenseness in Ignus' arms. He had his hands balled up into fists and he radiated with a kind of anger.

"I thought you had everything under control," Lucien said and Ignus chuckled, striking a nerve with him.

"Yeah, right."

"The hell are you laughing about?" Lucien asked angrily before getting up, ignoring the heart-wrenching pain coming from his body. His bandages grew soggy and he felt the thick wetness that came from tearing his wounds open again. Lucien stepped forward and all of a sudden, he and Ignus were at each other's throats. Katherine stepped forward, but Ignus simply shoved Lucien off him.

"You werewolves always think it's so easy, don't you?" Ignus cursed, "What the hell do you wanna do, huh? Wage a war?"

"If I have to, I will," Lucien said in a low voice and Ignus began to laugh.

"Your mate is an heiress and if you think werewolves are good at operating with their instincts you have no idea what she'll be capable of if they wake that up in her."

"You didn't even know jack-shit about her did you? What the hell did you even do for your group, huh? Didn't you just lead them right to her?"

"We all would've gotten to her at some point. We're not like you, we can't renounce members, we're bound together just like you are sure, but if it were so easy to just run from this clan we would've done it a long time ago," Ignus said.

"Can the two of you just calm down?"

"You didn't answer my question. Did you know jack-shit about her? Do you actually know what will happen with her if she tastes blood or if she does 'awaken'? Huh?"

Ignus didn't respond and Lucien shook his head. Katherine herself even remained silent as Lucien walked around in frustration, though she winced with every sound Lucien made, his body was literally falling apart. But she knew he wouldn't listen to her even if she tried.

"So what do we do now?" Lucien asked, Ignus breathed a heavy sigh and Katherine watched the two carefully.

"We-"

We found someone, Alpha. Katherine and Lucien instantly looked at each other.

A bloodhound? Lucien asked.

She says she wants to see someone. Lucien looked over at Ignus who had no idea of what was going on.

"There's someone still on the grounds," Lucien said and Ignus stared at him in surprise.

"Shit," he cursed, "Is it a woman?" Lucien nodded. Ignus shook his head and looked over at Lucien before breathing in a heavy sigh.

"It's her, isn't it?" A young voice asked and everyone turned to find Dalton making his way down the stairs.

"Not now, Dalton," Ignus began.

"She's our only chance," he replied and Lucien gave Ignus a stern look.

"Do you know who it is?" Lucien asked. Ignus didn't reply, so Dalton did.

"She's his mate."

"Not if I have anything to do about it," Ignus muttered, "It'd be better if we met her outside." Lucien raised a brow and turned to Katherine.

"Why's that?"

"Because I don't know if she's a spy or if she's honestly doing this out of the goodness of her so-called heart," Ignus said bitterly before climbing up the stairs, "Are you all coming or what?"

The four of them made their way through the forest where six pack members including Xander stood-by, encircling the lone woman. She had short curly brown hair and a pair of hazel eyes that looked nervously around her but they lit up as soon as she her eyes met with Ignus' who turned away from her gaze. Lucien ignored them to the best of his ability.

"Has she said anything?" Lucien asked turning to face Xander. He shook his head.

Nothing worth mentioning, Alpha. She only said she was surrendering. He mind-linked.

"And you are?" Lucien asked, looking straight at her. She looked back into his eyes and Ignus immediately cleared his throat, stepping forward to catch her attention.

"She's Medusa's reincarnation," he said bitterly, "so don't look into her eyes, she's not as innocent as you think she is." The werewolves all of a sudden shifted their weight uneasily between their feet and it wasn't hard to tell that they were all speaking to each other through their link.

Silence. Lucien commanded and everyone seemed to freeze. The woman chewed her bottom lip before looking over at Ignus.

"This isn't fair," she said and Ignus merely whistled and looked elsewhere.

"Such is life, now what the hell are you doing here?" Ignus asked, his voice so harsh that she shuddered.

"I came to help you," she said and Ignus rolled his eyes.

"Sure," he said with a shrug.

"Stop being such an asshole Ignus," Hera countered, walking forward but she was careful not to step in front of Lucien. "We're with them now, Celia, so if you're planning on doing or even saying anything stupid, I suggest you leave." Hera said, motioning to the pack. Celia swallowed a lump in her throat.

"He's constantly moving around," Celia said, "She's not gonna be somewhere you can find, not for a while."

"But do you know where they are?" Hera asked and Celia paused. Ignus let out an incredulous laugh.

"Really? And you chose to show up here?"

"Ignus." Hera scolded.

"He wanted to keep things under lock and key," Celia explained, "he has her, for sure, and I can- I can help-"

"Help get into our heads and warn him again? I don't think so," Ignus said indignantly, "But thanks for the information."

"I didn't have a choice," Celia countered angrily.

"Bullshit," Ignus cursed, "Everyone has a choice. It's not like he put a gun to your head." Lucien breathed out a sigh.

"Let her speak," Lucien said and Celia bit on her bottom lip.

"I-I can find her for you and tell you where she is... It'll take time – but you'll have eyes inside," she said, staring at the ground as if purposely avoiding doing anything that might raise suspicion.

"Why should we trust you?" Katherine asked.

"I just... I'm trying to make up for a mistake, a big mistake-" she said, her eyes looking over at Ignus who stubbornly refused to return her gaze. Lucien looked over at Hera who was studying Celia intensely.

"What exactly happened between you two anyways?" Lucien asked.

"I-"

"The man who took your mate is her brother," Ignus said with a smirk on his face as he looked straight into Celia's eyes, "Have fun convincing them that you're anything but a snake." And with that, Ignus turned and left, disappearing in the blink of an eye.

"You didn't have to be such an asshole," Hera said, slamming the door shut behind her. Ignus shook his head as he took out one of his own syringes and quickly poked himself in the arm before taking it away. He clicked the bones around his neck and sighed.

"I don't expect you to understand," Ignus said and it was Hera's turn to sigh.

"She's still your mate."

"Well she sure doesn't act like it," he snapped.

"Listen, like it or not, she's our only shot," she replied.

"Yeah, a bad one at that. We might as well search ourselves-"

"But he'll tell her- I'm sure."

"Yeah and then he'll easily slip into her head and figure it all out."

"Can you stop being such a pessimistic ass?" Hera hissed and Ignus shrugged.

"She didn't even do anything to stop him that time, what makes you think she'll act any different? She's a coward. A manipulative one at that."

"You just need to give her a chance," Hera said. "She knows more about this than you do." Ignus let out a frustrated groan. A knock on the door suddenly took their attention and they opened it to find Lucien and Katherine along with Desmond.

"That's the girl that marked you?" Desmond asked looking at Ignus who simply chuckled.

"Like I said, 'snake'," he said turning to Hera who shook her head. "Did you keep her on lock-down?"

"For now, yes," Lucien said, "But I need explanations."

"Yeah, I knew that was coming," Ignus said with a sigh, "You all might wanna take a seat, this is gonna take a while."

Chapter 26

"Could someone please remind me why it is that we've locked the poor girl in the basement?" Katherine asked as the group stood in the living room.

Lucien had a grim look on his face as he leaned against the wall, occasionally glancing outside, spotting the other pack members patrolling the grounds. Ignus, on the other hand was busy pouring himself a drink. After taking a sip, he turned around and faced Katherine, who had her arms folded over her chest and was looking expectedly at him.

"Oh, you mean Celia?" Ignus asked as he took another sip from his dark glass of bourbon. "Well, if her brother contacts her, he won't know what we're talking about so that's one. And I like the idea of locking traitors up in a basement... granted you all gave her food and water, which is more than I can say for what she'd be willing to do to-" Hera cleared her throat, interrupting him.

"What he's trying to say is that despite Celia's willingness to work with us, she's not exactly the best at keeping her head closed – especially since Ezra's her brother. Think of it like an Alpha's command...

except we can thoroughly look into each other's heads and Ezra just so happens to have the free-key into most peoples'." Katherine and Desmond's face contorted with what looked like disgust.

"How are you guys even able to handle each other?" Desmond asked.

"Well, most of us shut others out. Actually, Auden does it pretty well," Ignus said with a shrug. "I think she learned it faster than most of us do too. We're usually open books to everyone until we reach maturity- which is around the sixteen-seventeen threshold. Unfortunately, exceptions can be made when Celia's bloodline happens to be one of the most manipulative bastards in the world."

"Manipulative?" Katherine asked.

"We'll get to that later. Right now, we need to be on the same page," Hera said with a sigh, glancing over at Lucien. "He okay?" Katherine followed her gaze and sighed.

Earth to Lucien. Katherine mind-linked. Lucien's gaze went toward the room.

"You said we need to be on the same page. Go on then," Lucien said and Hera pressed her lips into a thin line before she opened her mouth to continue.

"Auden's mother, Aurelia, was the leader of our group up until four years ago, right now, her position is being held 'temporarily' by Auden's grandfather- Castor," Hera explained, "Before we knew about Auden, there were only two families that had pure-blood heirs and each one of these heirs had a chance to attain 'leadership'."

"Sounds more like 'the crown' rather than leadership to me, seems you guys have more of a monarchy system going on," Desmond said and Ignus chuckled.

"Exactly," he responded as he poured himself more bourbon. "We're kind of still stuck in the dark-ages."

"Anyways," Hera said, glaring at Ignus and walking up to him, "the two families had a total of three qualified heirs, before Auden." She said before taking the bottle away from Ignus and placing it aside. Ignus rolled his eyes before walking away from her and towards Lucien, where he joined him as they leaned against the window together.

"Three? Why so few?" Katherine asked.

"Because royal bloodlines like to in-breed and the more it happens, the less children they make. An inward rejection that royals refuse to acknowledge," Ignus said with a laugh, "hence their issues finding 'sane' leaders." Katherine grimaced.

"You're not exactly one to talk about royals," Hera hissed. "But that's besides the point, the matter is that among those three, you've already met two." Lucien raised a brow at that.

"What do you mean?" Lucien asked and Ignus grinned.

"Well, Celia's one of them and the other one is standing right in front of you," Ignus responded before Hera bit onto her bottom lip.

"You're a candidate?" Katherine asked. "Jesus you're like twelve."

"I'm sixteen and at the very least, I'm not crazy," Hera said, glaring at Ignus.

"So the other one is Celia's brother?" Lucien asked and the two bloodhounds in the room nodded.

"None other. His name's Ezra and he's a mind freak. Literally. That man weaves through our heads like no one else can," Ignus said with a shrug.

"But if that's the case then why are you so angry at your mate? Seems like she had no choice," Katherine said with a scrutinizing look in her eye.

"Because she's the only one left who can fight it and she didn't," Ignus said, gritting his teeth. "And since that's not something every-one believes, why don't we just ask her?" He asked before putting his glass down and looking over at Lucien.

Celia looked at the werewolves around her as she played with the bottom of the wooden chair she sat on. She then found her gaze landing on Ignus who refused to look at her.

"What exactly do you do for your clan?" Lucien asked. Despite the fact that they called it a basement, the place was really more of a fortified cell. There was nothing in it save for the chair Celia sat on and a single lightbulb that hung from the ceiling. The walls were made of concrete and the floor was the same. The only way out was a large metal door that led directly up a flight of stairs into the pack house.

"I'm a researcher, a doctor if you will," she said simply.

"Researching what?" Lucien asked.

"Look, we're bloodhounds, but the world doesn't exactly let mur-ders happen, and it certainly isn't as easy to cover our tracks, so I try to find substitutes and I'm the one that gives out relaxants that stop us from lashing out," she said, looking at Lucien straight in the eye.

"And what exactly can you really do for us?" Lucien asked in a straightforward manner.

"Considering how much I research, I can get direct access to your mate – she's someone we're all interested in and I'm the only one that can head the project," she said before glancing over at Ignus, "and if it's an issue of security, then simple, I can get her to contact Ignus and that should be enough. She'll be the only one to feed you information." Lucien looked to Ignus.

"You can contact her from these distances?" Lucien asked, a low growl interlacing with his voice.

"Yes. But before you ask, I already tried to contact her when we lost her. She's out and there's no doubt that Ezra's part of that," Ignus responded. "Either way, one little slip-up from little miss doctor here and our party's over."

"But it sounds simple enough, doesn't it?" Katherine asked. "What other chance have we got?" Celia looked to Ignus with a triumphant grin, but he merely tilted his head towards Katherine.

"Considering Celia doesn't know how to make a mind-maze for her brother, if she slips up this one teeny-tiny secret, we're done for."

"But they would never kill her," Hera interjected before looking to Celia for certainty. "Right?" She simply nodded and Lucien paused.

"And why not? How can we assume she'll be fine if she was aimed at during the attack?"

"Well... she definitely won't die as soon as you think. I can get you time as well as communication. Just keep me out of it and we'll be fine," Celia said, reassuringly, "I-I can't be trusted, I know that... I... But I can at least get you all to do what you must." Lucien then turned to Ignus.

"Why exactly did you approach Auden in the first place?"

"Well, better us than the others. She was going to be found no matter what, we told you this before," Hera said.

"But why exactly would you be any better?" Lucien pressed. Hera opened her mouth to speak but immediately found herself at a loss for words.

"Because we would've given her a choice," Ignus said grimly.

"A choice about what?" Lucien asked.

"Leadership," Celia said for everyone. "It's not like... we can force leadership," Celia said, pausing and looking around before continuing.

"But Auden was Aurelia's child. Even if she was hidden from us, she would've undoubtedly come back to our clan... We always do," Celia said, before looking over at Ignus. "And we can all agree that in the right hands, she would be better than Ezra."

"And a more fitting candidate than myself," Hera said. "If she's a real hybrid, she'll be able to effect change like no other leader before."

"And as Aurelia's only child... no one will be able to turn against her," Ignus added.

"I've been confused about this since earlier, but what exactly happened to Aurelia?" Desmond asked and everyone paused.

"She's sick," Ignus said simply.

"That's putting it lightly-" Celia began but Ignus shot her an icy glare that froze her words. Lucien gave Ignus a look of suspicion but when their eyes met, Ignus looked like he was making a plea to speak of it later. Lucien hesitantly let it go.

"Okay, fine. But wouldn't you all have some kind of problem with Auden being, you know, a hybrid?" Katherine asked, sensing the need to change the subject. Ignus shook his head.

"Do you know why Celia works to research alternatives to blood? Because we're trying to change. Auden's being a hybrid will only help that cause... and we're almost certain her werewolf blood will make her stronger, not weaker," Ignus said, unable to resist sneaking a glance over at Celia, whose eyes were right on his. Their gaze immediately stopped each other and Ignus had to fight his own instincts to close his eyes and look away.

"And what exactly were the others going to do with her?" Lucien asked.

"Train her. Re-wire her, even," Celia said. "And before any of you say anything... I just want to make clear, when we said that my brother- no, Ezra, could weave through our heads, there's a certain element about that that's real. If he manages to catch Auden off-guard, he can go through anyone and change them... with enough time."

"Wait a second, re-wire?" Katherine asked.

"Exactly what it sounds like," Ignus said, "if Auden isn't able to keep him out, and I doubt it, she's already good at shutting me off. But if he gets a way in... there's a chance Auden won't exactly be 'Auden' anymore."

"And you know this how?" Katherine asked, gritting her teeth. A silence fell on Ignus, Hera, and Celia.

"Ignus' si-" Celia began but she was soon interrupted.

"Let's just say we've seen it happen to the best of our families," Ignus said with a serious tone in his voice.

"Then it sounds like we'll have to trust your mate," Lucien said, without hesitation.

"Not that we have a better choice," Hera said, looking over at Celia and then at Ignus. It was clear how tense he was and Lucien could swear that the air was palpably heavier than it was before. Ignus marched over to Celia and it seemed like every vein on his arm was threatening to pop. He knelt down in front of her and Celia froze.

"If anything goes wrong, anything, I will tear you and your brother, limb from limb even if it kills me," Ignus said, his voice deep and filled with rage. Celia's lip quivered but not subtly – she couldn't stop shaking... And the rest of the room felt the weight of his words. Even Lucien felt a command over him stronger than that of his own Alpha command over his pack. Ignus stood up and rolled his arms back before turning around and leaving – slamming the door behind him. As Lucien slowly felt the weight lift off of him, he immediately looked around the room.

"We'll release you at sun-down," he said, turning to Celia before he marched off on his own, this time to talk to Ignus, in private.

It took Lucien a while to find the bloodhound. He didn't realize Ignus was exactly so good at hiding until the moment he found himself calling out to him. Then and only then was Lucien able to trace him by scent. He found Ignus by the lake, but he wasn't alone, he was with a pack of four dogs, all happily barking and licking Ignus' hands.

"Well that's not what I was expecting," Lucien said, knowing he had to be the one in a lighter mood. Ignus chuckled before turning to look at him.

"No one even noticed that they'd slipped in," he said with a smile.

"They're dogs, we may be wolves but it isn't a problem if a stray or two make their way in," Lucien sad, "Although I might be more than a little concerned now."

"You shouldn't be. No one else can summon these little guys," Ignus said as he rubbed the belly of one of the dogs.

"What do you do with them?" Lucien asked.

"Spy," he answered quickly.

"Spy?"

"I can see and feel the things they do... It's my family's special trait," Ignus said with a grin.

"Do you all have a special trait?"

"You could say that."

"And what was Auden's?" Lucien asked and Ignus paused for a moment before he turned his head and smiled.

"That family is a little less predictable. Royalty usually is," Ignus said before looking over at Lucien. "I've no doubt that Auden will be fine, physically anyways." Lucien rolled his eyes.

"Thanks for the reassurance," Lucien said with sarcasm.

"You're welcome."

"What do you think is the plan after he re-wires her head?" Lucien asked and Ignus paused as he rubbed the head of another dog. There was no ignoring the possibility and Ignus knew that if he were in Ezra's shoes, that would be his exact plan.

"I think you have an idea, don't you?"

"Not a good one."

"Yeah, well, if Ezra was good, we wouldn't be out here in this mess. His easiest plan would be to have her be on his side and if that's done... well his next steps depend on how obsessed he is with her... which is pretty obsessed if you ask me."

"But even if he could re-wire her head, it's not like she'd forget-"

"She might not forget you... But she won't think of you the same. At least probably not...," Ignus said with a sigh.

"Why didn't you let her mark me then?" Ignus stood up at that.

"Because she's not stable."

"But wouldn't it have been better to let her mark me than to let her be?"

"If she marked you and she couldn't stop, she might've killed you. There was a higher chance of your death, which would make it even harder on everyone else... We need you alive – if we want to maintain some part of her at least."

"Doesn't make sense to me. I would've rather risked it."

"Aurelia couldn't mark her mate when he was already mated to another and she didn't want him to try and reject what already bonded. Bloodhounds heal a lot faster than you do and even then our chances of survival aren't significantly higher. Imagine it like this," Ignus paused. "Say you find a starving dog locked away in a cage, it's snarling and it's been patient all its life, and then you make that dog bite you and it smells flesh and meat. Except now that dog may or may not possess a surprise gift or two."

"You're saying she'd go haywire?"

"She'd go crazy over you, had we had the time... I would've wanted to figure out a way to gradually introduce it to her. But like I said, starving dog."

The two of them stood in silence, the only sound filling the air were the dogs' panting and fooling around.

Lucien, would you mind heading back here with Ignus, the girl's got a weird request. Katherine's voice suddenly rang through. Lucien sighed and looked over at Ignus.

"Your mate apparently made a weird request," Lucien said and Ignus raised an eyebrow.

It wasn't long before they were back in the basement. Celia was now standing up straight with a fierce look of determination in her eyes.

"What do you want?" Ignus asked with nonchalance.

"I need an injury," Celia responded. "Otherwise Ezra won't believe me." Ignus paused for a moment.

"I told you it was a weird request," Katherine commented. "This is some weird S-and-M shit right here." Ignus chuckled before looking over at his mate and narrowing his eyes. Lucien stepped forward but Ignus shook his head.

"I'll gladly do it," he said with a smirk and Katherine gawked at him.

"Are you-"

"I'm going to feel it too, Katherine," Ignus said, "Isn't it only fair? Besides, if I don't do it, Ezra'll be even more suspicious." Lucien looked between the two bloodhounds and nodded his head.

"Go ahead," he said simply and Ignus nodded as he stepped forward, massaging his right hand with his left.

"I'm going to enjoy this," Ignus muttered.

"I know," Celia answered back with a fire in her eyes and the two of them found that they couldn't look away from each other's gaze. In a blink of an eye, Ignus took her arm in his grip and she refused to let out a sound.

"Oh I cannot watch this this is fucking gross," Katherine said as she turned around and left the room, dragging Desmond behind her.

"I don't think I'll stick around for this either," Hera said with a grimace before looking over at Lucien.

"Will she heal fast enough?" Lucien asked and Ignus grinned.

"She'll heal of course; I don't hate myself that much to feel that broken." Lucien nodded before he stepped back.

"I'll be right by the door." Once Lucien shut the door behind him, Ignus breathed out a large sigh.

"You're a real piece of work, you know that?" Ignus muttered.

"Oh, so we're on speaking terms now?" Celia asked and Ignus didn't respond.

Instead, a loud crack and a high-pitched scream filled the room... and Ignus barely even twitched.

"This is almost as painful as the mark you gave me," Ignus muttered and Celia gasped and groaned.

"Bullshit..." She cursed and Ignus grinned.

"I think two injuries would be more realistic don't you?" Ignus said sadistically and Celia groaned, writhing in pain on the floor.

"Do... it..." She said in between breaths and Ignus grinned before he walked towards her. He dropped down and their eyes met again.

"If you think this is pain, you have no idea," Ignus said and a deep ferocious growl resounded from his chest. "This is for Irena." Ignus hissed as he grabbed her.

Chapter 27

- -

Pain. That was all I could feel as I felt my nails dig into the sheets. My head throbbed and nothing but garbled screams escaped my mouth. It was dark – probably because the light had made my head throb even harder. I was hungry, thirsty, and in unbearable pain.

Make it stop. Make it stop. Make it stop. I repeated in my head. I clutched my stomach as my body convulsed. I could feel the dried blood that surrounded the area and I panted. The pain always subsided for only a few moments – as if my body really just wanted me to breathe before it struck me again like a tidal wave. I took a deep breath as I felt the pain quell. I processed the room around me as I breathed and finally had the composure to wipe the disgusting drool off my face.

I groaned as I sat up and observed the room as best as I could. It was large – tall ceilings, dark wooden floors, the curtains were closed, the door was probably locked, and the only source of light was a single candle burning on a table in the room. I looked at my hands, they were trembling from the pain I had experienced earlier. How many days had it been? I'd lost count.

My stomach, which had been stabbed, had only miraculously healed itself – and yet for some reason my entire body was in absolute pain. It was so painful that I couldn't think. I heard the door unlock and I felt a sharp pain sting my entire body. In walked the man himself – Ezra Gilden, who simply walked over to the bed and snapped his fingers before I was swallowed up by the pain again.

"I don't know how you do it," he said as I writhed about in the bed, biting into the sheets beneath me. "Somehow the wall in your head is as thick and sturdy as ever." I couldn't respond, instead I felt myself lose control over my body again as it twisted and turned, contracting and grasping for some kind of relief that didn't exist. I suddenly heard footsteps and Ezra came over and his hands caressed my face... I could do nothing as I felt tears fall from my eyes from the pain.

"You poor thing..." he trailed off before he placed his hands beneath me and lifted me off the bed. I felt my breath leave me in short quick pants as I shivered and shook in his grasp. I could just barely make out the shapes of people moving in and out of the room. I grit my teeth as I felt the pain soar throughout my body and my eyes closed as more tears streamed through them. It felt like ages before Ezra placed me down and I felt the sheets beneath me... They smelled clean and covered in... something else.

"Perhaps... even in your dreams you'll manage to defend yourse lf..." his voice said as I faded out of consciousness...

My eyes blinked awake and I found myself lying down in a large all-white bed, tucked in peacefully as the curtains were being drawn by a group of women. A man entered the room rolling in what looked like a tray of food and I suddenly faced a profound hunger in me.

Where the hell was I? I grimaced as I tried to move and found every inch of my body sore and in pain. Flashbacks of the previous days of pain and agony suddenly made their way into my head. That was probably why I had such a headache as my eyes adjusted to the light. The man, who was dressed in completely white attire, pushed the tray to my side as a woman with curled locks of brown hair walked – well, really, limped her way inside. She had a cane with her that seemed to help her movements and she adjusted a pair of thin silver glasses on her face.

She looked over at me and smiled – her eyes, a pale hazel color, suddenly reminded me of Lucien, and the dull ache in my chest suddenly bloomed into a kind of emotional pain... I bit into my bottom lip and suddenly felt how dry they were.

"Good morning," she greeted and I simply stared in her direction. As she took a few steps towards me, a snarl escaped my lips, freezing her in place and startling even me. Her smile faded from her face as the sound of footsteps made its way towards us. I didn't even have to look to know that it was Ezra and only then did it become clear why I snarled. I could sense the blood shared between them – siblings.

"All that pain and yet she still has the energy to snarl," Ezra said with a smile.

"Don't taunt her. She's still weak from her awakening," his sister responded. I opened my mouth to speak and yet nothing came out but a weak whisper of air.

"So it seems," Ezra said, the smile remaining on his face. "We're lucky Ignus didn't turn her sooner. A dog is easier to tame when they're young."

"Ezra-" she began but he simply raised his hand and it was like her voice had faded from her too. He walked towards me and I felt the air around me turn heavy. I opened my mouth – but not a single sound came out even as I could feel a growl well up in my chest. It was then that I felt it, it was a command – like that of an Alpha's – and yet, though a part of me felt like bowing, the other part of me, felt like resisting it but I couldn't summon the strength to- I felt his touch on my cheek and shivered as I tried to move against it, only to find myself moving towards him.

"You can't quite multi-task when you're this weak, Auden," he said with a smile. "But I will be patient... and you will be our greatest treasure." He said and I felt disgust well inside me as he ran his fingers down my cheek. I found my eyes looking over at his sister who simply stood there as if she was unable to move.

Ezra tucked my hair behind my ear before clicking his tongue, it was only then that his sister moved forward with a long silver pen-like object similar to what Ignus, Hera, and Dalton used... Ezra took it from her and sighed as he stared into my eyes and tapped the tip of the pen onto the center of my chest. A warmth bloomed from where he'd had it touch me and so did a hunger I'd never seen before. I felt my voice return as I let out a breath and as I turned to look over at Ezra, he smiled.

"Everyone has been wasting your talents, but we will not be the same," he said, "Celia, continue to hand her the prepared dosage, it'll be less painful than before that way... and feed her the normal stuff. We can't have her bloodlust released here."

"Understood," his sister replied. He stood up and I felt relief course through me as he moved away. Once he was gone, she looked to me and released a shaky breath that she'd probably been holding the moment he'd entered.

"I... promise I won't hurt you. So please... eat," she said as she walked over and began serving me food. I could barely even move and I was sure she realized it as she picked up a spoonful of food and put it to my lips. I nodded simply as I opened my mouth and ate.

"Auden,"a woman's voice called out. There was nothing around me but darkness, a suffocating and painful darkness. "Find me."

I opened my eyes – and as I blinked, a series of images flashed through my head. Directions. A straight walk, a set of large doors, three flights of stairs, three turns, and a code-locked door. I released a shaky breath. I heard a rustle beside me and found myself looking over at Celia, who had just tapped the pen-like object into left my arm.

"Sorry, did I wake you?" She asked and I shook my head. "You're looking better already." I nodded simply as I felt the heat from the contact travel through my body. I must've stared at it for a long time as Celia began explaining it to me.

"This is a bloodvac, or at least that's what we call it. It stands for a Blood Vaccine – even though it's not really a vaccine and I just think the name sounds cool... Anyways, it contains controlled doses of blood as well as other synthetic material to create the illusion of feeding. The more blood, the greater the satisfaction and impact," she said and I nodded. "My name is Celia by the way." She said as she extended her hand towards me. I lifted my right hand and she smiled as she took it and squeezed.

"You really do look like her," she said in a low voice.

"Like who?" I asked, my voice surprising the two of us. It was weak, soft as a whisper, and definitely hoarse.

"Wait, let me get you some water," she said as she turned around and picked up a pitcher on the nightstand. She poured me a glass. "Can you hold it?" I extended my hand and she rested the glass in it, testing to see if I could handle its weight. She released it and I managed to hold it up, though it did take more effort than it should've. I brought the glass to my lips and sipped quietly as she took in a breath.

"You look a lot like Aurelia," Celia said and I paused.

"Is she here?" I asked and Celia pressed her lips into a thin line.

"Are you hungry?" She asked, changing the subject. Deciding that I was too weak to interrogate anyone, I nodded. In a few moments, the double doors to the room opened and in an elderly man in a simple white dress shirt and black slacks from yesterday with a tray of food being rolled in. Celia took the glass from my hands and put it back on the nightstand before offering her hand to me.

"Can you stand?" I nodded weakly as I took her hand and lifted myself.

My legs felt weak as I lifted my back and took a seat on the edge of the bed. The old man pushed the tray towards me before adjusting its height, turning it into a breakfast table. I mustered up a smile for him as a thank you and he returned it with a curt nod as he lifted the metal lid off the plate of food, revealing a bowl of rice porridge. He then stepped aside before heading out the door.

"How long have I been here?" I asked, clearing my throat after speaking and picking up a spoon.

"It's been just a little over a week," she said and I paused before looking at her. She nodded simply with a soft smile as I took a spoonful of porridge into my mouth. I felt like all the hunger suddenly came at me as I ate spoon after spoon.

"You've never been injured like that before so your body had to take its time... Plus, you've only recently woken your wolf and your hound."

"What exactly did I injure?" I asked just after swallowing yet another spoonful.

"Well your stomach was punctured and you nicked part of your lung..."

"Okay... and I didn't internally bleed out because...?" Celia grinned.

"We gave you a huge dose of blood the first day – which we were lucky that your body didn't reject, probably because you really needed it." I nodded trying to process that information as I cleaned off the bowl.

"Do you want more?" Celia asked and I shook my head.

"I'd rather not surprise my stomach with all this food after not having any for more than a week," I said and she nodded. The man from earlier then entered the room, quietly covering up the bowl before pulling away.

"What's his name?" I asked as he disappeared once more.

"His name's Bo, he's been the caretaker of this residence even before Aurelia was born."

"Huh." Celia then suddenly moved close to me.

"You... can't hear anyone in your head, can you?" She asked and I bit my bottom lip.

"No but I can feel certain people trying to get in," I said and she nodded briefly.

"Do you think you can keep them out for an extended period?" She asked and I nodded.

"It really isn't that hard, so yeah," I said with a shrug and she breathed a sigh of relief.

"Good to know..." she trailed off before she paused, closed her eyes for a few moments, and re-opened them. If I wasn't mistaken, her hazel eyes had a subtle yellow glow to them now and she looked straight into my eyes. "My brother instructed me to come by every day to study you, I'll help you learn more about us and I'll be in charge of monitoring your... condition."

"Okay." I answered simply.

"There's a bathroom in here, just go through the door in the corner and you'll find it." I nodded and then Celia pressed her lips into a thin line.

"Be careful." She said simply before she took my hand in hers before getting up and leaving, shutting the door behind her with a soft thud. She mumbled something to someone, which meant there was definitely a guard at the doors. In the hand she'd held, she'd left me a note. At first glance, it looked like a prescription for medicine, but there was something written behind it.

Make sure to get rid of this. Flush it down the toilet. Can't burn it – brother will notice. Ignus told me to watch you. My brother can go through someone's head like it's a toy he can play, learn, and rearrange. Don't tell me anything important. Keep everyone out of your head.

Chapter 28

As it turns out, keeping everyone out of my head, wasn't as complicated as it seemed. What was, complicated I mean, was trying to figure out how to get the hell out of this place. It isn't easy when I couldn't reach out to Ignus, even though I had a feeling I could definitely pull it off- if it didn't mean letting Celia's weird brother into my head. She'd warned me enough and Ignus had acted all scary when I'd told him I was hearing things from him – so, fair enough.

The guy that brought me my food everyday – Bo – was actually really nice. He didn't usually make much conversation, but when he did, it made me smile. He'd comment on how much I'd been eating, ask if I needed anything, and so on and so forth. Celia, on the other hand, seemed to be desperately trying to keep her mouth shut. Which was a surprise to me, since we were talking earlier and she saw me at least twice every day to administer the BloodVac.

"Do you think it's gonna rain today?" I asked, looking over at Bo who had just started to pour me a cup of coffee from the press he'd brought into the room.

"Most probably. Spring isn't really the brightest of seasons. It'll be a while before the gardens bloom," he said, adding that small comment of his. I sighed as I looked back out the window. Over the past few days, I had at least learned more about the layout of this place. Ezra had given Celia permission to walk me around – but never outside. The closest to outside I could get was a glass room on the ground floor that looked out the greenhouse.

Ezra wasn't an idiot, that was for sure. To his credit, he used every up he had against me to make sure I stayed put, knowing as little to nothing as he could possibly give me. Not even my newly developed senses could help me get out of this mess. I couldn't make any progress into finding that room I'd seen either. Every step I took, every sound I made, and if I'd let it happen – every thought I had, was pretty much tracked down to a T. There wasn't a single place in here that was empty. There was always someone and they didn't have to even breathe for me to know they were there. I guess that was how bloodhounds worked so well. I could sense them throughout the building, which made me wonder how the hell Ignus and his group ever escaped in the first place.

I sighed as Bo placed the coffee on the table in front of me. I had been standing outside the windows all day and no matter what, I just knew that the trees in front of me were just as riddled with bloodhounds as this damned building was. I needed to find a way out of here. But at this rate, it seemed damn right impossible. I might as well be chained to the ground.

"Is there any way to spend time productively in this place?" I asked, folding my arms over my chest, and Bo smiled to himself.

"I don't think Sir Ezra would like you to do anything in particular," he replied and I rolled my eyes.

"Well, there has to be something I can do," I replied and Bo paused for a moment.

"There's a library on the ground floor," he said and I raised my brows.

"And?"

"I'm sure Sir Ezra wouldn't mind you in there and there should be enough books to your liking."

"I'm guessing computers are out of the question," I said and Bo chuckled.

"Need I respond?" I smiled at him this time. "You should drink it while it's hot." He said simply as he nudged the cup of coffee towards me.

"Right..." I trailed off just as Bo nodded his head and stepped back. I lifted the cup and just as I was about to take a sip, I noticed a slim piece of paper. Bo seemed to be deliberately avoiding me then. I took the paper into my hand and knowing I had to hide it somewhere, I tucked it underneath the long-sleeved dress I was wearing and into my bra. Better safe than sorry.

"When you see Sir Ezra again, you should ask him about the library," Bo said suddenly and I nodded but the sound of footsteps made me roll my eyes.

"Looks like he's here," I said as the doors swung open and the two siblings, Ezra and Celia made their way inside. Celia closed the doors behind them, while Ezra walked up to me, making me put my coffee down. I rolled the right sleeve of my dress up and Ezra grinned as Celia came forward and tapped the vaccine into my arm. Recently, they'd begun to send a numbness through my body that made my head hurt.

"Any headaches today?" Celia asked as I pulled down my sleeve.

"Not yet," I replied.

"It's a reaction to the increased doses we've been giving," Ezra explained and I knew he was trying to read my face since my mind was about as locked up as it could be. Not that I couldn't feel him poking around me to see if he could get in – he was always there. It was uncanny and sometimes it made me shiver at night.

"You'll get used to it soon. We're almost at a full dose," Celia said with a soft smile. I sighed before turning to look over at Ezra.

"Bo says there's a library here," I said and Ezra raised an eyebrow.

"Did he?" He responded, before looking over at Bo. The air suddenly felt heavy, almost suffocating, and though he did well to hide it, Bo had shivered.

"If I may..." Bo responded, his voice weak. Ezra nodded and the air lifted, if only slightly. "Miss Auden has had nothing to do. The library is the least entertainment to offer." Ezra sighed and the air became clear as he looked over at me before he seemed to have gotten an idea. He smiled at me, which honestly filled me with dread.

"Fine. I'll pick you up in the morning and escort you to the library. You'll pick out a book and then I'll bring you to my office."

"Ezra-" Celia began but Ezra simply glared in her direction, sending her into silence.

"Great," I said plainly. Ezra grinned before he turned on his heel. Celia gave me a nervous glance before she scurried away behind him while Bo fixed his tie, offered me a smile, and left me alone as well.

As soon as the door was shut, I made my way to the bathroom, locked the door, and ran the shower. I took the paper out, unfolded it, and read.

Ezra hears everything so even Bo can't have a clear idea. My dear child, there are only two minds he cannot enter. Mine and yours. Stay sharp and wait your time. I've showed you the way. -Aurelia

I clutched the piece of paper close to my chest. I had only one ally I could trust and even then, it seemed the world was against us. But if she could contact me this way or show me images in my head... then maybe... just maybe, I could learn a thing or two. I took a deep breath. One thing's for certain, I wasn't getting out of here any time soon.

I stripped down and stared at my reflection in the mirror. I'd tried hard not to think of Lucien especially when Ezra was so close by. It seemed to me that he could not only go through your head, but he had a keen sense of emotions – and something told me he'd use anything to his advantage. A pang in my heart throbbed as I remembered Lucien's embrace. I looked over at the mark he'd given me, the welts in my skin of his fangs had faded much faster than I'd ever seen before. Even my mother- well, step-mother, had a darker mark to her skin. But mine seemed lighter as if they were simply stretches of pale skin. Bloodhounds healed well indeed.

I sighed as I threw the paper into the toilet and flushed it down. Lucien would have to wait as I do. But the moment I get the chance, I'll run right towards him.

Chapter 29

Whenen you're in the library, Bo will recommend you a book. Don't be afraid to read it in front of Ezra.

I sighed as I looked through the books. Bo told me to read a history book in the furthest corner. I found it with ease, though I highly doubted it would've been of interest to me. Considering I couldn't converse with Aurelia herself, it's hard to tell her that I would've been more interested in medical books. Despite being my mother, we knew little to nothing about each other.

"And what's today's selection?" Ezra's voice asked from behind me. I turned and showed him the book.

"Volume one of Bloodhound History, huh," he said, seemingly unimpressed. "They're mainly just myths and legends."

"Considering I don't know anything about bloodhounds, I thought it'd be a good start," I said, thankful that there was an excuse I could use. I guess that was one reason she'd chosen it.

I followed Ezra to his office, which was further away from where I needed to be. I sighed as he took a seat at his desk and he motioned for me to sit at the chair right across it.

"Bo will come bring snacks in a bit," Ezra said and I nodded as I took my seat.

"Don't you think this is a little awkward?" I asked and Ezra raised an eyebrow as he brought out a computer. So there's gotta be WiFi. I thought to myself.

"Not at all. In fact, I'd appreciate it if you developed some kind of Stockholm Syndrome," he said without a single bit of amusement in his tone.

"Why did you bring me here?"

"Because I want you," he answered directly before pausing for a moment and looking at me with those piercing grey eyes. "Rather, I need you for something." It was my turn to raise a brow.

"For what?"

"Validation." He answered simply and that was it. He simply began typing away as I looked through the book in front of me.

To be fair, the book wasn't as boring as it seemed. Then again, myths and legends were always interesting. Werewolf legends were great too. Finding out about mate bonds and such... Not that I ever thought I had one, all things considered back then. I flipped a page and suddenly found myself pausing. A wave of drowsiness came over me as I read and soon enough, I found my mind drifting...

"Auden," a voice called to me. I found myself waking up and saw a woman in front of me, propped up in a bed. She had long brown hair, soft brown eyes, and pale almost snow-like skin. But it wasn't the healthy kind of look, it was a paleness that meant illness... Like she was a flower about to wilt. She smiled as I looked at her.

"Looks like Dante raised you well," she said simply. I opened my mouth to speak, but she placed a finger to her lips.

"Until I teach you how to 'speak', it's best not to try," she said with a soft smile. "For most bloodhounds, you either hear everyone's thoughts like a hive-mind... or you block everyone out. Some people are better at it than others, like Ezra. But even he isn't an exception – you, however," she said looking at me kindly.

"As my daughter, you are capable of far more... and I've a feeling you'll learn fast. It won't be long until you'll be able to talk to me..." She trailed off. "I thought we'd be able to meet in person, but with Ezra's methods, that'll be close to impossible..." She then looked into my eyes.

"Our world mimics that of werewolves sometimes. Our blood and our strength, base our place. But unlike werewolves, our familial powers are more important. Ignus' family has had great connections with dogs and will always do, Ezra manifested the power to go through minds and as a result of his own... experimentation, he's figured out that he can go much further by changing them to his advantage." I pointed to myself and she smiled.

"You, half-werewolf and half-bloodhound, will outrank us in physical strength. But as you already show signs of my power... I'm hopeful," she said just as she reached out to me. "I'll see you again soon."

I suppressed a yawn as I blinked my eyes, only to find myself sitting right across Ezra, the history book still sat in my lap and it was as if time had barely moved. I flipped through the book and glanced up, only to find that Ezra had met my gaze.

"What?" I asked.

"You were dozing off earlier."

"And you should get back to work," I said, refusing to make even more conversation with him.

I would definitely get out of here. No matter how long it took.

Chapter 30

"Lucien, I don't think this is a good idea," Katherine said as she fiddled with the end of her blouse.

"On the contrary, I think this is a great idea," Ignus counteracted and Katherine rolled her eyes. Lucien was dressed in a fine suit with Lana, Xander, Desmond, and other members of his pack following behind him.

"We won't find her on our own," Lucien said.

"And some of these guys would do anything to get their hands on a weakness," Katherine said, to which Desmond nodded his head.

"Speak carefully, Alpha," Desmond said and Lucien merely nodded his head as he entered the large conference room. Alphas and Betas filled the tables that formed a large rectangle around the room.

It was rare for Lucien to make a request and having made a desperate plea for help, he was answered by every pack he could grab a hold of. With a little help from his more powerful friends of course. Small or large there was a pack from every part of North America and that was just how Lucien wanted it. All of the werewolves stood up upon Lucien's entrance and once he got the head of the table, everyone simultaneously took their seats.

"Good evening. I know some of you came from places far away, some of you were busy, and some of you have never even heard of the Umbra Pack. I thank you for your time," Lucien said respectfully. "Let me get straight to the point..."

Lucien poured himself a glass of whiskey. He hadn't been out of his territory in so long, and he'd flown all the way to Seattle to meet with the packs.

"Alpha Lucien," Ignus' voice called from outside the room. "You have visitors." Lucien found himself raising his brows. Ignus was never that formal. He turned around and watched as the door to his room was opened and in walked a close friend of his and an unfamiliar woman with him.

"Alpha Cross," Lucien said with mock respect. The Alpha chuckled at him and Lucien immediately felt the other aura surrounding the woman with him. "Luna."

"You said this guy was chill," the woman said, smirking. Lucien grinned and found the Alpha in front of him chuckling as well.

"He is. It's been a while, Lucien," the Alpha said and Lucien chuckled as they got in for a quick hug.

"This must be your mate," Lucien greeted as he got a better look at the Luna. She had soft blonde hair and piercing blue eyes and Lucien noticed the small bump on her stomach.

"Congratulations."

"Thanks. Call me Elair. Luna's a bit much for Maddox's friends," she said with a smile and Lucien grinned.

"I was surprised you made it," Lucien said as he turned to Maddox, the Alpha himself.

"You barely ask for my help. We may be the big bad pack of the group, but Macabre helps its friends," Maddox replied.

"That and we aren't busy. Search parties are the least Maddox will have me do," Elair added. "Would you mind if I took a seat? I've been getting winded quicker than I should be." Lucien nodded and they all moved to the set of couches that sat across from each other.

"It's because of the children. I told you to take it easy."

"Mind your damn business, Maddox," she replied as she took her seat.

"Children?" Lucien mused and Elair nodded as she caressed her stomach.

Lucien watched the two of them with envy as Maddox caressed his mate's hands. It didn't help that they looked like perfection together. Years of knowing Maddox Cross, Alpha of the Macabre Pack, and finally he meets his mate. They looked like a portrait, with Maddox in his all black suit and Elair in her white dress.

"The person outside earlier, he wasn't a wolf was he?" Elair asked, surprising Lucien. They had all made sure that Ignus smelled just like one of them, which wasn't hard to do given how long he'd been living in the pack house.

"Bloodhound," Lucien answered and Elair paused before nodding.

"Not unheard of, I guess, pretty rare though," Elair said casually, surprising Lucien. "But having a bloodhound on our side makes this a bit of an even playing field."

"It doesn't-"

"Scare me?" Elair asked and she simply shrugged. "There are things much scarier than

"Looks like Macabre always has so little to fear," Lucien comment-ed and he suddenly noticed a certain darkness pass over the

"We've been through quite a bit actually. But that's not what we're here to discuss," Maddox said, clearing his throat. "A friend of ours can try to track down your mate... albeit in much less ordinary circumstances." Lucien

"Nothing is really ordinary when it comes to you and your pack," he said, earning a smile from the two.

"We're just extremists," Elair said with a wink before she hastily stood up. "I know what it's like to not be close to your mate. I know what it's like to be kept away from them." She said as she placed a hand on Lucien's

"We'll search for her like one of our own." Maddox said and Lucien could do nothing but bow as the two of them said their goodbyes and left. As soon as they were gone, Ignus crept his way inside and breathed a sigh of

"Never knew you were the type to make friends with such intense people," Ignus

"They practically sniffed you out," Lucien said with a

"Yeah, no shit, that Luna gave me a look that could kill," Ignus said as he brushed the back of his head. "But it's good to know we have strong people like that behind us."

"You think she's okay?" Lucien asked and Ignus breathed a sigh.

"Considering Ezra hasn't shown up all guns blazing, I think she's still putting up a fight," Ignus replied with a shrug. "Keep your hopes up Lucien." He added, noticing the sad look that glazed over Lucien's eyes. Ignus had learned the Lucien was good at hiding away, but it was the subtleties that let him down.

"Tell everyone we'll be leaving for home soon," Lucien said and Ignus nodded his head simply. By this time, Ignus had already accepted that he was basically like Lucien's secretary. "Have your hounds gotten anything?"

"You know I'd tell you if they did," Ignus said simply and Lucien nodded as he poured himself another glass of whiskey. Ignus took that as his cue to leave and he couldn't help but sigh as he closed the door behind him. Despite Lucien's exterior, he was an emotional mess, which made Ignus worry even more on Auden's behalf. Lucien had cut up a ton of Auden's clothes and dispersed pieces of it to almost every werewolf they came across. The Alpha meeting was no exception.

Lucien was desperate and it wasn't hard to see.

You okay? Hera asked and Ignus managed to smile.

Same as usual. Anything new?

I wish. Hera replied. Dalton's empty-handed. Thankfully Lucien's bond hasn't shattered.

Ignus didn't respond. Lucien's bond with Auden was their lifeline and even now, he knew it was as thin as a piece of thread. They didn't know when it would snap or if it was stronger than it seemed. Regret often swallowed Ignus up faster than anything. He'd dragged Hera and Dalton in his fight, broke things off with Celia, instigated contact with Auden, stopped her from marking Lucien, and his decisions made him doubt himself.

I can feel your pain, Ignus. Calm down. Hera suddenly said and Ignus shook his head.

Let me drown in it sometimes.

We've got bigger issues and an Alpha to console. Might wanna get that in your head first, otherwise Ezra will gain the upperhand.

Ignus shut her out. He didn't need a pep talk, he needed to think, it was the only way he could cope. He only hoped he wasn't wasting time thinking rather than acting.

Chapter 31

Minds are just like houses, Auden. Aurelia's voice said and I flipped a page of the book in front of me. Ezra was on a phone call, but considering the fact that he wasn't speaking, it was just plain weird.

Yeah, well, his is a locked up loony house. I replied before flipping another page. Aurelia did well to choose more... challenging books. I got frustrated often and reading about complex surgical processes did not help. As soon as Aurelia learned that I was a vet, she adapted her choice of books, though we had the occasional bloodhound history book, and since I figured out how to make an open line of communication with her a few weeks ago, we spoke quite often. She made for great company.

I didn't even have to be in this damn office to contact her. Our only problem now, rested on longer distance communication, which I couldn't exactly test out... and Ezra seemed to rub that fact into my face by using a phone.

"I don't understand why you'd read a book that causes such frustration," Ezra said as he hung up the phone.

"How do you have signal?" I asked, eyeing the phone on his desk. He smirked.

"I operate a nearby cell-tower. Sometimes it runs, sometimes it doesn't," he replied and I nodded before turning back to my book.

"I'm surprised you haven't cried," he said and I refused to look up at him. "I hear mate bonds are quite... heart wrenching."

"Sorry, I couldn't hear you over my intensely heart wrenching urge to leave," I replied, earning a smile on Ezra's face. Fucking weirdo.

"Still haven't given up? Not that you've made any attempts," Ezra said and I glared at him. "No comebacks?"

"How's it feel being locked out of my head? I imagine it must really suck for your ego," I said with a smile before closing my book and standing up. "You may have everyone else dancing around the palm of your hand, but not me, and that must really really suck." I hissed before shoving the book into his stomach as hard as I could. I heard him wince slightly as I turned on my heel.

"Where do you think you're going-"

"To my room. I can find my own way," I said as I slammed the doors shut behind me.

I had little freedoms granted now, like walking to my room and to the library by myself. Ezra still guarded me and I'd spotted more than a few bloodhounds hanging around to make sure I was going where I was supposed to. That was the first time I'd done anything like an outburst. Ezra would definitely find a way to punish me - at least Aurelia told me he would.

When I got to my room, I simply hopped into bed. I listened to the sounds around me - there were definitely a ton more people around. I took a deep breath, preparing to contact Aurelia, when the doors to the room opened and Ezra walked in, a hard look in his eyes.

"Get up." I did as I was told. "Follow me." I didn't bother making conversation. I simply walked behind him.

Celia was nowhere in sight and neither was Bo as we made our way through the halls. Although, there were four other people shadowing us, probably for safe measure.

"Do you know how much blood you're receiving nowadays?" Ezra suddenly asked as we walked past the library, followed by his office.

"Full doses, three times, everyday," I replied just as he turned a left and it suddenly dawned on me that we were heading exactly where I had to go.

We paused at the door and I realized that Ezra had to put in the code. Minds are just like houses. I took a deep breath. More than a few beeps later, the door clicked open and Ezra stepped inside. No luck getting that code... I thought to myself. The room was cold and unexpectedly silent, save for the whirring of a machine and a soft beeping noise that came between regular intervals. In a room almost identical to mine, lay a hospital bed, in which a woman lay down... Celia hung up an IV bag and as she proceeded to work, her eyes met mine with a kind of pitiful sadness. Ezra walked over stopped at the foot of the bed. I felt a sudden tightness in my chest and a dryness in my throat.

Ezra whispered something I couldn't bother to decipher before Celia backed away and walked with him to the door. They both stood there and averted their eyes as I stood at the foot of Aurelia's bed.

She was barely even skin and bone, much less healthier than how she looked in the vision I'd had of her before. She was dressed in what looked like a hospital gown, though I couldn't tell much since she had a blanket covering her from the chest down. Her soft brown hair was brittle and dry, a crease settled in between her brows, and despite her sleeping form, she looked to be in pain.

My breath began to shake as I walked closer to her, moving around to her right side. She'd been talking to me, teaching me, and writing to me, in this state? I looked over at her arms, they had gone purple and bruised, probably from the bloodvac's they'd give her, maybe other things...

I never planned on meeting you like this. Her voice said in my mind, and for a second, I was started at the strength of her voice. I know it's hard... but don't make a sound. Take my hand. I couldn't help but just... stare.

Don't think, Auden. I'll be alright. I took a moment to breathe and collect myself before I traced the bruises down her arm, each one sending a pang in my heart. I took her hand in mine. She was ice cold and if it wasn't for the heart monitor, I would've thought she was dead. I tried my best not to squeeze her hand too hard. I was worried that if I held onto her any tighter, she would break. But as soon as I had tightened my grip, her hand clasped closed around mine and a pain seared up from my palms to my arms.

Our time is coming to an end. She said and the pain ceased. I felt a soft touch on my cheek. But there was no one there. I looked over at her face, the crease in between her brows had gone, and she blinked her eyes awake. She didn't bother looking at me, instead she looked over at Ezra... and smiled... I thought it was just my imagination, but I watched as Ezra suddenly turned stiff and quivered in his position. Moments later, Celia dropped to her knees.

Ezra began to step forward in a strange, slow... almost unnatural manner. His jaw revealed a tenseness in his actions and I watched as he made his way to the foot of the bed. Celia's face looked freakishly pale as she watched her brother take out a blade from the inner pocket of his suit jacket. Taken aback, I tried to move and grab him, but Aurelia's grip held me firmly in place.

Trust me. She said simply but it was hard to watch as Ezra took the blade and to my surprise, brought it to his hand and drew it through. The smell of his blood wafted throughout the room and I watched as he walked around over to Aurelia, trembling as he offered his bloodied hand to her lips. I looked away. I couldn't watch. But when I felt her grip, loosen around my wrist, I couldn't help but look at the scene. Ezra trembled terribly under Aurelia's gaze. Her eyes landed on mine as she licked her lips clean. She pushed Ezra's hand away from her and I watched as her body pulsed with life, her skin turned supple, hair smooth, and she let out a relieved sigh. Her green eyes then turned a viscious red, as if sending a warning to me.

I didn't know if I was frozen out of fear or out of sheer confusion. Something was wrong and yet I couldn't understand why Aurelia would-

This is how you'll get out of here. Her voice said and I watched as she nodded her head towards Ezra and he moved away from the bed, settling back where Celia was kneeling.

"It's nice to finally meet you," she said, her voice was softer than I expected.

What you've seen me do is our bloodline's trait. Mind control. Though it seems like a powerful tool, I can no longer do it for very long. She then took my hand in hers. Consider my plans in action.

"For my blood, a gift," Aurelia suddenly said and it was like she was reciting a set of lines, "For my enemies, a weapon, and for our lives, a curse." As she spoke, red lines, almost like veins, appeared from the hand that held mine and I watched, as if in a trance, as they travelled and transferred over to my own skin. A burning sensation then began climbing up my arms and into the rest of my body, images flashed through my head and my breath hitched.

I felt a weight over my shoulders and I couldn't breathe. Aurelia refused to release my hand even though the heat had now changed into a scorching pain. I could feel tears stream down my face, my vision blurred, and all I could register was pain... and then I heard it. Voices. Jumbled and messy, like I was stuck in a crowd of whispers - and then before I could decipher any single one of the voices...

Silence.

This is the only way. Our plans live today. Aurelia's voice said and it was as if she woke me up. I was back in the room but Aurelia's grip on mine was no longer there, it was gone, and so was the health that had spread through her from Ezra's blood. I immediately looked over at the heart rate monitor. Stable. I breathed a sigh of relief, but just as I did so, I felt hands grab both my arms, forcing them behind my back.

"What the hell-" I began but all I had to do was look over at Ezra and the anger in his eyes.

"Take her to the basement." Before I could even try to set myself free, I felt a soft pressure on my neck and I was gone.

Chapter 32

Ezra sat on a steel chair across me. My feet had been chained with large clamps that made sure it was difficult to move around and my arms were restrained with tight metal cuffs that had been chained together so that my wrists were never more than six inches apart. A single light bulb hung above, making sure I had enough to still see his stupid figure.

"What did she show you?" Ezra asked and I chose not to respond. It seemed to anger him as he immediately tried to empower me with that stupid bloodhound aura of his.

"You'll never figure out how to use it. Not here, not with me around," Ezra said and I smirked.

"Is that why you put me in here?" I asked and he chose not to respond. "What do you even want from me? Why not kill me and get it over with-"

"Only you can pass that trait," Ezra walked over to me and put a finger to my head, "Only your bloodline." His grey eyes were cold and terrifying.

"And you want me to pass it over to you?" I asked and he smiled, a twisted smile that filled me with disgust.

"Not me... My bloodline," he replied and I laughed in his face.

"Fuck you."

"We will... I just need you docile," he said and I suddenly felt nauseous as he trailed his hand down my face, I snapped my teeth at him in response, but he merely pulled his hand away. "I will get what I want from you... You will give in. With time."

"Go to hell."

"And you'll join me." He said with a triumphant grin. "I always get what I want, Auden. This time will be no different."

I took a deep breath. I needed a Bloodvac, I could feel the hunger for it course through my body. As Aurelia had advised... I would have to give into that desperation. It was now or never.

I hated playing the waiting game. It felt like I had been practically playing it the entire time I was here... and now I had to wait in a cellar as my hunger gnawed at me. Aurelia hadn't contacted me for the past few days, which was a given, considering what we were going to do. Ezra hadn't showed up and I was a little grateful. I was way too weak to deal with that shit-bag and my body was showing it. I could barely lift my arms to move, my lips had chapped, and the cold concrete floor didn't help the shivers that constantly ran throughout my body.

I knew I had to wait for Aurelia and that it would be a struggle... but plans always did sound better before they actually took place. There wasn't even much to do to keep my entertained, which I guessed was the point. Chained to the wall, I had nothing but a single light bulb for light, a heavy metal door across me, and luckily enough, a working toilet just within my reach.

I didn't have to even sniff the air to know I was filthy, but that was the least of my concerns. The hunger had started to cause... certain changes to my body. I'm pretty sure bloodhounds didn't normally have heat sensing vision... and that I shouldn't be able to tell the heart rate of a living being standing three feet behind a heavy metal door in front of me. I also shouldn't probably be drooling at the sound of their heart beating... probably.

The sound of footsteps approaching snapped me out of my trance. Whoever was guarding me had stepped aside to make way for a visitor – and I knew by the scent that it wasn't Ezra. I heard something heavy get lifted from the door before it slowly swung open, creaking and settling with a loud thud as it hit the back wall. I closed my eyes.

I couldn't even see them as people if I tried. I just saw blood-bags and their smell was way too enticing...

"How are you doing?" Celia's voice asked, I couldn't help but let out a weak laugh.

"What are you doing here?" I countered, refusing to open my eyes. Aurelia had told me what the symptoms would be and I had a vague idea what my poor bloodhound instincts wanted me to do...

"I... I couldn't let him just starve you-"

"You should," I replied.

"Why won't you look at me? Is there something wrong with your eyes?" I heard her heel click as she took a step forward and an involuntary growl escaped my lips.

"You're a scientist, right?" I asked and I heard her release a shaky breath. "It doesn't take a scientist to figure out that dangling a steak in front of a dead-hungry wolf is a bad fucking idea."

"I just-" I opened my eyes and stared straight into her eyes. Celia froze up in front of me and I breathed a sigh.

"The amount of self-control it takes for me not to try and pounce at you... is astounding," I said as I began to grind my teeth against each other. Celia grabbed hold of her arm, seemingly steadying herself before she reached into her pockets and pulled out a small cloth bag. She put it down on the ground, right before her feet before she kicked it forward. It landed with a soft clink in front of my knees.

"These are for you... They're pure bloodvac's... Synthetics won't do you any good, you need real ones if you want to survive..." she trailed off.

"He'll kill you if he finds out," I said and Celia shook her head, avoiding my gaze and I shook my head. "Unless he already knows."

"I-"

"Get out," I said and when she didn't move, I let out a fierce growl that had been building inside me. She practically wobbled as she stepped away... and I took a breath.

I'll call you when I need you. I linked and she froze. Don't worry. You won't wait long. I didn't need a response. Instead, I watched her leave, and smiled as I managed to watch the heat of her body lead the way to my escape...

I looked at the bag she'd left for me and picked it up. Bloodvacs, six of them. More than enough to satiate the bloodhound inside me... I took them in my hands.

It's time. Aurelia's voice called and I just knew this was all a part of her plan.

"Let's hope this fucking works," I said, my voice barely even a whisper as I took the vaccines in my hands, pulled my arms back behind my head, bones clicking at the sudden movements I'd decided to make, and with as much strength as I could muster, I hurled them towards the concrete wall. All six shattered at once and I felt my hunger build inside me. A feral growl escaped my lips as I smelt the blood from the vaccines... I felt my teeth elongate and I bit down on my lips until blood escaped them to stop myself from screaming.

My bones ached and pierced my being. I felt like I was being cut up and spread as I slowly felt the shift come through. I remembered Aurelia's explanation.

As a half-blood, you're two halves will always oppose each other... but they won't when they have a common goal... To feed. I... would never recommend using that as a learning method. But under these circumstances, we have no other choice. Your instincts will tell you how to use all of your powers, bloodhound or werewolf. And with a little help from me and my allies, I will get you out.

I fell to the floor and the smell of blood embraced me. My vision began to come and go... Blood. Meat. Hunger. Blood. I reached out towards the area where the bloody scent was coming from... and when I looked, I no longer had any restraints... or hands.

Pure black paws sheathing claws that I had no idea had been digging into the ground had formed. Blood. I sniffed the air and grimaced before standing up on all fours.

Hunt.

Chapter 33

Celia couldn't stop trembling. She had just gotten back to her office and was organizing the Bloodvacs according to doses. As she tried desperately to place them into their containers, she couldn't help but recall the look in Auden's eyes and the voice with which she spoke.

I'll call when I need you. Don't worry. You won't wait long. Celia held her breath. What if Ezra heard? What the hell was Auden planning? A knock on the door made her shudder in fear before in walked Ezra himself.

"I'll be going away this evening for a meeting," he said and Celia nodded her head stiffly. He gave her a long discerning look. "What's wrong?"

"Nothing," she said, her voice low like a whisper. He walked towards her and Celia's heard thudded loud against her chest. Ezra lifted a hand and Celia immediately flinched before he rested his hand at the top of her head. Memory after memory flipped through Celia's thoughts and yet, to her surprise, nothing about her encounter with Auden showed through.

"Still scared of me," Ezra said, sighing. He then ruffled Celia's hair, choosing to ignore how much his sister trembled underneath his touch. "Don't do anything stupid. I have a meeting with grandfather. I'll return in an hour or two." And with that, he turned around and left.

Celia let out a huge breath, her heart pounded against her chest... He didn't know. He didn't know she'd visited Auden... and he didn't find out about what Auden told her. Something was different. Auden was different.

Nice thought process. Auden's voice said and Celia jumped in her seat. I need to know if you're ready to leave this place for good. Are you? She froze. She was tired of Ezra's mind games, tired of being mind-read every day, fearing some mistake... She was afraid of what her brother could do... and she just wanted to be free from it all. She took a deep breath, slowly releasing it before she made contact.

How can I help?

Celia had packed as well as she could. She took every necessity – Bloodvacs, research notes, and other whatnots into a backpack, making sure to pack clothes for both her and Auden. To be safe, Celia took a handgun too. She looked at herself in the mirror. Her hair's natural curls looked all over the place, she pulled it into a tight bun and shoved her feet into a pair of sneakers. Breathe, Celia... breathe... She told herself.

I'm ready. She said, hoping Auden heard her.

So am I. But first, contact Ignus. Auden replied and Celia grimaced. She promised she'd try to let Auden figure out to contact them... and she could only imagine what Ignus would think if she warned him.

Don't worry about that. Auden interrupted. Contact him. Then head to the cellar – I'll meet you there.

How will you get out? What do I tell him? Celia asked, but she knew she wouldn't get a response. She looked at herself in the mirror again and pulled the right sleeve of her sweater, revealing the mark on her neck.

Ignus. Celia called out. She closed her eyes and prayed for a response.

So the princess calls. I thought I'd hear from Auden.

No time. Something's happening. Auden told me to contact you. So... be ready. Celia said and she hoped he'd say anything... But he didn't. Celia couldn't help the feeling of dejection that hit at her heart. She covered up her mark. She had to go.

She was probably a hundred feet away from the entrance to the cellar from the ground floor, when she felt an overwhelming aura consume the air around her. Celia found it difficult to breathe, to see, and to move forward. It was an unfamiliar aura, definitely not her brother's – definitely not any of the usual hounds at the estate... so there could've only been one person it was coming from.

Where are you? Celia called out and as she slowly managed to make it in front of the doorway to the cellar... she froze. The door had been torn down to pieces and the dark staircase leading down the cell felt ominous. Celia swallowed a lump in her throat.

"Auden?" She called out. She was greeted by a loud growl as heavy padded footsteps, followed by the soft sound of clicking crept up the darkness.

The first thing she saw were claws, huge, black, claws... and then fur... and Celia could swear her heart had stopped as a giant wolf appeared in front of her... On instinct, Celia found herself drop to her knees and bow her head, the aura of the wolf overpowering her very being. The wolf huffed, seemingly giving Celia permission to rise. So she did, and she was met with a pair of chocolate brown eyes...

"Auden?" Celia said again and the wolf rolled its eyes.

Any idea where Bo is? Auden's voice asked and Celia hesitantly shook her head. Auden's wolf was bigger than any that Celia had ever encountered – and she'd seen a good amount of them. Auden probably stood seven feet tall, she had a mane of long black fur that covered her upper half, but from her lower jaw all the way down to her stomach, she was a golden brown color. Her claws were long and black and Celia immediately found herself looking over at Auden's mouth. She didn't smell of blood. But Celia knew there had to have been at least four guards that would've been alarmed-

They're all down there. They're fine. Auden said.

"R-right."

Do you have everything you need? Celia nodded. Then get on. Bo's waiting outside.

Auden knelt down and Celia hesitated before she stepped for-ward and climbed over Auden's ginormous form. She gripped Au-den's fur tightly and tried to mentally prepare herself for the trip.

Are you gonna run the whole way out? Celia asked.

Yeah.

Want a vac?

No. Not yet. Auden replied, surprising Celia. Sorry Celia, but I'm gonna have to search your head for the way out, we'll get out quicker if you don't have to tell me where to go. Celia didn't respond and Auden turned her head, to get a glimpse of her.

May I? Auden asked and Celia had thought it was obvious. Actually... she had never been asked.

Of course. Auden barked in response and Celia smiled before she felt the wolf beneath her rear back and launch herself forward.

Auden sped through the hallways, using Celia's mind as a guide to get out of there. Celia, on the other hand, kept reaching out to Bo, making sure all was going well. She didn't exactly know what the plans were, other than making a run for it, but she knew that they had a bit of time before everyone found out. Ezra was out, which meant that the estate would be quiet and calm. That didn't mean there weren't people loyal to him, though.

He's out? Auden asked, interrupting Celia's thoughts.

Yeah. He said he had a meeting with our grandfather.

Grandfather? Auden asked as she suddenly stopped at a corner and everything became dead quiet.

What's the problem? Celia asked, looking around.

People. Auden replied before she lay down on all fours.

What are we doing?

Waiting... Auden said and Celia gave her a look of confusion. Two men suddenly appeared from the corner and as if they were invisible, they walked without even noticing the giant fur ball that had laid down.

There's no way they didn't see-

Aurelia. Auden said simply.

What? Celia asked.

That's all I'll say for now. Auden replied before she got up and eyed the wide doors in front of her.

It'll take us forever if we take that route. Celia said and she knew Auden was chuckling as the wolf beneath her huffed.

Window. Auden responded and Celia raised her brows. Brace yourself. Without another warning, Auden reared her body back, curling up and forcing Celia to grab hold, as she launched herself at a window, crashing it open before landing with a thud onto the cool grass of the garden outside.

You okay? Auden asked. Celia checked her hands and felt around her neck for any cuts.

I'm good. Auden let out a soft bark in response before she took off. Celia reached for the gun in her bag and prepped it.

How many guards in the forest? Auden asked.

Ten at several different points. It'd be best to sneak past them. Celia turned off the safety on her gun and grabbed on as Auden pushed through the forest, weaving herself expertly around the trees. Celia would've been lying if she said she wasn't impressed... Auden was travelling faster than any werewolf, which meant that her bloodhound instincts had mingled with her wolf's... but she was definitely running on just that – instinct.

Auden, you're gonna need a bloodvac soon. Celia said.

Not yet.

But- Auden let out a growl and although Celia first thought it was targeted at her, it took her a second to realize that they'd been found out.

"Lookie here..." A woman said, her eyes aglow as she stepped out, along with two other bloodhounds behind her. "Two traitors... one big reward." She said, looking straight at Celia.

"Let us out, Quinn, we don't want any trouble," Celia said, holding the gun in her hands.

"I could let the whole place know you're escaping-" Quinn began but she froze as Celia felt a heavy aura swallow her whole, making it impossible to speak and even hard to breathe.

Celia watched as the three bloodhounds trembled in front of them. Auden let out a snarl before she lurched forward, trapping Quinn down in between her two front paws. Quinn let out a short squeal before fear swallowed the rest of the noise in her voice and she curled up on the ground below Auden's huge form. The other two bloodhounds flinched and though they tried to step forward, Auden merely let out a loud growl and the two found themselves unable to move.

Auden didn't let up on the aura, she exuded such immense power that Quinn let out soft noises of fear, quaking and shivering beneath her. Celia watched as Auden began to salivate, her wolf's drool falling to the ground, grazing Quinn's skin...

Auden, we have to go. Celia said, afraid but aware she had to get them out of there. She was met with silence. Celia watched over Auden's shoulders as the heaviness around them lifted and the bloodhounds began to breathe normally. Quinn immediately began to release heavy breaths before she gave Auden a cold hard stare and a smirk – Celia felt her heart drop – but just as she was about to panic, Auden's jaw expanded.

Epilogue

I was running. The wind whipped through my fur, my eyes focused on paths, and my mind focused on one thing and one thing only - escape. There was no time to think about what I could've done differently - no time to think about my rationale. Escape. That was my priority and there was more on the line than just my life, Celia's frozen grip on my back was proof of that - the fact that I even made it out of estate was even more proof. I only had to rely on one more person to get out - Bo.

How much further? I asked Celia. When I didn't get a response, I stopped in my tracks. My paws dug into the soft dirt beneath them and I took a moment to catch my breath. If I could've looked at Celia, I would've. But since she was on my back, I merely called even louder.

Celia. Her hands loosened their grip around me for a brief moment.

Yeah? She answered timidly. Why are we stopping? I shook my head. We couldn't waste time, so I sniffed the air around me instead.

At first, it was hard for me to get passed the strong rusty-iron clad smell that had wrapped around the entire upper half of my body - but then it became easier. The smell of pine separated from that of the other trees, the dirt, the subtle traces of bloodhound scents... and then there it was - a familiar scent of his - the smell of coffee from the brews he made daily for both my mother and myself. I felt a pang in my heart. Don't think. I reminded myself. Just move.

So I did.

Bo had been waiting for us at what looked like an unguarded gateway. Though, judging by the bodies that peeked out from the small guard houses on either side of the gate - it had definitely been guarded before he got there. Bo bowed his head as soon as he saw us and I lowered my legs down, allowing Celia to climb off of me.

Whose car? I asked, looking over at the black SUV that had been parked at the gate.

Your mother's. He replied, before offering a kind smile.

"I have water and a few towels prepared inside, we should get moving," he said aloud, I noted the look he gave me, probably examining the blood that had begun to cling to my body. His gaze didn't last too long though as he turned on his heel and opened up the trunk. Bo had moved around the seats, giving me ample room to sit, and I watched as Celia unloaded some clothes from her bag and rested them in the car.

"I'll leave the bloodvacs there too, take three, just for stability - I know you just... you know, but this will do more to satiate you," she said and I could tell she was still shaken by what had happened earlier. I gave her a light bark before I placed my front paws onto the car and hopped in.

Once the drive began, I clung onto the flooring as my body began to shift back into its human form. The pain was barely there now - probably because I had fed - though my body felt sore, it was nothing compared to the first time. Bones clicked and re-shaped, my fur receded, and though I let out a whimper and a yelp here and there, I soon found myself looking at my hands, my fingers covered in dirt and my mouth and chest damp and crusty from dried blood. I grabbed a towel from one of the chairs, sighing in relief at its warmth as I wiped myself down. I pressed it against my face and then my mouth. I remembered the feeling of flesh in my mouth, the strength that it took to bite down, my fangs that had dug in... Forget it. Not now. I continued to wipe myself down, I remembered the smell of iron, the tangy taste of it, the feeling of it dripping down...

"Are you okay?" Celia asked, bringing me out of my thoughts.

"I'm fine," I replied quickly as I proceeded to clean up. I knew she was genuinely concerned but also relieved that I, at least, looked human now. "Do you have a towel up front?"

"Yes, I've already cleaned up," she responded as I took her bag and pulled on the clothes she'd prepared for me. Now clean and dressed, I took out three bloodvacs and, without hesitation, pressed one after the other into the crease of my elbow on the left arm. Relief and calm washed over me, the adrenaline wore off, and rationale kicked in.

"Where will we be heading?" I asked.

"Miss Aurelia told me to take you to a safehouse of a friend's. From there, I suppose Miss Celia will be able to contact her mate."

"Her mate?" I raised an eyebrow and I noticed Celia shudder.

"Ignus," she said simply and I lurched forward and looked at her face.

"Ignus is your mate?" I asked and she nodded stiffly. It was only then that I noticed the mark that rested just behind the folds of her shirt. Celia seemed to notice my gaze, since she began to fiddle with it, raising the collar up a little higher.

"That idiot was mated to you?" I asked, trying to lighten up the situation. Celia nodded and offered me a small smile before she took it back and assumed a more serious expression.

"My brother should be heading back any time soon," she said, glancing at the watch on her left wrist. "How are we-"

"You needn't worry about that Miss Celia, we're about to take a detour," Bo said before he turned the car towards a dirt path. "These paths were used by Miss Aurelia quite often in the past." I folded my lips into a thin line.

"Will she be alright?" I asked.

I was met with silence.

"She will do her best to survive and that is the most that we can hope for. Having met her, the two of you have made a connection between blood - you will know how well or how worse she is doing of your own intuition," Bo responded and I simply nodded.

"What about our tracks?" Celia asked, looking over at the rearview mirror.

"These paths are still used often by other hounds - mainly for supplies. There are four cars scheduled to leave today - as Miss Aurelia's private vehicle, this car will be noted missing later, giving us about an hour more for our escape," Bo said, just as he began to speed up.

"So everything was planned out?" Celia asked.

"Miss Aurelia has had plenty of time to plan," Bo said with a smile. With that, I turned back and took a seat, fastening my seatbelt as the terrain turned a little rougher.

I stared out the window, the trees whipped past behind us, the occasional shudder of the car made me jump in my seat - and I suddenly remembered my first day with Lucien. The way I grabbed onto his wolf as he ran forward weaving through the trees and bushes. I placed my hand on my chest. I knew that I'd meet with him soon enough. I just had to be patient.

It took us about an hour and a half before we finally pulled into a city - the bright streetlights and tall buildings were no better signifier of that. We were in Oregon, surprisingly enough. Bo pulled up to a tall building and presented a card to the guards on watch, he then drove down into the basement parking area.

"Has Ignus said anything?" I asked Celia and she shook her head.

"I'll provide him with more information once we get inside to the safehouse," she responded. Bo unloaded some things of his own before leading us in.

"So who exactly does the safehouse belong to?" I asked as we got onto the elevator.

"You'll see," Bo replied, making me raise my eyebrows but choose to say nothing. It was only in the elevator that I was able to catch sight of my reflection. I didn't look particularly unhealthy, which was to my surprise. Celia seemed to catch onto my thoughts.

Royal blood thrives best on our own bloodline. She linked.

"I won't inquire much about the details of your escape, but Miss Auden, did you feed on someone?" Bo asked.

"I did."

"She was being taunted - anyone would've-" Celia began and I gave her a smile that interrupted her speech.

"It was a moment out of my control, that was it," I said and Bo nodded.

"I only meant to ask to remark that you are doing surprisingly well. Though I have no doubt that the constant dosage of bloodvacs have something to do with that," he said, smiling over at Celia just as the elevator doors slid open.

We took a long walk through the hallways before Bo stopped at a single door and knocked - though he did it in quite a peculiar way. He stomped his right foot down first before knocking twice on the door and sliding the palm of his hand from the right to the left side. It was only then that the door swung open.

"I'm surprised it took you so long, my friend," a man answered. He was tall with long silvery hair and golden colored eyes. The man wore a sleek and clean white suit with a black tie and his eyes immediately examined us. He stopped as his gaze landed on me.

"So it is her," he said, walking over to me and extending his hand. "My name is Mikhail, a friend of a friend of your mate's. I will put you into contact soon enough. Another pack here has been anxiously looking for you - on behalf of your mate's request of course." He said with an unsettling smile.

"Lucien's request?" I asked.

"You could say that he used every bit of his influence to find you," Mikhail said. "But please, do come in," he said, before gesturing to go inside.

The apartment was definitely an upscale one, despite its simple and modern look, there was something expensive about the black wooden floors, glass surfaces, and white marble that made up the majority of the decor. The windows came down from the ceiling to the floor, offering an almost bird's eye view of the city.

"Okay, first off, you need to calm the hell down and-" A woman's voice said from inside the apartment, and soon we found ourselves in front of a tall, blonde-haired woman, with her right hand on her phone and her left running through her hair.

"No, that is not how you- okay, okay, I'll tell River to help out, but just breathe for now and make sure Sera's okay, got it?" she said before hanging up her phone. It was only then that she realized that there were more people in the room.

"Oh, shit, are these them?" She asked and Mikhail nodded. She walked towards each one of us and seemed to assess us further than Mikhail. "No clear injuries but you all might wanna go ahead and take a bath. We've got rooms for each one of you."

"I'm sorry, who are you?" I asked, genuinely curious. She smiled, her blue eyes staring right into me.

"Elair, Luna of the Macabre Pack," she greeted, extending her hand towards me. I shook it and smiled back. "My mate, Maddox will be better at communicating Umbra, so hang tight. We'll get you back soon enough."

"Sorry, I have a question too," Celia said from beside me. Elair raised her eyebrows.

"Go ahead."

"How do you know Bo?" She asked and Elair looked over at him.

"I don't, but Mikhail and his master does, apparently," she answered with a casual shrug, Mikhail smirked at her response before he stood by Bo and whispered something inaudible even to my hearing. Bo nodded his head in response.

"I have a few things to discuss, so I'll excuse myself," he said, bowing his head. I do advise you, Miss Auden, not to contact your mother any time soon. He added before turning and leaving with Mikhail, heading into another room.

"So," Elair began, "let me show you to your rooms."

Celia dismissed herself quite quickly, leaving me alone in my room. I took a shower just like Elair had suggested and found myself resting my forehead against the shower wall. I tried to think of something, anything... but nothing could take my mind away from what I'd done mere hours earlier... A sickening feeling filled the pit of my stomach and I found myself rushing out of the bathroom, my hands gripping the sides of the toilet as I felt the urge to vomit... but nothing came out.

Nothing.

A part of me was disgusted - sure. But a greater part of me - was satisfied. I got up, headed back into the shower, cleaned up, dressed, and headed to bed.

There was no taking back the past. No regretting escape.

Not when I had so much more to deal with.

Not when I was still so far from home.